Keefe thought quickly. He didn't want to tell her just yet who he really was. He searched the pocket of his shirt. Finding nothing, he was forced to ask, "Could you give me something to write on? I'll leave you my pager number."

"You don't live in the building? You could just give me your apartment number or…" She hesitated, not wanting the man to get the wrong idea. Sure, she'd thanked him for his assistance with Damien, but she wasn't in the market for a new man. "Just a sec, I'll get you some paper."

Keefe sensed the hesitancy in her. At least they'd moved from sworn enemies to janitor-tenant relationship. Things would break, she'd need him.

"Listen," he said to her as he handed over his pager number. His voice dropped to a low, co-conspirator whisper. "This number is not for all the tenants in the building. I hear that the owner is looking for a second janitor. I'll only be doing emergency jobs."

"So what are you going to be, like the head janitor?"

Keefe rubbed the back of his ear, trying to decide if she was being condescending, sizing up the amount in his bank account by the title of his job. For now he'd let it go. "No, not the top janitor, just I'm not available or qualified to handle all the things that could go wrong in a building this size."

"So a man that finally admits he's not king of the universe. How refreshing."

This time Ashleigh was smiling; she was teasing him. He smiled back, not answering, the lock done but not wanting to leave, just wanting to talk to her a bit longer. But he had no excuse, no reason for lingering. "See you later." He smiled at her again and left before she asked him to.

RSJ 2008

THE WEDDING GOWN

DYANNE DAVIS

Yasmine Ide
Best of Luck
in your
wedding DyDa

Genesis Press Inc.

Indigo Love Stories

An imprint Genesis Press Publishing

Indigo Love Stories
c/o Genesis Press, Inc.
1213 Hwy 45 N, 2nd Floor
Columbus, MS 39705

Copyright© 2003 by Dyanne Davis
The Wedding Gown

ISBN 1-58571-120-9
Manufactured in the United States of America

First Edition

Visit us at www.genesis-press.com
or call at 1-888-Indigo-1

DEDICATION

Dedicated To Jackqueline Toreas Jackson-my own baby sister, who embodies every traditional trait that being the baby sister entails. If I had been given a choice, I would have chosen you. So, with all my love to the keeper of my secrets, this one's for you.

CHAPTER ONE

Wedding gown for sale. Cheap. Brand new, never worn. Reason: Potential groom turned out to be a two-timing jackass!!!

Ashleigh pushed the thumbtack firmly into the sign and stepped back from the laundry room bulletin board. *There*, she thought, *that should do it.* She could of course have called Damien a lot worse things than a two-timing jackass. In her opinion she'd been rather nice. She was thinking about all the other less nice but true things she could have called him when the notice fluttered in a sudden breeze as a door opened and closed somewhere. Ashleigh frowned. Damien was trouble even when he was just mentioned on a sign. Obviously she needed more than one thumbtack or it would rip loose.

As she glanced around for more thumbtacks, her eyes fell on an open toolbox sitting on the counter. *Probably the janitor's*, she thought. And right there, poking out of it and just begging to be used, was a staple gun. With only a moment's hesitation, she grabbed it and zapped three quick staples into her notice before it balked at spitting out a fourth. Opening it, Ashleigh saw that it was completely empty. She peeped into the toolbox for more staples to refill it but saw only other tools. Darn it! She thought about just forgetting it. After all, it had only been a couple of staples. Big deal! The janitor would have run out the first time he tried to use it. Yet it bothered her. She was the one who'd emptied it. She'd not only appropriated someone else's property, but she'd rendered it momentarily useless to that person. How many times had she herself gotten angry when someone borrowed something of hers and returned it needing something before it could be used?

With a sigh, she examined the staple gun again and saw that it used staples the same size as those in her desk upstairs. The solution was annoyingly simple: She could go get her staples and refill the staple gun — maybe even before the janitor returned from wherever he was. *Then get to it*, her conscience ordered. So, without further ado, Ashleigh headed for the elevator. She'd satisfy her conscience and do a good deed at the same time.

Keefe read the notice posted in the laundry room, amusement creasing his handsome face. He wondered for a moment if this was a joke. He glanced casually once again at the notice and saw what he'd missed initially, an e-mail address. He knew instantly that the woman was serious.

Cheap, he thought, wondering how cheap it would be. Some people thought five thousand dollars for a gown was cheap. He wasn't one of them. Of course his sister would think his even considering buying her a second-hand gown would be cheap, meaning him not the gown.

And she would consider it used, worn or not. He could just hear her scolding voice now. "But Keefe, you promised. Why do I have to buy a gown someone else chose? It's bad luck, Keefe. Did you ever think of that?"

Just to be sure, Keefe read the notice once more. The potential bridegroom was a "two-timing jackass." Well, that couldn't be because of the gown, he assured himself as he pulled a pencil from behind his ear and scribbled down the e-mail address. It was at least worth looking into.

Ashleigh stopped short in the doorway to the laundry room. A man had his back to her, reading the notice she'd posted. It must be the janitor. She was just about to confess and offer him the box of staples when he suddenly laughed.

"What's so funny?" She asked.

"Excuse me?" Keefe answered, turning to confront the hostile voice.

"I said, what's so funny?" She shoved the staples into her pocket. To heck with her conscience. Any man who found her notice funny didn't deserve a good deed. For that matter, why was a man reading her notice?

Damn, she's fine, Keefe thought to himself as he eyed the woman standing before him. His eyes were drawn to her breasts and stayed a second or two longer than was decent. He was aware of that. And if he weren't, the glare the woman shot him from her brown eyes reminded him of that fact in a hurry.

"I was reading the notice about the wedding gown. Why? Is

there something wrong with that?"

"Why are you reading that notice anyway? It's for *a wedding gown, a woman's wedding gown.*"

Keefe took a step back better to peruse the woman looking at him with such disdain. Having done that, he began inventorying himself, making it obvious what he was doing. It was clear what the woman standing before him had just implied.

His eyes flicked over his attire, jeans and a tee shirt. Nothing about his clothes implied he would be into wearing women's attire. He continued scrutinizing: tool-belt around his waist, hammer on the counter near him with a half box of penny nails spilled out in varying spots. Just as he thought, everything about him appeared to be in order.

"Excuse me, miss, but is there something about me or my demeanor?" He raised an eyebrow, daring her to answer before he even finished the question. "Is there something about me that would have you questioning my manhood before you've even introduced yourself to me?"

"You're looking at a notice to buy a wedding gown."

"And that fact alone tells you what? That I want it for myself?"

"Well, it tells me one of two things. Either you're gay, or you're a cheap bastard who wants to buy his girlfriend this gown because he thinks he can get a bargain."

The woman was beginning to irk him. Fine or not, he wasn't in the mood to charm a man-hating female. Nope, too many women in the world that loved men for him to go to such trouble.

"Why is what I do or read any of your business?" He watched as the woman's eyes lifted. He saw her blink as though she hadn't expected him to say anything.

"It's my gown," she answered at last.

"Oh."

He wanted to apologize, to tell her he was sorry things hadn't worked out for her, to tell her not to become bitter, but while he was contemplating how to begin, the woman turned and walked out of the laundry room, leaving him standing with what he knew was a stupid expression on his face. Damn, he hadn't even gotten the woman's name.

You do have her e-mail address, his subconscious screamed at him, so make use of that.

"I'll be glad when I find a buyer for the gown." Ashleigh turned to her friend. "Did you hear me?"

"I heard you," Nicki answered, "but I don't know why you're doing this. Every time he messes up you just take his sorry ass back. Why, girl? I don't understand. The man definitely must be good at something 'cause he's not worth a damn."

Her friend's remarks didn't anger Ashleigh even though indirectly she was being called a fool for putting up with Damien's BS. Instead, she laughed.

"No, he's good at two things: making me feel sorry for him and making me wish there was some way I could help him. And his voice, don't forget his voice. When he sings to me I melt."

Ashleigh's voice drifted away as her eyes closed in memory. Two seconds later they popped open when a hard object whacked across her head.

"What the hell are you doing?" She glared at Nicki.

"The last thing you need to be doing is thinking about how

good the brother makes you feel. You have to forget all that, put it behind you. Try and focus on the fact that not only did he screw that hoochie, he had the nerve to do it on your dime. How could you be fool enough to let him use your charge card?"

"I hope you don't think I authorized him to go and shack up in a hotel." Ashleigh shuddered. "Maybe I wasn't clear when I said, 'This card is to buy what you need.' Do you think I should have added, except some hoochie?" She started to laugh and found she couldn't stop. Even after she fell to the floor, Ashleigh continued laughing hysterically. "Thanks, Nicki. What was I thinking? Believe me, this will be the last brother that I spend money on. Tell me how in the world I ever allowed that to happen in the first place. I can't believe I'm now one of those women that's talked about on talk shows or on court TV. 'The Woman Who Took Care of Her Man.' God, what a fool I was."

"At least you woke up before it was too late."

"Not exactly," Ashleigh said, looking sadly at the wedding gown concealed in the heavy plastic bag. "I wish I had woken up before I made that." She jerked her head in the direction of the gown.

"Be thankful you made it yourself. You're only out the labor."

"That's not true. The suppliers don't give me free material because it's for my personal use." Ashleigh shook her head. That's probably what any prospective buyer would think. Three had already said as much and thought she should just hand the gown over. She'd replied that it was cheap, not free.

"Listen, Nicki, that gown would sell easily for seven or eight thousand dollars. It doesn't matter that I made it myself. I used the best material; the seed pearls are hand sewn. Everything about that damn dress is double stitched. With my time and material it's worth over four thousand dollars. Not only am I not making a dime on this dress, I'm not even getting back all the money on material."

"So what, Ash? It's worth it to get rid of Damien, isn't it? To not have him standing around anymore with his hand out, you're going to profit on the end of this relationship. Hell, if you kept taking care of the brother, you'd be outdoors within a year. He's a user, a real leech. I told you that the night we met him."

"I know, but... I just thought you were... Well, you know what I thought."

"Yeah, we both know what you thought. You thought I wanted him and I'll admit maybe a little of it was jealousy, but when he went after you, I had time to breathe, to see what Damien was really about. You should have listened. The only thing the brother had going was that oh so fine silky voice of his and that tight little butt and that sexy body." Nicki grinned. "And apparently he kept you happy in the bedroom."

Not so much, Ashleigh thought but she wouldn't tell Nicki that. She would look like a bigger fool than she already did. Not only didn't Damien rock her world, he didn't even create a quiver. And for the last four months he hadn't touched her at all.

So why the hell had she stuck with him for so long? Why had she opened her home and her bank account to such a loser? Because he could sing.

That was his dream, and one she believed in. In the beginning, she had been honored that he included her in his world, allowed her to help finance him. After all, they were building a future, they would be rolling in dough, but first they just had to get past the lean times. And she could help. Why shouldn't she?

"Okay, girl, you're thinking about that sorry ass brother again. Forget him," Nicki quipped.

"He wasn't the one that I was thinking about," Ashleigh lied.

"No? Then tell me, who were you thinking of?"

Ashleigh thought quickly of the man she'd met in the laundry room. The one who'd made her angry when he'd laughed at her sign. "I met the new janitor in the laundry room. He has a bad attitude."

"What did he do?"

"He laughed at me, right in my face. He ticked me off." Ashleigh caught Nicki's smirk. "What?"

"All of that emotion because some brother laughed at you. I don't buy it. Exactly why was he laughing?"

"He was laughing at my sign for the gown." Ashleigh hated admitting it because she knew what was going to happen, and sure enough it did. Nicki laughed.

"It's not that funny."

Nicki took a couple of deep breaths in an attempt to still her laughter. "Okay, Ash, I'm sorry. I just got this picture of the brother and it cracked me up." She smiled, biting her lip as she did so. She couldn't let go of the picture in her head. She decided to try again. "He was laughing, why?"

"Who knows? But I put him in his place, hinted that I thought he was gay, and you know what that does to a straight brother."

"Yeah, don't I know." Nicki grinned and the women laughed together. "So we have a new janitor," Nicki said, ignoring Ashleigh's knowing smile. Nicki was a bit man hungry; it was no secret. Everyone knew it. "Hope he's better than the last one the owner sent."

Ashleigh nodded in agreement. "I'm surprised that for such a nice building we can't get a decent janitor."

"This new guy, did he look like he knew what he was doing?"

Ashleigh eyed her friend, trying to determine if she was speaking only of the man's janitorial skills. "I don't know. He had a hammer and nails, but like I said, his laughing at my sign pissed me off. I forgot to tell him to come and change my locks."

"Girl, you know you're going to have to pay for that."

"Who cares? I just want to make sure Damien can't get back in."

"So this new janitor, what's his name?" Nicki asked, never one to lose sight of new prey.

"I don't know."

"You mean you were so damn rude to the man you didn't even ask his name or tell him yours?"

"No, why should I? It wasn't like we were having tea; it wasn't social. Like I said, there was something about him I just didn't like."

"Like what?"

"Like the fact he's another poor brother with a low paying job. I'm not into that, not anymore. Next man I'm with, gots to have money."

"I didn't know you were looking. There must have been more to get you all hot and bothered. The brother must be fine, huh? Come on, Ash, tell me he's fine. Right?"

"I don't know. I suppose he looked okay. Like I said, I wasn't interested in his looks. I mean, we're having a cleansing to get rid of one man. Why on earth would I want another one so soon?"

"To scratch that itch."

"You are so nasty." Ashleigh laughed at her friend. "Maybe you should go in the laundry room and find the janitor since you're always so horny. Then maybe you can keep your nose out of my business."

Ashleigh threw a pillow at her friend. They could say whatever they felt to each other. They'd grown up together, lived next door to each other since birth and had been best friends for a lifetime. They'd both moved from their hometown of Sawmill, Georgia, to

Chicago. The only thing they hadn't been able to do was live together. So they'd done the next best thing. They'd gotten apartments in the same building. They could spend time together yet have their own space. It was insurance for a friendship that neither of them wanted to lose.

CHAPTER TWO

"I don't want a gown someone else picked out, Keefe. You promised to help me with this wedding. You made the offer to buy the gown, now you're trying to back out."

Just as he'd expected, his little sister was not taking to this idea very well. Hell, he'd tried presenting this to her as a good opportunity, but now he was feeling every bit as stubborn as she was.

"I'm not made of money, Mia."

"You're not broke either, but you're always poor- mouthing. God, Keefe, when you die you can't take it with you."

"At the rate that you're going if I don't die soon there will be nothing left to take."

"Forget it, Keefe, I'll buy my own gown. Just forget it."

The pounding sensation began in his temples. Women. Sometimes he thought the world would be better off without them. They always wanted something from you; usually it was your money. For women everything came with a price tag. If you had enough money you could buy them what they wanted and perhaps receive some momentary peace.

"Is it because you think I have money that you won't even look at the gown?"

"No. It's because you made me a promise."

"Asking you to take a look at the gown isn't breaking my promise. You don't know how much the gown is selling for or whether you'll see it and fall in love with it. It was just an idea. You don't have to bite my head off. I swear, you women, you want one thing: a man to spend his money on you."

He wished he could take back the words but it was too late. The sudden chill in the room was evidence of that fact.

"I'm sorry, Mia."

"Forget it, Keefe. I don't want you to buy my gown, not now."

"I shouldn't have said that. I was thinking about Mom and Treece. I didn't mean to compare you to them. I really didn't."

"But you did. So you must think that about me too. Anyway, give me the e-mail address, Keefe. I'll contact the woman with the gown and make an appointment to see it. But if I like the gown, I'll buy it myself."

"No, forget it. It was a bad idea. Let's go to some of those bridal shops you wanted to go to."

"Look, Kee, don't try to humor me. I don't want your help, not any longer."

"I want to help," Keefe pleaded, wishing for once he'd not allowed his relationship with women to color his conversation with his sister. She was the only female in the entire universe who didn't want anything from him. The only one he could trust.

Hell, the whole thing had been his idea from the beginning. He'd coerced her into allowing him to help with the expenses. The only thing she'd asked of him was that he walk her down the aisle. Now he'd probably screwed that up as well.

"Mia, I really am sorry."

"I know you are, but I won't have you putting me in the same category as you do all women. Give me the address."

He dipped his hand into his pocket, his eyes never leaving his sister's face, a face so like his own: pecan coloring, dark brown eyes fringed by a massive amount of black lashes, usually smiling eyes now marred by the sparkling of tears. He couldn't believe he'd been the one to put them in her eyes.

"Mia, please."

"No," she answered as she took the paper from his outstretched hand and headed to the corner to turn on her computer. She typed in a few words, then sent the message off, leaving the speaker on.

"It's going to take time to hear from her," Keefe offered. "You may as well try a few shops while you wait for her to get back to you."

His sister merely arched her brows in a derisive manner, dismissing him. For twenty minutes he fiddled with his fingers, wondering how on earth he could possibly make things right.

"You've got mail."

His eyes turned toward the sound of the speaker. His gut told him it was the wedding gown woman. His sister headed for the computer, then called out to him, "It's her." To his surprise, he felt a little excitement. Then, reluctantly, he admitted to himself that he'd had ulterior motives in getting his sister involved with the owner of the dress.

"What did she say?" Keefe badgered. "Has she sold the dress?" For a moment he thought she wasn't going to answer.

"She told me if I'm interested to give her my number and she'll call me. She also wanted to know how I found out about it. Don't you think that's a little strange? I mean, you did say she had a notice in the laundry room of your building. Why is she being so paranoid? How does she think I got her e-mail address?"

Keefe cringed inwardly at his sister's analyzing look, wishing she didn't know him so well.

"I talked to her for a few minutes. For some strange reason she took an instant dislike to me. I don't think you should mention me.

Just tell her that a friend of yours who was in the building saw the notice and gave you the information."

"So you want me to lie?"

"Not lie. I do consider myself your friend."

"Hrrump. That's splitting hairs, you're my brother."

"What? You don't consider me to be your friend?" Keefe teased, sensing his sister's mood was lightening and she was no longer angry.

"You're my best friend, Keefe," she smiled broadly, "and I think I'm your only friend. I'm the only person alive who can stand your pompous behind." With a flourish Mia typed in her phone number and the half-truth that a friend had given her the information about the gown.

Less than five minutes passed before the phone rang. The caller ID flashed "unknown caller." Keefe and his sister both smiled at the extent the woman was going to in order to maintain her privacy.

"Hello, this is Ashleigh Johnson. Is this Mia?"

"Yes it is. Thanks for calling back so quickly. Listen, I'm sorry to hear that things didn't go so well for you. I'm a little curious, though, about why you posted the ad."

Keefe heard the laughter, even from where he was sitting. He turned his head in his sister's direction. Surely this laughing from the other end of the phone couldn't be the same surly woman he'd met. This woman sounded downright pleasant. This woman was one he'd want to meet, especially since he already knew how she looked.

He felt the beginning of a bulge that embarrassed the hell out of him. How the hell had he allowed that to happen and in the presence of his little sister?

He walked away, wanting to hear the rest of the conversation, but knowing his ardor demanded he go somewhere and cool off a bit, forget about the woman on the phone, forget about the lush round behind and the firm breasts that he could see his lips clinging to even now.

Stop it, Keefe, his inner voice scolded. *That's not the way to get rid of a hard-on.*

"Okay, big brother, I'm going to go and take a look at the gown," Mia yelled to him.

"You don't have to do that. I'm sorry I said anything. I'll buy you whatever gown you want."

"No, Keefe, the woman sounds interesting, I want to meet her. I want to know how she put you in her web so quickly."

"What the hell are you talking about...no one has me anywhere. You're crazy."

Keefe was sputtering; he backed away from his sister. "Leave me out of this. You want the gown, go look at it."

"So... Is she cute?"

"Cute is what you are." Keefe smiled into Mia's eyes, then laughed. "Okay, yes, she's beautiful, but I've never seen a woman with so much attitude."

"Who do you think you're fooling, Kee? You're interested in the woman.

"What are you talking about? I talked to the woman all of five minutes. I don't even know if I like her, let alone want to date her."

"Please, Keefe, you're protesting a bit too much. I know the signs. You don't fall often but I think you're almost there."

"All I said was..."

"I know what you said and how you said it. I also saw your eyes light up. That's interested."

"Who's the oldest here?" Keefe smiled again at his sister, glad to have this woman on his side. He knew he could always depend on her. She would have his back at all times.

He hugged her close. The two of them against the world. They had each other, always had, and always would. She was the only woman who'd never lied to him.

Still, he wanted more, for both of them. The odds of finding it weren't good. Look at the divorce rate. Hell, why was he thinking of divorce? The gown, he realized. That dammed wedding gown had him going way past the wedding day straight to divorce court.

"What's her name?" he asked.

"Ashleigh Johnson."

"When are you going over?"

"I told her I could be there in a couple of hours. She's having a group of her friends over. She said they're going to have a cleansing and said I could participate if I wanted."

"A cleansing?" Keefe frowned, wondering what the hell he was getting his sister involved in.

"You know." Mia stopped. "Sorry, you wouldn't know. You're a man." She ignored the scowl on her brother's face. "Do you want me to tell you what it is?"

"No, Mia, I was just asking for my health."

He fumed for a couple of minutes, hating the silly grin on Mia's face, the you're-dying-to-know-and-I'm-not-going-to-tell-you look. He sat until he could take the suspense no longer. "Okay, Mia, tell me. What's a cleansing?"

"You have to promise never to divulge this to another man as long as you live."

"Okay already, tell me."

"Not until you promise."

"Damn it, Mia, I promise. Now tell me."

"Well, when a sister wants to make sure she rids herself of a no good brother, no offense, she burns every picture of him and smudges everything that he ever came in contact with."

"You mean smudge as in putting a dirt mark on things?"

"No, Kee, smudge as in getting a small bundle of mixed herbs, lighting it and saying some words to keep the brother away."

"Sounds like witchcraft to me. How do you know about this?"

"Excuse me, Kee, how old do you think I am? I'm your baby sister, but that doesn't mean that I'm a baby. I read."

"Have you ever done it?"

"Not to get rid of anyone, but I participated in one in college."

"Did it work?"

"Not really, but we had a heck of a party the night we did it. We ordered pizza, drank beer and wine and got wasted. It was a lot of fun."

"But it didn't work, you said."

"No, it didn't work. Three months after we cleansed the guy out of my friend's hair she had the nerve to tell us she was pregnant by the fool."

"So why do you women keep doing it if it doesn't work?"

"It's a girl thing. It makes us feel powerful and in control, and it *can* work if the woman is strong enough not to listen to some weak line."

"So the whole thing depends on the woman's will power?"

"Of course."

"Then why bother with the incense, the smudging, the whole charade? Why go through with all of that?"

"Like I said, you're a man. It would take forever to make you understand that we do what we can to feel in control, to just get by until the pain goes away."

"Why would she ask a stranger to come to something like that? It should be personal, for friends."

"That's part of it. You depersonalize it. You invite women you don't know. The more womanpower you have, the more female energy to counteract the bad vibes from the man. The women take power from each other. It actually helps when you know you never have to see some of the people again. You can exchange energy and not have regrets about it."

Keefe stared for a moment over his sister's head. At least she seemed to know what she was doing. She didn't seem afraid that she was going to something that was over her head.

She was right. Twenty-three wasn't a baby anymore. Hell, she was getting married in six months. In his mind he knew he had to let her go, allow her to grow up. In his heart he only hoped he had the strength to do so after a lifetime of taking care of her. It would be hard not to be her knight.

Thinking like this was getting him nowhere. He had to move the subject to something he could handle. "How much for the gown?"

"Two thousand. Ashleigh said it's a seven-thousand- dollar designer original."

"Two thousand dollars for a dress that's going to be worn once? That's…" At least he had the good sense to cut off the words before anything else came from his mouth. "If you like it, it's yours," he promised.

"Good. By the way, Mama called. She said she would love to come to the wedding, but she's going to need money for a dress, a place to stay, and her fare here. She thought maybe you could let her stay in one of your empty apartments."

"Hell no!" Keefe exploded, pushing away from his sister. "Hell no."

"I want her to come. It's my wedding, I want my mother to be there."

"Then let her stay in your apartment."

A grin broke out on Mia's face. "I already told her she can. I was just yanking your chain."

"Don't. Not about her. You know how I feel."

"I know. But Keefe, she *is* your mother. One day you'll have to forgive her. You're never going to be happy until you let go of the past, our past, Keefe. Remember that. I shared the same life as you, but I've found a way to go on, to be happy. I want to be happy. Don't you? Don't you ever want to love a woman without wondering how much she plans on taking you for?"

God, women. How could you shut them up? From one blowup to another. Drama. Always drama. Mia had not lived the same life as he had. He'd been there to protect her, be her buffer. When it came to someone being there to protect him, he'd had no one.

He gritted his teeth, glancing toward his sister. She had to be deliberately trying to work his nerves. Why else would she bring up their mother to him, especially so soon after they'd made up?

The muscles in his jaw tightened, and he could feel his teeth clench. "Mia, are you baiting me?"

"What are you talking about?"

"You know damn well what I'm talking about. Don't play games."

"Are you talking about Mama?"

Her voice dripped with fake syrupy sweetness. Anyone not knowing her would think she was innocent of the crime he'd accused her of. But he was not anyone. He knew her as well as she knew him, and she was guilty as hell.

"When did she call?" he challenged. "Don't lie."

He watched as her lips parted and her eyes closed. If he were anyone else, he knew she would lie, but not to him, never to him.

"Alright, she called a couple of weeks ago, but I thought you deserved to think she wanted to stay with you, after you compared me with her."

"I didn't compare you. You're nothing like her. You're decent and kind and she's nothing but a leech. That's all she ever was."

"No, she's more than that, Keefe. She's our mother."

"That's where you're wrong. She was never a mother to either of us. She had us, period. We don't owe her a damn thing. So don't let blood influence you; she'll only hurt you. Again," he added.

Mia glanced at her brother, pain and sadness filling her eyes. "I didn't invite her only for me, Keefe. It's a gift I'm giving you. Maybe you can find the courage to take it."

"That's a hell of a gift. Why don't you just keep it?"

"I don't think I will, big brother. It's your chance to be free. I want that for you more than I want my own happiness. You've been everything to me; you deserve to live your life now. If it hadn't been for Treece, I think you would be."

"Don't start with me. That was a long time ago."

"Yes, but she's the one who put the final nail into your heart, big brother. If it weren't for her, who knows, maybe you could be with a woman right now, instead of arguing with me about it."

Only his sister could get away with mouthing off like that to him. Anyone else and he would write them off. Opinionated women. What a pain in the ass.

"Keefe, stop daydreaming."

"I can't help it. It's the only way I get to have a say." He ducked a moment before his sister's hand shot out, narrowly missing him.

"Okay, enough. I won't say anything, but just tell me this, Keefe. What was it about this woman that has you wondering?"

He wasn't wondering, was he? He tilted his head to the side, observing his sister for a moment before he answered. "Well, her note was kind of funny. I think it takes a woman with real balls…" He glanced at the disapproving look on his sister's face and amended his words.

"I think it takes a strong woman to write that kind of note. It intrigued me, she intrigued me, but make no mistake, I'm not wondering about her."

"She must have found you handsome and charming. All of my friends want to get with you. Just say the word."

"The word is, no thanks. I don't need your fix ups. As for Ashleigh Johnson, she didn't fall for anything about me. She thought I was a gay handy man."

"Handy man? Where on earth would she get that idea?"

"Handy man you question, but gay you don't even acknowledge?"

"The woman had to have been messing with your head. There's nothing about you that would ever make a woman think you're anything less than…" She stopped and started giggling.

"Go ahead," Keefe pressed her, "anything less than what?"

"Look, Keefe, this brother and sister thing can go only so far. I'm not about to tell you the things my friends say about you. Suffice it to say they think you're hot, and believe me, they're not into trying to turn any guy. They want them ready, willing and able."

She laughed again as she walked away from her brother, embarrassed to be having this conversation with him.

"Hey, you want me to drive you over to look at the dress?" Keefe grinned, not even trying to hide the fact that he wanted in on the search for the gown, or his hope that maybe after the abrupt first meeting, the laughing woman on the phone would be more agreeable.

"I don't know. If she hated you on contact, I don't want her to associate me with you."

"Look, I'll drive. I *am* paying for the dress." He took his sister's hand, pulling her out the door. When he felt the gentle squeezing of her fingers on his, he relaxed. The moment had passed. Things were as they should be with Mia.

He'd never before accused her of being like their mother, and he never wanted to again. She was nothing like the woman who had given birth to them.

"Wishes do come true," Ashleigh said, turning from the phone toward Nicki. "The woman I just talked to, Mia Black wants to see the gown. I invited her to join our cleansing." For a moment Ashleigh frowned, a puzzled expression crossing her face.

"What's wrong?" Nicki asked.

"I don't know. Mia doesn't live in the building. How did she hear about the gown?"

"Did she mention how she'd heard about it?

"Yeah, she said a friend told her about it. Do you think I should be worried?"

"What's the big deal? This is a huge building. Anyone could have seen the notice you put in the laundry room."

"You're right. It's just…I don't know, it's just a funny feeling I have." Ashleigh didn't want to mention the janitor again. She was afraid that Nicki would make more of it than need be. But the more she thought of the man's handsome face laughing, the more the funny feeling intensified. She felt a blush coming on when she realized that even in her anger she'd not failed to notice that the man was exceptionally good-looking.

"Forget your funny feeling. You do want to sell the dress, right?" Nicki smirked.

"I know what you're thinking, and you're wrong. I'm not having second thoughts. If Mia likes the dress, it's hers." Ashleigh said a little prayer. She wanted, no, she needed Mia to like the gown. Getting rid of the gown would be her first step toward a new life.

"Keefe, don't you dare say anything to mess things up."

"What's this? A couple of hours ago you were calling me cheap, feeling insulted that I would even suggest that you look at the gown. Now you're warning me how to act?"

"Now it's different," Mia smiled. The dress has some history that makes it special."

"Just don't forget you might not like the dress and it just might not fit you."

"No way, big brother. You are cheap, but you're not blind, and I know that you figured it would fit or you would not have so quickly counted up the money you would save on the dress. Now hush, Keefe. I don't know if you should even be here with me. I mean, these things are usually hostile to any male within shouting distance.

"I have legitimate business. I don't want to start off on the wrong foot with my tenants. I was thinking of introducing myself to all of them anyway, hear about their complaints and their needs."

"I'll bet," Mia answered as she rapped three times on the door. "What do I say if she asks how I got in?"

Keefe never got a chance to answer as the door opened and the woman he now knew was named Ashleigh peered out at him. She glared for what appeared to be forever before taking notice of Mia standing in front of him.

"I'm sorry, it's so noisy inside I didn't hear you at first. You must be Mia." Ashleigh completely shut Keefe out as she spoke to his sister. "I see the janitor let you in and showed you to my door. Good."

Keefe stared at her as she extended an arm toward Mia, pulling her in and at the same time closing the door on Keefe.

Mia couldn't speak, and the look on her brother's face was more than likely expressed on hers. She was pulled into the room, into a group of chattering women.

"Ashleigh, wasn't that the janitor? Get him to change your lock."

"Now?" Ashleigh stared at Nicki, then at Mia.

"No time like the present."

Mia looked toward Ashleigh's friend, her tongue unable to move. She wanted to tell them all they'd made a mistake; that the man they were talking about was her brother, the owner of the building, not the janitor.

It seemed that everything was spiraling out of control. Ashleigh was shouting her name and she had to mentally shake herself before she could concentrate enough to hear.

"Mia, please ask the janitor to come back."

"But…" Mia sputtered, "he's not…"

"Mia, please hurry before he gets away. You have no idea how hard it is to get things fixed around here."

Mia moved toward the door. She had to be dreaming. She opened the door, prepared to go down the hall and collect her brother, have him come in and tell the women the truth. His scowling face wasn't down the hall. He was standing in front of the door.

Her mouth opened in amazement. "She wants you to fix her door."

"Yeah, I heard."

"Keefe, tell her the truth."

"Not on your life, little sister. I'm going to have some fun."

Before she could plead with him, Ashleigh had come alongside her. "Thanks, Mia," she said, once again bringing her into the room. To Keefe she cocked her head toward the door. "I need my lock changed."

"Excuse me." Keefe stood there, anger fueling him at the arrogance of this rude woman standing in front of him. "Do you know how to ask?"

"Don't you get paid for this? You're the janitor, or should I call your boss and tell him he's sent us someone else who refuses to work?"

"Listen, miss…"

"Johnson."

"Miss Johnson, there has to be a reason for me to change your lock. My employer will not just okay such a change without a good reason."

"Look, I don't expect your boss to foot the cost. And if you go and get it and do it quickly and quietly without interfering with my party, I'll give you twenty bucks."

"Twenty bucks, really? Well, you should have mentioned the twenty in the beginning," Keefe answered, flashing his white teeth at her. "And don't forget the money for the lock."

Ashleigh walked away from him, hissing underneath her breath as she went to get her purse. Mia stood perplexed in the center of the room, eyeing him uneasily.

He smiled in her direction before turning toward the other women in the room who were eyeing him with open-mouthed curiosity, if not hostility.

One thing about Mia, she was never wrong. A woman's cleansing was not the place to be for a man, but he intended to stay. He wanted to see the smug look washed off Ashleigh's face when she realized he wasn't the janitor.

"Excuse me, what's your name?"

Keefe turned to face the woman with the sky-high weave and the pouty lips. God, where the hell had women ever got the idea that lining their lips with that god-awful black color was sexy?

He looked the woman up and down. She oozed sexuality, big plump breasts, wide hips and a slutty attitude. Just the kind of woman he'd dated for the past year. A woman who wanted only sex and nothing more.

Keefe's eyes darted in his sister's direction before returning to the woman standing before him. She was so obviously displaying her wares that he found her amusing. From the look in his sister's eyes, he knew she understood that he wanted Ashleigh to be taught a lesson. He'd play the game a little longer.

"My name's Cole. What's yours?"

"You can call me used to be cold, but now I'm burning up."

Keefe laughed aloud. The lusty woman had an unexpected humor about her. He smiled deeply at her. "And is 'hot' what you want me to call you?"

"No, Cole. You can call me 'ready.' What's your last name, Cole?"

Keefe felt his entire mouth pulling into a grin. The woman was a barracuda. The entire room was watching them, probably waiting for the manhunter to strike him down. "Cole Hunter," he answered, thinking himself clever in using the handle he'd just assigned to her.

"This isn't a social visit with Mr. Hunter, Nicki," Ashleigh interjected.

Keefe had seen her approach, but was determined to ignore her despite the sudden pounding in his ears, the slight flaring of his nostrils that he prayed only he knew about. While the rude woman bugged the hell out of him, there was something about her that intrigued him. He hadn't failed to notice that she had caught his name.

"Here," she muttered, snappishly handing him a fifty. "This should cover the cost of the lock. Don't buy me anything cheap, and bring me a receipt. I'll pay you the twenty when you're done."

Keefe took the bill from her outstretched hand, being careful not to touch her in the process. He turned to Miss Hot and Lusty and smiled, closing Ashleigh's money into his palm.

"See you ladies in a few." He smiled and walked out the door. He wished he were a fly on the wall. He knew his name would be mentioned. In this instant, however, he didn't need to be a fly. He had his own personal spy. He grinned. His sister would tell him everything.

"You were kinda rough on that guy." Mia smiled at Ashleigh. "Does he remind you of your ex?" She watched as Ashleigh's head snapped toward the door, hoping she'd given herself enough of an opening that Ashleigh would leap right in and tell her what she found so offensive about her brother. If she didn't have a darn good reason for treating Keefe so coldly, she wouldn't buy the gown. She didn't care how beautiful it was.

"I'll tell you why she's so cold to the brother. He's fine, that's why. And our Ashleigh has a weakness for fine brothers. Now that she's on the warpath, any good-looking man will be her target."

Mia smiled. "So you think he's good-looking?" Now this was better, this was the way it should be.

Ashleigh glared at her friend. "Nicki, would you please shut up? I must be making a horrible first impression on you, Mia. I know I'm being a bitch, but I can't help it. Right now, big mouth Nicki is right. I guess I'm taking out my anger on that guy since I can't take it out on Damien's sorry ass."

Mia pushed a little more. "He seemed nice enough to me. It must be something more than his looks."

"A little earlier today he was reading my notice. The one I put up in the laundry room about the gown. There was something about him that, shall we say, sent up warning flares. I watched him for a moment. Then he laughed at my note, and it pissed me off. I could see Damien doing the same thing if he read it."

"What do you mean you could see him doing the same thing? The brother did! Don't lie. He laughed in your face when you called off the wedding. When you told him you were selling the gown, he damn near bust a gut. Girl, if you can't be honest on the day of his cleansing, then I say this whole thing is a waste of time." Nicki folded her hands across her ample bosom, her hips stuck out in a don't-give-me-that-crap sort of pose.

Ashleigh frowned as she looked at her lifelong best friend. Only she could get away with this behavior but still it reminded her of the reason they'd been unable to live together.

As much as she loved Nicki, she could not take her constantly sticking her nose into her business and just blabbing whenever the mood struck her. Did she really have to put all of her business in the street in front of strangers? Some things should remain private.

She turned from Nicki to Mia, ignoring her friend's rudeness. "Mia, I'm sorry, would you like to see the gown now before we do the cleansing or would you like to just wait?"

Mia thought quickly of her brother. Keefe would be returning from the store anytime and if she could keep him from being caught in the cross hairs of the women in the midst of the ritual she would.

"I'm game for the ritual," Mia answered. "In fact, I've been looking forward to it."

"Then let's do it."

Nicki took Mia's hand and reached out her other to Ashleigh. "Let's burn the bastard."

A medium-size black cast iron pot had been placed on the center of the table and all around were tiny bottles containing liquid. Mia knew there were different fragrances in the bottle. She glanced curiously at the intricate pattern of black candles, then focused on two strategically placed white candles.

"What are those for?" She turned to Ashleigh.

"One's for you. You're starting a new life and at the moment even though all of us here, with the exception of you, are angry at men in general, the white candle is to wish you happiness in your relationship and purity in your marriage."

"And the other one?" Mia asked.

"It's for me, a symbolic wish that I find happiness and purity also."

"Oh," Mia smiled. "That was nice of you to think of me, thanks."

"You're welcome." Ashleigh answered. Something in Mia's voice,

her face, her smile, caught her attention. She looked vaguely famil-
iar, like someone she'd met before, but that couldn't be. She'd only
met her less than an hour before. She smiled at Mia, a little sad that
the beautiful woman with the warm brown eyes would be wearing
the wedding gown she'd dreamed of her entire life.

CHAPTER THREE

The cleansing ritual was well underway when the door suddenly opened and a tall, light-skinned brother stepped inside and halted abruptly, apparently surprised to see all the women.

Mia took a long look at him. Attractive wasn't a strong enough word. He was sporting long braids obviously freshly done and his clothes, she observed as her eyes inventoried him, were impeccable.

"Excuse me, ladies. I didn't know Ashleigh had company."

His voice. Mia stared into his sun-kissed eyes and felt her soul melting at the sound of the man's voice. Wow, she thought, and prayed she'd not said it out loud.

She watched Ashleigh's body as the man came near her. She almost appeared to be afraid of the man, though for the life of her, Mia couldn't see why. The man was obviously a brother practiced in the art of love, not fighting. He had every woman in the room drooling. Including her. Unashamedly, she listened to their oh so public conversation.

"Damien, how did you get in? I took your key."

"You know me," Damien drawled, "always prepared. I had a spare. Just thought I'd give you some time to cool off, you know. I came to make everything right."

He flashed his brilliantly white, capped teeth. You know I can't stay away for long. Come on, give me a hug."

Ashleigh stepped away from Damien. She felt herself weakening. Lord, please, she prayed. Damn that slow ass janitor. Why the hell couldn't he have changed the lock already?

"Come on, Ash, let's go in the bedroom."

Damien's voice was melodic. His eyes with a mischievous gleam lighting them hinted of what he wanted to do to her. A smile played wantonly across his face. And Ashleigh trembled.

It was as if they were alone. The room felt as though it had tipped and was now spinning. Damn. If Damien could bottle up what he had and sell it, he would never have to worry about his music career taking off. He would be rich beyond his wildest dreams. She wished him well. She really did want him to have his dreams, but she didn't have enough money in her bank account to fulfill them.

"Leave, Damien, you're not welcome," Nicki said.

Ashleigh turned her head in her friend's direction a second before flinging her hand out, palm up toward her friend. "Chill," she glared at Nicki. "I've got this." She turned back to Damien. "She's right, Damien, you're not welcome here."

"What are you talking about? This is my home. What are you gonna do, diss a brother in front of all your friends? Where am I supposed to sleep tonight? You want me to go to a shelter? Is that what you want?"

"Frankly, Damien, I don't give a damn. I only know your head will not be lying near mine tonight, or ever again."

Ashleigh backed farther way, her legs beginning to feel weak. She had mixed emotions about her friends being there.

She would be embarrassed as hell when this was over. But she knew if they weren't there, Damien would probably be whispering in her ear how sorry he was in that oh so sexy voice. The women gave her strength, but she didn't know for how long.

"I'm not leaving, Ashleigh. You can go ahead and have your little party. I'm staying, or you can come into the bedroom with me and work this out."

"Damien, there is nothing for us to work out. Don't you understand? It's over."

"If you want me out, you'll have to call the cops. I'm not leaving on my own."

Ashleigh stopped moving, glaring at Damien. He'd said the one thing he knew she wouldn't do. She abhorred the thought that so many black men were locked away. She would never be a party to sending another one behind bars.

"Damien, you're crazy if you think there's anything left to salvage here."

"We're getting married, Ash. I made a little mistake. Dang, woman, you know how hard it is. You love me. You're my woman. Do you think I like having things like this, you making all the money? You know how hard I've tried; I just can't catch a break."

Ashleigh's eyes were filling with tears. The words were the same ones Damien had spoken to her every time he'd cheated. Those words, along with the sultry voice, had always made her forgive him.

What if she was wrong? What if he really only slept with other women because he was depressed that he didn't have a job? What if he really did love her?

"Ashleigh." It was Mia calling to her. "Ashleigh, would you mind very much if I looked at the gown now?"

Ashleigh could have kissed Mia. This was just what she needed to bring her out of her trance. As she was about to answer Mia, she caught Damien looking Mia up and down, checking her out. Ashleigh could almost hear the words he was thinking, *fine piece of ass*.

"Come on, Mia, in here." As Mia followed she bellowed over

her shoulder, "Damien, get the hell out. And go get a job."

"So that's the two-timing jackass?" Mia asked.

Ashleigh looked puzzled for a long moment before she remembered her sign. Then she laughed. "Thanks, girl, I owe you one. You saved my life."

"Were you going to cave?"

"Did you hear the man's voice?"

"Oh yeah, I heard," Mia answered. "I wouldn't blame you. I would have caved myself. What does he do?"

"Not a damn thing. That's why he has such a good game. He has nothing but time to work on it."

Ashleigh fumed for a moment, then took Mia's question seriously. "He's a singer. He's been trying to make it for years now but he just hasn't gotten the break he needs."

"How long have the two of you been together?"

"Two years, four months, one day." Ashleigh looked at her watch. "And seventeen hours."

"You're still counting the time?"

Ashleigh smiled, "I didn't think so, but apparently he's not out of my system yet. He's so damn talented." She caught Mia's raised brow. "I don't mean that. He can really sing and I do believe in him. I mean, with a voice like his, for him not to be hooked up, what's wrong? Life isn't fair and I guess that's why I keep taking him back. He's right, it's hard as hell for a brother to make it."

"Not all brothers," Mia interjected. "My brother had a hard time. No one handed him anything and he made it. He never used what wasn't given to him as a lame excuse."

"You've got a brother?" Ashleigh asked.

"Yes, he's the greatest. I could introduce you to him. He'd never have his hand out."

Ashleigh stared at Mia. In a matter of minutes the young woman had summed up Ashleigh's love life, making her wonder about the innocent remark. In a way she'd been insulted by this stranger yet she didn't feel insulted, more like the woman was looking out for her. Besides it was true. All the men in Ashleigh's life so far had taken advantage of her. And they'd all had their hands out.

"No thanks, Mia. I'm definitely not in the mood for a man. I haven't got rid of this one yet."

Ashleigh went into her closet, pretending to herself that a little piece of her heart wasn't breaking. It wasn't because she wouldn't be married to Damien. It was because she was about to give away her dream. Damn Damien anyway. She gave the gown over to Mia, her hand lingering lovingly on the folds. "Here you go, here it is."

"My God," Mia exclaimed. "This is absolutely beautiful. I wish I could meet the designer. I've never seen such fantastic work."

"You're in luck." Ashleigh stuck her hand out. "I designed and made this one myself. She smoothed out an imaginary wrinkle and picked away at a piece of lint that did not exist. Her eyes closed in longing and remorse. "Go ahead, Mia, try it on."

For a moment Mia's hand stilled. "You made this, Ashleigh?"

"Yeah."

"Oh God, I don't know if I can take this dress. It's something special, isn't it? You don't want to let it go. Some have a dream house, some a dream gown. This is your dream gown, isn't it, Ashleigh? Tell me the truth."

A tear slid unbidden from Ashleigh's eyes. She couldn't prevent it. "Yes, it is. But Mia, if you like the gown you would be doing me a favor. I need to get rid of it. I can use the money. Plus, don't you see that with the gown around I might be tempted to do something totally stupid, something so bad for me?"

"I hope Damien isn't going to turn you off from love forever," Mia answered. "There are lots of good guys out there."

"Harrumph, I think from now on I'm going to be like the brothers, just a quickie, then bam, I'm outta there. No commitments, no chance of getting hurt, that's it."

"You shouldn't have any problems finding anyone. The guy who was here a little while ago couldn't take his eyes off you."

"You mean the janitor? Mia, please, I told you I'm done with broke ass brothers looking for another mother to take care of them."

"But Ashleigh, what if he isn't?"

"Listen, Mia, if it walks like a duck and quacks like a duck, it's a broke brother."

Mia looked at the gown. "Ashleigh, you could be wrong, the guy could be just the right one. Who knows? He may only be moonlighting as the janitor. He could own this entire building."

"In that case I'd want him even less. I hate liars more than I hate a leech and if the brother turns out to be a liar, I wouldn't give him the time of day. A guy needs to be up front, keep it real.

"Ashleigh, why are you selling the gown? You could keep it. Maybe the next guy will be the right one."

"Mia, I appreciate what you're trying to do, but I'll handle it, okay? I'm selling the gown because I need to purge the memory of Damien from my system. Now come on, try on the gown and let's go model it for my girls. They've never seen it."

"You mean never?"

"No, not even Nicki. I wanted them all to be knocked out when they saw me wearing it down the aisle. Look, Mia, you don't need me. Get dressed, then come on out. Okay?"

Ashleigh practically ran from the room. *Damn Damien*, she thought again. Damn him. Her dream gown was lost to her forever.

She saw the way Mia had looked at the gown. She was going to buy it. Why hadn't she told her it cost more? Why had she made it such a good deal?

Keefe didn't know if the situation he found himself in was funny or not. He'd been interviewing men for the position of janitor of his building and he was now playing the part. He looked down at the bag containing the lock for his tenant's apartment. Oh yeah, this was going to be a lot of fun.

He knocked on Ashleigh's apartment door. This time when the door opened there were no smart words, no looks from the women. The entire atmosphere of the house had changed. The women were sitting subdued. He looked around for his sister, knowing something was wrong. For a moment Keefe cursed himself for having left his only sister with a group of strange women.

"Where is she?" he asked the busty, hot woman someone had called Nicki.

"Ashleigh? She's in the bedroom with Mia. Mia's trying on the wedding gown."

Keefe shook his head, blinking. Ashleigh was not the one he was inquiring about, but at least he knew his sister was safe.

"Hey, man, who're you here with?"

The voice pulled him. It sure as hell hadn't come from one of the sisters in the room. It was too sultry, too sexy and too damn deep.

He turned quickly, seeing the reason for the women's subdued tones. They were sitting mesmerized around a tall, muscular-looking brother who was lounging on the sofa as though he were at home. The *jackass*, he thought. No one but.

The man smiled lazily at him before stretching to extend his hand to Keefe.

"Hey, brother, nice to have another man in this den of femininity. Do you know my woman?"

Keefe was sure he knew whom the man meant, but decided not to play his game.

"No, brother, I'm afraid I don't know which of these fine sisters belongs to you."

"None of us," Ashleigh snapped as she suddenly appeared.

Keefe grinned at the man standing in front of him, wishing that Ashleigh had stayed out of the room for a moment longer. The woman had a bad habit of appearing out of nowhere. He didn't have time for much thought because Ashleigh was pointing her finger in his direction.

"Damien, this is Cole. He's the janitor of the building," Ashleigh explained. "He's here to change the lock on my door so no unwanted visitors can get in."

Damien turned from Ashleigh back to face Keefe. "Man, you're trying to lock me out of my home?"

Keefe noticed some of the man's friendliness had faded but he still didn't appear to be a threat. In fact, his voice had sort of a whiny quality…just like… Just like his mother's. Damn, were all whiners destined to plague him today?

"Listen, man, I'm sorry but the lady requested it and, my brother, she is the one paying the bills."

Keefe didn't know how he knew what he said was true but he felt it in the very marrow of his being. The man was a user, pure and simple. He'd been around enough users in his life to spot one a mile away.

Keefe's glance slid to Ashleigh, and he cast her a look of pity. He'd thought she'd be stronger than that. The tough, take-no-shit veneer she wore was a cover. She was a doormat. And that he didn't need.

"So what are you going to do, kick my ass out?" Damien inquired, flexing his shoulders, rolling his head a little.

You didn't have to go there, Keefe thought, but it was too late for thinking he'd been challenged and, like it or not, he had to answer. His gaze took in his sister's worried frown and he forced a smile to his own lips.

"Well, I don't plan on leaving this apartment until after you, and I have a legal right to be here. You, on the other hand, my brother, do not."

"Are you threatening to call the cops on me, man?"

"No threat." Keefe smiled. "This is all in your hands, your choice, and you look too smooth to want a woman who's kicked you to the curb. I know a brother like you has to have some woman in reserve."

He saw the slow smile on Damien's lips. That did it; the egomaniac was hooked. All Keefe had to do was smile in return and let the man sink himself even farther.

He caught a movement to the left side of his body and glanced over. Ashleigh was trembling. He thought of her and wished, almost, that he'd not placed the guy in a position of bragging, of having to prove his sexual prowess with the ladies. Ashleigh would be the only one hurt.

"For sho, man," Damien grinned in agreement before turning toward Ashleigh. "I'm outta here."

"How is it?" Mia's voice was hesitant as she walked back into the

39

room.

Keefe watched Damien as his head turned in the direction of Mia's voice. He heard the audible intake of Damien's breath and he witnessed, along with everyone else, including Ashleigh, the riveting look he was giving Mia.

"Wow, baby girl, you look beautiful," Damien crooned as his eyes fastened on Mia.

And in a horrible instant, Keefe realized the slime had fallen just that quickly for his sister. He stood there helpless, watching as Mia's eyes focused on the man, her sweet and innocent smile turning into something more, something he'd never seen on his sister's face. She wanted Damien's attention. It was as though the man had put her under a hypnotic spell. Damn, what was he supposed to do?

Damien began walking toward Mia, appearing to be in a trance himself. Keefe watched as Mia blinked, then looked around the room, her gaze lighting on Ashleigh before she glanced toward him.

Keefe hoped his frowning face alone would be enough to dissuade her from attracting any more of the man's attention. Hell, she was supposed to be in love. That was the reason they were here, so she could buy a gown for the man she loved, the man she was to marry. Keefe was getting a bad feeling about all of this. He didn't like it one bit.

"It's not me, it's the dress," Mia offered, her eyes never leaving Damien's face. "Ashleigh made it. Anyone wearing it would look good in it."

"I don't think so, in fact I know not. It's not the dress that makes you look beautiful. It's you that makes the dress look beautiful," Damien answered Mia. "The man you're going to wear that for will be very pleased."

Damien turned to Ashleigh. "I agree with your decision to sell the gown. You may not have known it when you designed and made it, but this gown was meant for her." He glanced again at Mia. "No one but her would do it justice." With that he turned and left.

Keefe stared at Ashleigh. She was sad, that was evident. There was no way in the world she could have hidden that.

His stomach knotted up as he continued looking at her and he stifled the groan that wanted desperately to escape. Damn. The last thing he needed was to become interested in a woman on the rebound.

Her gaze lifted and he waited for her rude comment. One more nasty word from her and he'd allow his brain to take over. His hormones wouldn't control him. He squared his shoulders waiting for her acid tongue, his jaw as hard and firm as steel.

"Thank you," Ashleigh all but whispered.

His eyes flicked over her. For a moment he wanted to jab his fingers in his ears just to make sure he'd heard right. "What did you say?" he asked softly, his eyes never leaving her face.

"I said thank you. That could have gotten really ugly. You handled it as only a man would and for that I'm grateful. Damien left here still feeling he's the man."

"Yeah, but that thing with…" He inclined his head toward his sister. "He was drooling over her, that was nasty."

"Nasty but true," Ashleigh answered him as she also looked toward Mia. "Cole, you have to admit Mia's beautiful. Don't you think so? And please don't lie. I detest liars."

Keefe knew she was testing him. He took a long look at his sister's smiling face as she blushed, accepting the women's compliments, all of them telling her the same thing the slime ball had said. She was beautiful. There was no denying it. His lips pulled into a smile as he watched her. He was so proud of her, his baby sister.

He turned back to Ashleigh, the disappointment evident on her face. "If I said anything other than the truth you'd know I'm lying. Of course she's beautiful, but there's one thing your boyfriend got wrong. You would look just as beautiful in that gown."

Keefe grinned wickedly at Ashleigh, true admiration coloring his words. "You're fantastic. That dress is beautiful."

She smiled and he was lost. He knew exactly how Damien had felt when he looked at Mia. Ashleigh's smile warmed his heart, made him forget that she was not even technically on the rebound. Her hurt was fresh; she was still bleeding from the wound Damien had just inflicted. Still, he couldn't stop the pounding of his heart or the adrenaline pumping through his veins.

Just as quickly as the feeling flooded his body, Ashleigh turned from him and said to Mia, "Mia, one thing Damien is never wrong about and that's beauty. He may be a two-timing jackass but he was right. That dress was made for you. You look gorgeous. And if you still want it after all the drama I've put you through today, I'll give it to you for fifteen hundred. Just my way of saying I'm sorry you had to witness all of this." Having gotten the words out, Ashleigh's hands fluttered to her side.

"Ashleigh, this is your dream dress, of course I love it. The moment I stepped into it I felt special, like Cinderella. If you're sure you want to sell it to me I definitely want to buy it."

"Then consider it yours."

"Thanks." Mia couldn't help smiling. She was trying her best not to glance at her brother. For now he would remain Cole. Still, she knew she would capture his attention with her next words. "But not for fifteen hundred dollars, Ashleigh. I wouldn't be able to take it from you for that. I would feel as though I'd caught you vulnerable and cheated you. Three thousand and not a penny less."

"Three thousand," Keefe roared, unable to keep his tongue. "Three thousand dollars for a wedding gown that's just been offered to you for fifteen hundred?"

He'd taken a step toward Mia when all the women in the room turned in one synchronized movement to stare at him.

"Why is this your business?" one of the women inquired. "Look, you may have helped with that dawg but this is not your concern."

Mia laughed at him. "Don't worry, Cole. My big brother is buying this gown. He owes me and I know him. He would never approve of me taking advantage of anyone, so Ashleigh gets three thousands dollars."

Keefe watched in horror as Mia stuck her hand out and Ashleigh took it. The women shook on the deal.

Keefe knew what was coming next as Mia sashayed across the room, the dress billowing out behind her. She was going for her purse and her checkbook tucked inside. The joint account they had for emergencies.

This isn't an emergency, he thought as he tried not to look at his sister gleefully writing out a three thousand dollar check from their account. Not a dime of the money was hers.

A thousand dollars more than the original asking price, fifteen hundred more than what she could have gotten it for. Oh yeah, he should have known he was going to have to pay for his earlier comments.

CHAPTER FOUR

"Hey, baby girl."

"My name's Mia."

"Okay then, hey Mia. I see you bought the gown. You did look good in it."

Mia glanced up toward the building she'd just left, wondering if anyone could see her standing outside talking with Damien.

"You serious about getting married? I mean now, after meeting me?"

Her laugh came quick. This brother was good. She'd say that for him. What a line. She'd never heard anything so weak.

"What do you think?" She pointed at the heavy bag she was holding. "I just bought a wedding gown."

She felt her body shiver as Damien's eyes slid over her. "What are you doing here? You left Ashleigh's apartment over an hour ago."

"I was waiting for you."

"Why?" Mia asked, her pulse racing. She should not be standing on a public street almost flirting with this man who'd just two-timed his girlfriend of two years. A leech, a man with no job, no visible means of support. She was getting married.

She clutched the bag tighter. That voice. She couldn't help it; she felt the magnetic pull toward the man. All she wanted was to fall into his arms and kiss him senseless.

"Want me to give you a ride home?"

"I have my own transportation." She thought of Keefe and

smiled inwardly. He'd nearly had a stroke when she'd upped the price. Served him right, she thought. It would also serve him right if she took off with this cad.

"Could we go somewhere for a minute, talk, get a drink?"

"I'm getting married," she answered softly.

"I know," Damien answered, "but I think I've fallen in love with you and by the way you were looking at me upstairs I think maybe you felt something too."

"I can see why Ashleigh dumped you. Man, you're a true dog."

Mia watched as Damien's gaze rested on her lips before he answered her.

"I am. You're right, I am a dog and she had every right to dump me. But I wasn't deliberately playing her, and I didn't mean for her to get hurt."

"You mean you didn't intend to get caught but you did and now you're looking for another meal ticket. First, I'm engaged and second, I don't take care of men. I won't support you or pay your bills."

"That's cold."

"Cold but true. Now what is it you want?" Mia frowned at him, trying her best to get her body to behave. Lord help her. She wanted this no good man standing before her.

"I want you," Damien answered honestly. "I want to make love to you. I want to taste every inch of your delicious brown body and start all over. I want to lick you from bottom to top. I want you in my bed, I want to wake up with you beside me and go to sleep with you curled in my arms. That's what I want."

Mia felt wetness between her legs. This shouldn't be happening. Damn that super sexy voice of his. It was entwining her in a cloud of lust. She was drowning and drowning fast. She needed something to hold on to, to pull her back up. This man was everything her brother had warned her about. Still, she wanted him.

"You know, Damien, you have an awful lot of nerve talking to me that way. I know what you're about. You sleep around; even you admit it. As for myself, I'm engaged.

She held her ring finger out to him for emphasis. "And even if I weren't, I'm not into sloppy seconds. And I definitely don't do booty calls. So, as you can see, I'm not interested."

"You're interested alright."

"Excuse you."

"You're interested, or you would have walked away by now. You're interested; make no mistake about that. We both are, so stop playing coy and go with me to have a drink. You can always leave. I promise you the one thing I'm not is violent and I never take a woman by force."

Mia ran her tongue across her lips. She looked away from Damien and back up toward the building. How could she even be anticipating going somewhere with him?

"Like I said, Damien, I'm not into paying for men. Do you have money for the drinks?"

He smiled slow and easy before pulling his wallet from his tight fitting jeans. He opened it up and announced unashamed, "I've got twenty-two bucks. We can go to Mickey D's," he teased.

"Is that money from Ashleigh?"

"I don't know," he answered again honestly, "probably is."

"Let me store this dress in my car, then make a call." She was doing it. She was actually going through with it. Mia punched in her brother's cell number, guilt hammering away at her. God, she'd never lied to him, thought she never would.

"Hey, I'm going to store my dress in the trunk. I'm so psyched from everything I just want to go for a walk."

"You'd don't have to do that. I'll come down and take you home."

"No, that's not necessary. I want some time alone." Mia felt a burning sensation hit her stomach and rise to her gut. If her brother didn't hang up soon she would throw up. He would hate that she lied, that she was turning out to be like their mother.

A lone tear slid down her cheek and she clicked the phone off. She had a choice; she knew it. She could send Damien packing right now and the guilt would go away. She wouldn't have to lie to her brother. She wouldn't have to think about her fiancé. She wouldn't have to be like her mother.

That was strange, Keefe thought as he pocketed the phone back into the holster on his belt. Why would Mia call him to tell him she wanted to walk?

Damn, how insensitive of him. He was her ride. He should have told her to just take the car and he would find his own way home. Now he had one more thing to make up to his baby sister, one more thing to feel guilty about. He felt eyes watching him. Ashleigh's eyes. When he turned in her direction, her head jerked toward the lock. He got it. She wanted him gone.

"Your lock is done." He smiled at her. "Any more repairs that you need while I'm here?" He ignored the smirks of her friends who were lingering still.

"No, none." Ashleigh answered, "though I would like to know if you're living in the building and how I can reach you if I need you."

Keefe thought quickly. He didn't want to tell her just yet who he really was. He searched the pocket of his shirt. Finding nothing, he was forced to ask, "Could you give me something to write on? I'll leave you my pager number."

"You don't live in the building? You could just give me your apartment number or…" She hesitated, not wanting the man to get the wrong idea. Sure, she'd thanked him for his assistance with Damien, but she wasn't in the market for a new man. "Just a sec, I'll get you some paper."

Keefe sensed the hesitancy in her. At least they'd moved from sworn enemies to janitor-tenant relationship. Things would break; she'd need him.

"Listen," he said to her as he handed over his pager number. His voice dropped to a low, co-conspirator whisper. "This number is not for all the tenants in the building. I hear that the owner is looking for a second janitor. I'll only be doing emergency jobs."

"So what are you going to be, like the head janitor?"

Keefe rubbed the back of his ear, trying to decide if she was being condescending, sizing up the amount in his bank account by the title of his job. For now he'd let it go. "No, not the top janitor, just I'm not available or qualified to handle all the things that could go wrong in a building this size."

"So a man that finally admits he's not king of the universe. How refreshing."

This time Ashleigh was smiling; she was teasing him. He smiled back, not answering, the lock done but not wanting to leave, just wanting to talk to her a bit longer. But he had no excuse, no reason for lingering. "See you later." He smiled at her again and left before she asked him to.

"You're glowing."

"Am I?"

"Yes, you must really love that gown."

"The gown?" Mia looked away from her brother. "Yes, the gown. It is beautiful, isn't it?"

"I have to agree with you there, but what was the deal with you paying twice what she wanted?"

"I didn't think it was fair to just take it from her. Ashleigh is a dress designer. This is her dream gown; she's been planning it in her mind for years. She told me she spent forever making sketches. She worked on this until it was perfect."

"Yeah, too bad she didn't find the perfect guy to marry. Can you believe it? That guy was scum, pure and simple."

"No one's all bad."

"He is."

"Keefe, you don't even know him."

"I know enough. Why are you defending the creep? Because he told you you were beautiful? Don't you know he did that to hurt Ashleigh? Hell, he'd sleep with anything that breathes."

I want you. The sound of Damien's voice purring in her ear wouldn't leave her. She thought of the time they'd spent in, of all places, McDonald's. Five hours she'd spent with him and the time had flown by. He wasn't all bad as Keefe thought. He was funny and sweet. There was more to the bad guy than her brother thought.

"Are you saying I didn't look beautiful in the gown, that he was only lying?"

She was deflecting her brother's attention away from her defense of Damien. She commanded the tears that weren't far away to come. She felt horrible manipulating Keefe this way, but she had to. She didn't want him asking questions about Damien. But it was all wrong. God, it was so wrong.

"Mia, I'm sorry, that wasn't what I meant. That was the one thing the guy was right about. You looked beautiful and I'm glad you bought the dress. James will never forget the way you look in it when you march down the aisle to marry him. I just meant Damien didn't have to hurt Ashleigh that way. He didn't have to be so crude. Hey," he continued, "when is that fiancé of yours going to come home? It's been awhile now."

"Who knows?" Mia answered. "He was due leave two months ago but with everything's that's going on it was cancelled. I don't think any sailors are having leave for a long time."

"What about the wedding? He'll be able to come home for that, won't he?"

Mia smiled sadly at her brother before answering. "Six months is a long time. I don't know what's going to happen."

"You're worried about him, aren't you?" Keefe pulled his sister into his arms, making room for her on the sofa. "Don't worry, he's going to be okay. I promise, nothing's going to happen. "You're going to marry him as planned."

Puzzled, he wiped away at the tears that continued to flow. His sister didn't generally cry and now she was crying as though her heart were breaking. He thought of the gown; that damn gown. Ever since he'd mentioned it both of their worlds had been turned upside down.

He did have one thing to be thankful for: his sister was marrying a man he approved of. She'd never become involved with scum like Damien.

"Keefe, why are you so late?"

Keefe kissed his sister quickly on the cheek. "I'm not that late. Besides you've canceled dates with me three times already." He looked at his sister. "What's up, Mia? Are you doing something that I should know about?"

Keefe eyed his sister carefully, sensing that he'd hit on something. She was speechless and for Mia that was indeed a first. She was blushing, her brown cheeks made rosy from her embarrassment. Keefe squinted closer. "Mia," he called to her.

He watched as some type of metamorphosis took place within his sister. She was standing before him, his little sister, and for some strange reason she didn't seem as innocent as he'd always imagined. He was scared. "Mia, is something going on with you?"

"I might ask you the same. Look at how you're dressed. Coveralls? Why don't you just wear jeans? You're still trying to pretend to be a janitor and you're asking me what I'm doing."

She was trying to turn the tables. He knew it but still she had a point. Besides, he didn't know if he was ready to deal with a secret that his baby sister was hiding.

"Ashleigh paged me; she had a leaky faucet. What was I supposed to do?"

"Hello… call the janitor."

"Yeah, but she paged me."

"Keefe, how long do you think you can get away with this game? Besides, I don't think Ashleigh's ready to date yet."

"How would you know?"

Mia turned away. She shouldn't have said anything. Now how was she going to get out of this one? "It's too soon, Keefe. Besides, if you want a shot at her you need to tell her the truth."

"Mia, I'm tired of gold-digging females, you know that.

Ashleigh intrigues me but I don't want to rush into anything, you know."

"Listen, Keefe, if she was with Damien, how can you think she's a gold digger?"

He shrugged. "Some of the things I've heard her say to her friends. She's looking for a man that's loaded, someone to take care of her."

"She didn't really say that." Mia paused, staring at her brother. "Did she?"

"Those were her exact words."

"Well," Mia continued, "she has a good reason for feeling like that, but still I don't think you should keep lying to her."

Keefe could feel his own attitude changing. He was no longer in a cheerful mood. Damn Mia, she was forever making him face things he didn't want to face. "Listen, Mia," he said after glaring at her. "She has her reasons and I have mine. I don't want another woman in my life who's interested in the size of my bank account."

"You're talking about Mom."

"Of course I'm talking about Mom. Who else would I be talking about? She was forever chasing after some man with money and she'd drop him as soon as she met another one who had a little more."

"Keefe, you're going to have to get over all of that, learn to forgive her."

"God, Mia, what's wrong with you? You're awfully quick these days on forgiving. You go ahead. I can't just forgive that easily."

"Keefe, nobody's perfect, everyone disappoints us sometimes."

He glanced at his sister, certain now there was something else that was beneath the words she'd spoken. But he was positive he didn't want to know her secret.

"You're wrong, Mia, you're perfect. You're the one person I know who will never disappoint me."

CHAPTER FIVE

"Ashleigh, why do you keeping coming up with these lame ass excuses to get Cole into your apartment? Why don't you just give the man the green light, let him know you're interested?"

"I didn't tell you I'm interested. Besides, he hasn't said a word to me.

"Even if he did you wouldn't give him the time of day, all because of that no good Damien."

Ashleigh turned to look at her friend. "I guess you're right, but I can't afford to take the chance again of falling for someone who's headed nowhere. You're the one who's been telling me that I was crazy to be sticking with Damien. Now I agree. I was crazy."

"Crazy in love?"

"Not really, not in the last year or so, but I did want to see Damien make it. He's had such a hard time."

"Yeah? Tell me something. Why couldn't he have tried harder to make a living, a gig singing every now and then? He's too damn old. It's time he gave up dreaming and started making a living."

"I don't know why you of all people would say something like that. If we'd listened to our parents we wouldn't be here now. They thought we were dreaming, that we needed to just get good jobs in the mills, find some guy and get married, stop dreaming. Remember?"

"Yeah, I remember, but so what? We didn't listen to them; we followed our dreams. Now you have your shop, and I have a good job on Judge Tony's show. Before long I'll make associate producer. But that doesn't mean we have to take in every stray cat that comes along wanting to be fed."

Ashleigh laughed at that. The thought of Damien being a stray cat was funny. She couldn't imagine him homeless. "Even after everything that's happened, I still like the guy, not love, so don't go getting crazy on me, but I do like him."

Nicki grunted, "Speaking of that mangy dog, have you heard from him?"

Ashleigh nodded her head. "Yeah, he called."

"What did he want, another chance?"

"No. He told me he was sorry that he'd hurt me. He promised one day he'd make it up to me."

The women looked hard at each other, then clinked their glasses together. "He's good, I'll give him that. He's very good, Ash. And the brother is fine."

"That he is," Ashleigh sighed. "But this time I really believe it's over. He sounded different." Ashleigh looked toward her friend who was glaring menacingly at her. "I know. I know what you're thinking. What are we doing wasting our time talking about Damien?"

"Yeah, when it's perfectly obvious that you've got a thang for the janitor."

Ashleigh could feel the heat of embarrassment rising through her body. She wasn't interested in Cole but she would admit to being heated when around him.

"Have you taken a good look at him? There's something not quite kosher there. I mean he's...he's...

"Fine?"

"Not that, well, I guess he is," Ashleigh laughed, "but he's something else. I can't believe he's a janitor. He's intelligent, cultured. He could be so much more."

"Ashleigh, don't do that. Don't go down that road again. No more trying to make guys over either. He's what you want or he isn't. You can't fix him, okay? And that crap about him being intelligent so he shouldn't be a janitor, do you know how that sounds?"

"I know, but I didn't mean it like that and you damn well know it. And as far as Cole is concerned, I'm not thinking of fixing him, I was just wondering." Ashleigh laughed. She was wondering alright. She was wondering why it had been such a long time since she'd made love, since she'd wanted to make love. She had almost thought something was wrong with her; that the sexual part of her had died. Now she knew that wasn't true. She was very much alive.

"You're going to have to bite the bullet and tell Ashleigh the truth," Mia blurted out to her brother, feeling like the hypocrite she was. Here she was lying to him and she was reprimanding him on honesty. If that didn't beat all.

"I know," Keefe answered, "I'll admit I like her."

"Then why haven't you told her?"

"First, she was rebounding, or did you forget that no good Damien?"

"Don't," Mia interrupted, "just tell me why you haven't said anything to Ashleigh. Its not like I'm telling you to marry her or anything." At the mention of marriage Mia could feel a flame of regret. She licked her suddenly dry lips. Oh God, what was she doing? Finding Ashleigh another man would never make up for what she was doing, and her brother, would he ever trust her again when he found out?

Mia squinted her eyes shut. What she was doing to Keefe was far worse that anything she'd ever imagined their mother had done. If her big brother never learned to trust women again, the fault would be traced back to her.

"Keefe, I'm sorry to be always sticking my nose in your business. I just want you to be happy, that's all. And you...you've had this thing for Ashleigh from the moment you met her. I'll stay out of it, okay? If that's what you want I won't say another word." His laughter surprised her.

"You stay out of my personal life? You couldn't do that on a bet. Besides, I like you meddling, Mia. I can count on you to tell me the truth. You're always looking out for me, no hidden agenda, so your meddling is okay."

"In that case stop wearing those awful coveralls. Ashleigh thought you were the janitor when you were wearing jeans. Please, go back to the jeans."

"Deal." He tore off a paper towel from the holder and rolled it in the palm of his hand before playfully tossing it at Mia.

"Do you think she's going to flip when she finds out I own the building?"

"I'm not sure, but the one thing she said that stuck in my head was that she hates liars."

"Yeah, I know." Keefe looked over his sister's head, wanting to dismiss the strange way she was behaving whenever they talked of Ashleigh. He'd noticed it for the past few weeks and he knew for sure it wasn't his imagination.

"Mia, is there something about Ashleigh that you don't like?" He watched her closely, determined to see if he could figure it out.

"Why are you asking me that? If I didn't like her, I wouldn't be telling you to ask her out." Mia's hand went to her hair and she found herself twirling strands of the curly locks around her finger. She couldn't bring herself to meet her brother's gaze.

"That's the reason, Mia." Keefe shrugged, pointing to her playing with her hair. "You won't look at me when you mention her name. Why?"

"I guess I feel guilty about having her dress." Darn, the lie had come out as easily as all the rest. She was going to have to take her own advice, tell Keefe before it was too late, before he found out for himself that she'd been lying to him for over a month. And poor James. What was she going to tell him? A "Dear John" letter when he was so far from home would be undeniably cold and heartless.

"Mia, what's wrong?"

Her brother's voice, soft and caring, brought the tears she'd been fighting. "I want you to be happy, Keefe. I want us both to be happy, to be in love and have someone love us. That's all that I want."

She felt her face being pressed into her brother's chest. As he tried to comfort her, his words at first were muffled by her tears. Then as she calmed she allowed herself to hear him.

"Mia, it's going to be okay. I should have known how worried you are about James. All this talk on the news every night, how could you not be worried? There's always another war to fight. I'm sorry I've been so insensitive, worrying about trying to get a woman to go out with me, worrying that she's seeing dollar signs and here you are worried if the man you love will come home alive. Mia, you're so brave, so brave," he crooned. "I'm so proud of you."

His words made her cry all the harder. When he found out he would know she was a fraud, that she wasn't brave at all. She was a coward. A coward who didn't want to risk losing her brother, have him look at her with the same distaste that claimed him whenever he spoke about their mother.

Mia thought about James and how he was going to be hurt. Then she thought about Damien and the way he made her feel and she shivered. From the tips of her toes to the top of her head she shivered. She clung to her brother, not wanting to let go of this moment in time. One day soon it wouldn't be like this. One day she would be forced to tell her brother the truth. She loved him, she owed him that much.

"Ashleigh, would you like to go to dinner with me tonight or any night this week?" Keefe stood with his wrench in his hand waiting for Ashleigh's answer. The silence was getting to him, so he tucked the wrench into the back pocket of his jeans. He was nervous as a schoolboy as he caught the flicker of indecision that flashed in Ashleigh's eyes. Then his nervousness turned to anger. He'd seen that look before, the calculating look of a woman measuring him by what he possessed. Damn her. And damn Mia for pushing him to ask her out. He'd been planning on telling her the truth on their date. Now to hell with her.

"Cole, doesn't your boss have a policy against you dating the tenants?"

"Why do you think he would care who I date?" Keefe glared at her, hating that he'd ever told her a lie about his name. Sometimes it was hard to remember who the hell Cole was. "I'm an adult, Ashleigh. No one can tell me who to date." He watched her. Her delicate brown fingers were engaged in some kind of rhythmic dance.

Say yes, Ashleigh's heart screamed to her, *say yes, give him a chance*. Then a much louder voice drowned out the voice of her heart. This one belonged to her friend. *Ash, don't be a fool. The guy looks mighty tasty. Go ahead and take a bite. Just don't get attached to him.*

Ashleigh looked into the hazel eyes of the man standing before her. She appraised him, his short-cropped hair and immaculate dress. She smiled as she thought about it. Every time she'd seen Cole he appeared to have just stepped from a barbershop. The obviously brand new jeans fit his muscular frame like a glove, yet he seemed more suited to silk shirts and silk ties, Armani suits and…

Ashleigh stopped, embarrassed to have been daydreaming. She admitted to herself that a date might just give her a chance to see Cole in a silk shirt. At the thought of that possibility she almost said yes. Almost. "Listen, I'm sorry, Cole, I was just wondering about something."

"What?" he asked, thinking she was more than likely going to ask if he had a wife or a girlfriend.

"Why are you a janitor?"

Keefe bit his bottom lip. There it was. He took a step away, wishing he'd ignored Mia's meddling. "What's wrong with being a janitor?" he asked.

Ashleigh saw the instant change in him, saw him bristle. "There's nothing wrong with it, but you're intelligent, you could be so much more."

"You know, you sound like a snob. I asked you out for dinner and I didn't ask you to pay for the meal. If you think that's the problem, then let me put your mind at ease."

That was both a dig at her previous relationship and acknowledgement of the fact that Ashleigh was proving to be exactly the kind of woman that Keefe had promised himself he would never again become involved with.

"Sorry, Ashleigh, I shouldn't have asked you out. I forgot I'm having dinner with my sister tonight."

"Your sister?"

There was a spark of interest, making Keefe wish he'd never mentioned his sister to Ashleigh.

"What's your sister's name?"

For a long moment Keefe simply stared at her. He wasn't going to lie about Mia being his sister, but he felt no compunction to be straight with Ashleigh. After all, he could see their relationship was going nowhere. So he gave her a half grunt and a partial smile. "My family's not up for discussion." Then he turned and started walking away. "Ashleigh, I think it's better from now on if you just called the regular janitor to handle your problems," he said over his shoulders.

Ashleigh watched as Cole walked away from her, knowing she'd hurt his feelings, something she'd never intended. She'd have to make it up to him, and not just because she wanted him. He was a nice guy. She'd give him some time to cool off, then she'd call him. She'd repair the damage.

"Cole, I'm really sorry if I hurt your feelings. I'd like to make it up to you."

Keefe put his hand over his cell phone and whispered to Mia, "It's Ashleigh," before taking a breath, readying himself to refuse her request for further janitorial services.

"That won't be necessary," he said to Ashleigh.

"I think it is. I'd like to make it up to you by cooking dinner for you. How about tomorrow night?"

"I'm busy tomorrow," Keefe answered her. "Thanks anyway."

"How about Friday? Are you busy then?"

"Yes, I have a date on Friday."

"Do you have a date on Saturday also?"

"I'm afraid I do, Ashleigh, but thanks for calling." He ended the call and turned to his sister, smiling at her wide-eyed expression. He thought of not telling her what the conversation was about but knew he'd have no peace until she got the information she wanted.

"What was that all about, Kee?"

"She wanted to make up for what she thought hurt my feelings. She wanted to make dinner for me."

"And you said no?"

"Yes, I said no."

"Why?"

"Because I don't need her crumbs. I asked her out, and she made it obvious that she doesn't want to go out with me. I'm good enough for her to have a kiss off dinner in her apartment but not to go out with in public. Someone might see her with the janitor."

"I don't think she's like that. Really, she seemed nice, not like she judges people by their job. Maybe she's gun-shy." Mia looked down, not wanting to say it, "Maybe she's like you, Kee. Maybe she doesn't want to be hurt."

Keefe looked at his sister, wondering if Mia could be right. "Well, it's too late now, I said no."

The phone rang again and Keefe and Mia looked at each other. "It's her," Keefe said to Mia's look as he answered his phone.

"Cole, I really am sorry," Ashleigh said. "Just come over and let's talk about it. I miss seeing you. I was hoping we could continue being friends. Come on over, okay?"

"Tomorrow," Keefe answered, hating that he was still answering to the name of Cole. That he would rectify. "Ashleigh, I don't know if we're ever going to be friends but my friends don't call me Cole, they call me," he stopped, glanced at his sister and smiled, "they call me Kee."

"Kee, but why? That has no connection with Cole."

"Would you please just call me Kee? I think I hate the name Cole."

"Okay, Keeee. She said his name in an exaggerated singsong. "Seven tomorrow night?"

"I'll be there at seven. And Ashleigh, it's only two e's."

Keefe smiled at his sister. One lie down and one to go. "I'll tell her the truth tomorrow." He noticed the look that came into Mia's eyes when he uttered his last words. A strange piercing touched him and he felt pain and sadness intermingled, emotions he'd never had concerning his baby sister.

"Mia, you're keeping something from me. I can feel it. You need to tell me what it is. You know I'll do everything I can to help you." He saw the look in her eyes rapidly change to fear.

"Mia, you're scaring me now. Stop it." He rapidly ran down possible things that could be affecting his sister. James was away; she couldn't be pregnant. It couldn't be money problems; she had full access to his bank account. Then Keefe smiled; maybe she'd spent too much money and was worried about it. That could be the reason for her behavior, he thought, though his heart told him it was something far more serious.

"So what did you do, go overboard on shopping, spend a little too much, and now you don't know how to tell me?" He was teasing her, hoping to make that frightened look in her eyes go away.

"I wish it were only that," she answered at last.

Another stab to his heart. He swallowed, saying a quick prayer before asking his next question. "Are you ill?" God, what would he do if anything ever happened to her?

"Not in the way you mean. I'm crazy, I must be."

The crushing pain that had been close to consuming him lightened its grip. He was curious when a smile pulled at his sister's lip and turned into a full grin. "Mia, tell me. I'm imagining the worst things possible. Just tell me and get it over with."

"Okay, you asked for it. I'm not sure if I want to marry James."

"What? You're kidding. When did this happen?"

Mia was watching her brother's features closely, waiting for signs of revulsion to set in, for him to compare her with their "love 'em and leave 'em" mother. "I don't know for sure. It's just that I keep thinking about it and I don't know that I'm ready to get married. I don't rush home anymore to see if there's a letter waiting for me and I don't get that same feeling when I don't get his letters." She saw her brother lower his eyes, not wanting to look at her most likely, not wanting to see what was probably in her eyes, that she was falling in love with another man.

"Mia, couldn't it just be that it's been so long and… and… I know that you're afraid of what might happen. I think you just don't want to deal with losing him."

"I don't think that's it, Keefe."

"Mia, how can you do this to him? It's so wrong. He's away fighting for our country and now you decide you don't love him."

His eyes closed and he felt fingers around his throat tightening as he allowed the pain of what he saw in her eyes to register. His baby sister hadn't just stopped loving her fiancé. She'd found a replacement. He thought of all the dates with him she'd missed in the last month. Hell, she'd been crazy in love with James when she went to Ashleigh's and paid way more for that damn gown than he'd wanted to pay. A chill traveled up his spine as he remembered the way Damien had looked at Mia and Mia had looked at him in return.

It couldn't be. He stood staring at her, the tears streaming down her cheeks. There was something else strange about that day. Mia had left him there at the apartment building and gone home alone. He didn't want to think it, didn't want to know. How the hell could he start a relationship with a woman knowing his baby sister was banging the woman's no-good ex?

"Kee, let me explain," Mia begged, knowing that her brother knew. She'd watched him watching her and the instant he knew she saw the pain she'd inflicted on him, saw the shudder of disgust he'd tried to shake off.

"I don't want to hear any more, Mia. I think we've talked enough for one night. I don't want to know."

"I don't like lying to you, but I didn't want you to hate me. I love you more than anyone on the face of this earth. I'll do everything in my power to keep your love."

"Then stop whatever you're doing and stick to your plans to marry James. He's a good man, he loves you and you love him. You're lonely, Mia. That's my fault. I've been so busy hanging around Ashleigh that I haven't spent enough time looking out for you. Don't worry, all of that's going to change. I'm going to stick to your side like glue until James returns and you're married."

Mia laughed, though she found nothing funny. "What about your date tomorrow night, or is it a date for three?"

"I'll cancel the date. You're what's important right now."

"Big brother, you can't be with me every minute of every day. It would be impossible. Besides, I want you to keep that date." She bit her lip, knowing he now knew the reason for her tears.

"I think I'll just go home, Mia. I'm getting tired."

"I thought we were going to a movie?" Mia asked, knowing full well that neither of them was in the mood for a movie.

Keefe bolted for the door, not kissing his sister goodnight, just wanting to stop looking at her. He didn't want to know what he knew. He stood outside her door, his heart breaking. When they were little he had been the one who had tucked her in and read bedtime stories to her, the one who had kissed her goodnight.

Now by choice he'd not done what he'd done her entire life. He turned and knocked on the door. Mia answered, tears streaming down her face. Neither spoke. Keefe leaned in and kissed her forehead. "Good night, baby sister."

CHAPTER SIX

Keefe knocked on Ashleigh's door; kicking himself for coming over, for letting himself in for the hurt he knew was coming. He could feel the hot breath of doom shadowing him, yet here he stood waiting to begin a game with fate that he could not win.

"Cole, I'm so glad you didn't change your mind about coming." Ashleigh was smiling at him and wonderful smells of cooking were coming from the apartment. That settled it. He'd at least get a meal out of it before he dropped his bombshell. His stomach was growling; he was famished.

He stepped into the room, noticing that Ashleigh was appraising him. He took a step back and looked down at his own body. "What...what's wrong?"

"Oh nothing," Ashleigh answered, not knowing how she could tell him that she'd pictured him arriving in one of the Armani suits and silk shirts she'd imagined him in. "I just thought that maybe you'd come dressed for dinner, not for work."

So that was it. He'd not known exactly how he should dress for her and had decided at last to go with another pair of jeans, a decision that he would have normally checked out with Mia. But after last night he'd decided to go this one alone. Besides, he knew his sister wanted to talk, to confess her sins to him and he wasn't up for it. No, he'd rather pretend to be an ostrich and keep his head buried in the sand for the moment.

"Are you saying you don't like the jeans?" He shrugged his

shoulders. "This isn't a real date, so why pretend?"

Not like the jeans? Not like the way his behind looked in the denim, how they made his long legs appear even longer and oh so muscular? No, she definitely had no problem seeing him in jeans, unless you called the fact that every time she saw him in jeans she felt a tightening in the pit of her stomach that made her want to see him out of the jeans as quickly as possible.

Ashleigh could feel the beginning embers of desire and with the slightest help from Cole, oh excuse her, a little help from the man who now wanted her to call him Kee, and it would turn into a raging fire.

"There isn't anything wrong with what you're wearing. I was just curious, that's all." She hesitated for only a moment. "There's something else that I'm curious about, your jeans. They're always new. Why? Are you paid enough money that you never have to wear the same ones twice?"

Keefe lowered his eyes and watched Ashleigh from underneath his lashes, calculating the chances of her knowing who he really was, wondering if she was totaling up his net worth in her head. "Is money of interest to you?" he asked at last.

"Money is of interest to everyone. Nothing's free in this world, Cole."

He quirked his eyebrow up and she amended the name. "Listen, why after a month are you telling me to call you by another name? Is something going on with you that you're not telling me? I have a strong suspicion that you're not who you seem to be."

"And would that be good or bad?"

"That would depend on who you turn out to be."

"If I turn out to be rich?"

"I wasn't speaking of your wallet, but your character, but I feel as though you've just attacked mine. I'll let that one go because I think I know where your hostility is coming from. You thought I was judging you earlier, not going out with you because you're a janitor."

"Oh, Ashleigh, I didn't think it, you said it."

"But I have a very good reason, Cole." This time she didn't amend the name. "You met one of them. I have this bad habit of hooking up with the wrong people, brothers with no income. I just can't go down that road again. Besides, my mother always told me that it's just as easy to love a rich man as a poor one. So I've decided I've had enough of loving the poor men."

"Then why am I here?"

"Because I like you and I don't want you to think I'm a snob or anything, and I do owe you for your help with Damien. You're a nice enough guy; it's just…

"It's just that there can't be anything between us. Is that what you're saying?"

Ashleigh had said enough. She valued honesty and had thought that this man she'd invited for dinner would value it also. Maybe she wouldn't mind, she wasn't sure, but maybe if they could at least have one hot and heavy date the hunger she had been feeling for months could finally be satisfied.

"How about a glass of wine? I made lasagna." She walked into the kitchen and returned with the wine, knowing that his eyes would be on her cleavage; she'd exposed enough of it. His not wanting to forgive her little misspoken words would be forgotten in a matter of moments.

She's horny, Keefe thought as he watched Ashleigh walk into the kitchen. He'd insulted her and she should have thrown him out. He'd all but called her a gold digger and now she was heading for him with a wine glass. So was that it? A janitor was good enough to screw in her apartment, in private, just not good enough for her to go out with. *Okay,* he thought, *if that's the way she wants to play it, then to hell with telling her the truth.* Keefe took the wine glass from her hands and frowned. Women. Damn them.

Dinner had been good. Keefe had to admit that he'd expected one of those already cooked frozen deals but she'd made it from scratch with plenty of meat and no vegetables. What kind of nonsense was vegetable lasagna anyway?

He glanced at his watch. It was getting late, and he knew he should be going. After talking with Ashleigh he'd decided not to just take her to bed. He did like her and he was going to leave her apartment knowing he hadn't taken advantage of her blatant need.

"I guess I should be going," he said as his eyes scanned the apartment for a loose knob, anything he could fix that would keep him there legitimately a while longer. At last he spotted a door that appeared to be off center on her entertainment center.

"Someone put that door on wrong," he observed, pointing it out to Ashleigh.

"Yeah, I know, but I haven't been able to get anyone to fix it for me."

"Why didn't you ever ask me?"

"It's not part of a janitor's duties to fix the tenants' furniture."

Keefe swallowed, bristling at knowing that that was all she thought he was capable of, repairing things. Hell, she'd not even thought enough of him to think that he would do her a simple favor and repair the damn thing. It would only take five minutes and a screwdriver. He would fix this one last thing for her and then she could go to hell.

"Give me a screwdriver and I'll take care of it before I leave." He didn't look directly at her. He didn't want to gaze at her soft smooth skin or look at the way her breasts moved beneath her sweater and he didn't want to see the roundness of them peeping out at him from the vee of her sweater. No, he didn't need to see any of that. He just wanted to fix her door and get the hell out of there.

Ashleigh walked away from Keefe, thinking she'd ruined things and not knowing exactly what she'd done. For a couple of hours they'd had fun. She would like to do it again, but he'd turned suddenly cold and no longer seemed interested. And the way he was avoiding looking at her, especially at her bosom, suddenly made her feel slutty, like—oh damn, she thought, like Nicki. Nicki did look slutty, but she loved her just the same. Now she was feeling slutty and she didn't want him thinking about her in that manner.

Ashleigh stood watching Cole, the way he talked, his lips stretching out as he smiled, the way his hands moved when he worked, and yes, she'd admit she'd done quite a bit of staring at his behind, wondering why he was now hiding it beneath those looser fitting, albeit new, jeans. Why the heck he wasn't wearing the same kind of jeans she'd first seen him in was a mystery, much as the man himself.

Who'd ever heard of a janitor that no one else ever saw? Not a single person that she knew in the building had ever had Cole to repair a darn thing in their apartments. No, the only janitor anyone had ever seen was somewhere between sixty and infinity.

And him—Ashleigh hoped he never put on jeans. He wore coveralls most days, and on those occasions when he didn't, Ashleigh made sure to rush past him in the elevator or corridors. On the days he wore pants the weight of the tools pulled the pants down under the equator. She didn't need or want to see the crack of his behind. She had thought of asking Cole to make sure the man wore only coveralls, but changed her mind when she thought she could be causing the man some problems.

Curiosity had gotten the better of Ashleigh and she'd teamed up with Nicki to try to find out information on Cole. Despite Nicki's extraordinary snooping abilities, they'd had no luck. It was as if he didn't exist. Ashleigh knew better than that. He did exist. And he was squatting in the middle of her living room with just the most minuscule beads of sweat running down his body. One at a time. She knew that for sure. For with her eyes she'd followed each drop into his shirt and she'd had to stop herself from opening it up to see where it went after that.

"Can I help?" she asked as she kneeled down on the floor beside him. She was well aware that she was staring at his lips, willing him to kiss her, and finally he took notice. She saw the look that came into his eyes, the indecision, and she waited, hoping.

Keefe finished up the door and turned toward Ashleigh. She was kneeling next to him, so close that he could smell her scent. He breathed deeply, trying to place the fragrance. He was pretty sure the clean smell was soap. His imagination went into full tilt as he thought of Ashleigh stepping from her shower, water and soap lingering on her body.

He felt himself begin to stiffen and remained where he was but turned his head slightly. Damn, he thought to himself as he dropped his gaze and sat on his haunches. He found his mouth was in line with Ashleigh's breasts, brown as berries and probably just as juicy. He lifted his eyes and saw the desire in her eyes. She was staring at him, her tongue swiping her lips, her look uncertain. She smiled at him and he smiled back, then stood, holding out his hand to her.

For a moment they stood staring at each other, neither saying a word. Without touching her, he leaned into her just the tinniest bit in case he was wrong, in case she wasn't sending him signals. She tilted her head toward him and kissed his lips. God, were her lips soft. He loved the feel of them. They weren't greasy from an over-application of lipstick or lip-gloss. He wondered about that. The color of her lips appeared to be a rich berry color, much the same as the color of her breasts. He'd thought for certain that she wore lip-stick. Kissing her he knew she didn't. It was all 100 percent pure Ashleigh.

She parted her lips and he heard her sharp intake of breath. Her tongue slid into his mouth and he melted, pulling on her tongue gently with his teeth. Though he'd wanted to taste her for so long, he planned to take it slow, not push her. Those were his plans, but then again plans were meant to be broken. Heat filled his body. He wanted her. He heard the metal hinge of his zipper being pulled down and a moment later he felt warm hands reaching through the opening of his underwear to stroke him. If that wasn't a go-ahead, what was?

She'd gone for it, tucked her head just beneath his and kissed him.

And at the same instant he'd given up his battle and was kissing her. She smiled inwardly as they kissed, wondering who got the credit for making the first move.

His lips underneath hers had just the right amount of firmness, reminding her of the story of the three bears. Truly, his lips were just right. She couldn't resist reaching her hand down to make sure that everything else was just right also.

There was a distant noise in her head, fuzzy and incoherent as if someone were calling her from a distance, from so far way that she couldn't make out the exact words. But she felt the urgency and instinctively knew it was a warning that her brain was trying desperately to send her to stop the kiss right now, end it before he thought something more would come of their relationship.

God help her, she was getting what she hadn't had in months. The embers were flaming back to life, and like the phoenix, she was rising from the ashes. She felt her body shiver and pure lust overrode her good sense. He lifted her in his arms and she didn't object. She wanted him to make love to her; she wanted to make love to him. She'd worry later about telling him they could only have sex. A relationship between them was never going to happen. He carried her to her bedroom, a place he'd been on several occasions to fix little odds and ends. Now he was going to fix the most important thing in the room: her. Surprised, Ashleigh heard herself whimper. She'd never been a very vocal person when it came to lovemaking. She must have needed the touch of a man more than she realized.

Cole laid her on her bed, stared at her for a moment and whispered, "You're beautiful Ashleigh, inside and out." She searched his eyes and saw no sign of deceit. He meant it. Besides that, there was no need for lying. She was more than willing.

He smiled at her and that smile stirred more than her loins. It tugged at her heart. She realized then that it wasn't just the touch of a man her body had been craving, but the touch of a special man. Her heart was proclaiming that Cole could well be that special man.

She shivered as Cole's fingers went under her sweater. Her heart fluttered again, something that had never happened once to her in all her time with Damien. Indeed, during the last few months of their time together, she had not wanted him at all. She just hadn't known how to let go.

"What are you thinking about, Ashleigh?"

Her head turned a little to the right before she answered. "Who said I'm thinking of anything?"

"The eyes are the windows to the soul, Ashleigh, and yours tell me that you're not here."

Damn, she thought, he might not have Damien's sexy voice but he sure had the right words. She smiled at him. *Why did they still have their clothes on?* she wondered. She wanted to feel him on top of her, then beneath her and inside of her before the voices in her head drove her crazy. She wanted to enjoy this man fully and completely just once before she moved on to the new life she was carving out for herself.

Feeling he was moving too slowly, she raised her upper torso and ripped off her sweater, leaving the bra for him to figure out.

As he bent his head and kissed her, his hand finally found the clasp and stripped the bra away. The look of adoration he trained on her breasts made the juices that had been buried so long deep inside of her begin to flow. She felt the wetness and a moan that she swallowed. To think that he was able to do that to her with only a look!

The next instant he caressed her breasts. The softness of his touch didn't surprise her. She'd never thought he looked like a man who did manual labor. When he took her breast into his mouth, she couldn't hold back the moan.

Trailing hot kisses all over her, he moved lower and lower. When his tongue darted quickly into her navel and swirled, Ashleigh felt her body rise from the bed. Some part of her wanted to stop him because she knew that this man was making love to Ashleigh the person, not just her body, and she couldn't have that.

Even as she reached this conclusion, it was too late. She felt his fingers, warm and loving, as he gently removed her silk panties. Ashleigh felt another tug of her heart at his tenderness and her body shivered in desire. Oh God, help me, she thought, lest I fall for this man big time.

His hand moved between her legs, and he looked up and smiled. "I love the way you feel," he said. "Your skin is so soft." Then he nibbled her inner thigh, and said, "You're so sweet. You look and taste like brown juicy berries. Are you this sweet all over?" He had a twinkle in his eye as he said, "Let's see." Then his head disappeared between her thighs and she felt his tongue slide into her body and she thought she would die of the pleasure. Then just as suddenly he was smiling at her and announcing, "You are that sweet all over."

When he moved from the bed and Ashleigh's hand reached out to pull him back, he smiled wickedly. "I think we'll both enjoy this better if I take off my clothes. I know I will." He smiled again.

Ashleigh was so damn hot, moaning and groaning like a common whore, that she hadn't even noticed that Cole was completely dressed. She turned her gaze on him as he slipped off the shirt. That he was beautiful was her first thought. God, how she loved the color brown. She couldn't think of anything that looked exactly the color of Cole's beautiful brown skin, but it sure looked yummy. She looked at the hair on his chest, long and straight, and from where she lay, it looked as soft as the down on the back of baby ducks.

Her eyes moved lower. His stomach was rippled, the muscles firm, looking both hard and soft at the same time. Not the body of a weight lifter but definitely the body of a man who took pride in it and kept it well toned. She hated an over-abundance of muscles. Again she was reminded of the three bears. *His body is just right.*

He was smiling wickedly at her. As he slid the jeans down his hips she sucked in a breath and closed her eyes for an instant in awe. "Wow," she said aloud before she could stop herself. The man was beautiful. His legs were as she'd known they would be. God, were they long and powerfully built. Michelangelo's David had nothing on Cole. Matter of fact, if the marble statue could, it would probably run and hide if it got a good look at the living work of art here in her bedroom doing a slow erotic striptease for her.

She'd known his penis would be magnificent, and she wasn't disappointed. It was long and thick and, thank God, he'd been circumcised. As he walked toward her, she got a much better look at his magnificent tool. Taut and shiny, it looked so silky she wanted to touch him, to taste him. She couldn't believe it. She who didn't particularly care for oral sex was actually wanting to taste this man standing before her.

Again she shivered and a longer tugging of her heart pierced her. Damn, it wasn't just horny attraction she was feeling for Cole; she was falling in love with him. This couldn't be happening.

He was standing at the top of the bed, an embarrassed look on his face. "Ashleigh, do you have any condoms? I'm afraid I didn't come prepared."

Her hand shot out to the nightstand and she handed him a condom. But the simple fact that he'd not come to her home to score, that he was a decent man, resurrected the voices in her head.

Shut up, she muttered to the voices telling her to stop. She wouldn't listen, not now, maybe later. Right now she had to do as her body commanded. She had to taste Cole, see if he was as sweet as he looked.

Her eyes closed and her head bent down. In her hand, heavy with need and soft as a baby's bottom, his silken skin was stretched taut over what appeared to be an unbreakable rod of iron. She took him in her mouth, tasted him, felt desire shiver throughout his body and she shivered in return, knowing that she had done that to him. "You taste good, Cole. Sweet."

He surprised her by laughing. "I don't think I ever had anyone tell me that before, but thank you, Ashleigh. Now if you don't mind, as good as this feels, you're doing too good a job. I want us to go a long time," he said, then walked away from her and crawled into the other side of the bed.

For the second time Ashleigh felt like a common whore. On the one hand she was glad that what she'd done had pleased Cole, but she sure as hell didn't want him thinking she was so good at it because she was quite experienced.

What does it matter what he thinks of you? You're going to dump him anyway. That's your plan. Remember? Use him and lose him.

Then Cole took her in his arms and his lips found hers and she melted. This wasn't what she'd wanted, not the tenderness. She'd wanted hot, quick sex, without involvement. But she was helpless to stop.

I shouldn't be here, Keefe thought as he slipped into the bed and took Ashleigh into his arms. Damn it all to hell! He was falling in love with her. He should have known. All the warning signs were there but like a fool he'd ignored them.

Hell, he knew the reason she was in bed with him right now. She was lonely and horny and she needed a man and he just happened to fit the bill. He'd thought he'd go along with it, screw her brains out, then dump her before she could dump him. He wasn't an idiot; he'd gotten the comments she'd made to him about his being a janitor.

But he'd tasted her, something he rarely did, and with that taste came a yearning and an awareness of the feelings he didn't want to have for Ashleigh. And he'd looked into her eyes and he could swear that he wasn't in her bed just because she was horny but because she wanted *him,* not just a handy male body.

When she'd taken him in her mouth he could have ended things right then and there. He'd been poised on the brink of climax. But when he opened his eyes it wasn't lust he read in her eyes but caring. She cared about him and the knowledge had made him pull away. If he'd allowed her to continue what she was doing, he wouldn't have lasted a second longer. The short walk around the side of the bed had given him the time he so desperately needed to regain control of his raging hormones.

He circled his arms about her and buried his lips in her neck, tasting the sweet nectar that was Ashleigh, anything to stave off the inevitable. He didn't want to rush things and just the thought of touching her, of putting his fingers into her moist wetness made him shudder.

Then the moment came when he could resist no longer. He had to touch her. He put a finger into her sweet moistness, felt her body tense and curl around him, pulling him in deeper. She moaned as his thumb rubbed back and forth over the essence of her woman-hood. He wanted to taste her again, feel her juices as they ran over his tongue. Oh God, he wanted her. Keefe kissed his way down her smooth belly and then, oh sweet heaven, he dipped his head and feasted on her womanly essence as though starved.

Her body bucked wildly beneath him and he felt her nails digging into his back, and her hips shoving hard against him.

But she wasn't trying to push him away. She wanted this, wanted what he was doing to her. And then she came. Oh how she came and her whimpers of delight filled him. He was torn between wanting to mount her and wanting to stay right where he was, lapping away at her juices. He decided to wait it out. When he felt her limbs loosen, he came up, found she'd torn the condom from its package and was looking at him, holding it just out of his reach. Then she pushed him down on the bed and kissed her way from his chest to his groin, sucked him greedily, brought him to the edge, then stopped and put the condom on him.

"Ashleigh, you don't know what you've started," he murmured.

"Oh, but I do," she answered and slid onto his erection and rode him, smiling down at him as he lay on his back. When he saw that she was about to come again, he switched positions. He entered her slowly, wanting to remember all the sensations of their first time together, ignoring her hips trying to push him on. She was so damn hot and so was he. The climax was building in him and try as he might he could no longer control it. Besides, he didn't want to stop it. He bent lower to kiss Ashleigh, knowing that in a matter of moments they would be riding the crest of desire together. He pushed himself into her harder, faster.

"Ashleigh," he groaned as he came.

He held her close and as she reached orgasm he heard her moan,

"Cole, Cole."

Keefe froze. As she came down from her climax, a look of utter contentment on her face, he could tell she wasn't aware of his distress. Why should she be? She'd only moaned his name. Only it wasn't his name. It was time to tell her everything.

They lay together, her on his chest trying hard to catch her breath, him trying to think of the best way to tell her. He didn't want to make love to a woman and have her call out another man's name, even if that name was supposed to be his. He wanted to hear her call his name, his real name, as she came.

At the same moment they both spoke.

"I have something to tell you, Cole," Ashleigh said.

"My name's not Cole, Ashleigh, it's Keefe. I'm Mia's brother."

"What?"

Ashleigh sat up, pulling the covers over her body, feeling betrayed. The best sex she'd had in…hell, the best sex she'd ever had and it was with a man who'd lied about his identity. Damn, when would she ever learn?

"Mia, the woman who bought my gown? You're her brother? Why didn't you just say so?" She glared at him. "Now it makes sense," she said. "I wondered how she'd found out about my dress. Now I know. The janitor was her brother. But I don't understand the lie. I would have sold it to her anyway. I can understand why it disturbed you that she wanted to pay more than I asked. I mean, with what you probably make, you couldn't really afford it, could you?" she asked in an accusing manner.

Her tone of voice was making him angry. If she'd been upset only about the lie, that he could understand, but there she went with that class shit again. Who the hell did she think she was, the queen of England?

"You said you had something to tell me. What is it?" he asked, knowing from the look in her eyes what it was going to be.

"Listen, I told you I don't like liars. But that really isn't the reason for what I'm about to say. You're a nice guy and all, cute, mannerly, smart and some woman would be lucky to have you. But I can't become seriously involved with you. I mean, if you want to come by occasionally for…"She shrugged her shoulders. "But there can't be any more than that. I want to tell you the truth right up front. You see, I do believe in honesty."

"Since you said this wasn't because of my lie, why are you saying this?" He wanted to make her come right out and say it.

"Look, Cole…I'm sorry, Keefe, or whoever the hell you really are. We have different goals. I'm looking for a man who's already arrived, not one who's still trying to get there."

"Do you have any idea at all how that sounds?"

"I know how it sounds."

"That would make you what?"

"A woman who knows what she wants."

"Should I leave money on the nightstand?" Keefe asked as he climbed from the bed, "because it sure as hell sounds to me like you're for sale."

"I suppose you think insulting me is going to make me have a sudden epiphany. Well, I had an epiphany. I'm not taking care of a man with only a plan. I don't care how great the plan sounds. I'm not investing in dreams, Cole, sorry, Keefe."

"That's good because you haven't bothered to even ask me if I have any dreams."

"Why should I? I know what you do for a living. You're a janitor and regardless of your dreams I can't allow myself to fall for you, no matter how good you are in bed."

Keefe pulled on his jeans and closed the zipper with an air of finality. "I hate gold diggers, Ashleigh."

"I'm not a gold digger but I'm also not a charity. You don't make the money that I do and I don't ever plan on being the one to do the paying anymore."

Keefe laughed, the sound harsh and dry. "So you're saying that if I had money this little speech would have never happened." He watched as she shrugged her shoulders.

"There would have been no need," she answered at last, "but you don't have any, so this conversation is moot."

"That's where you're wrong, Ashleigh. I was going to tell you, but you didn't give me a chance. I'm not the janitor but even if I were, I don't think I'd like to see you again."

"Then who are you, what do you do?"

"I own the whole damn building," he answered. "Is that a big enough dream arrival for you?"

"I don't know. You've lied about everything else, why not about this?"

Keefe was past angry. She should be ashamed of herself for thinking the way that she did but no, she was still standing firm. He shouldn't prove a damn thing to her but he did. He pulled his wallet from his back pocket, drew out a card and threw it on the bed.

Keefe Black, Real Estate Investor, the card read. "Is that real enough for you, Ashleigh?"

"Why?" she asked as she looked at the card. "Why lie?"

"Like you, I'm sick to death of taking care of moochers." With that he stomped out of her bedroom, out of her apartment, and out of her life.

CHAPTER SEVEN

Ashleigh hugged the pillow close to her body. She'd screwed up big time. Keefe Black had slammed her front door more than ten minutes ago and still she heard the sound reverberating through her skull.

What happened? she wondered. Her body was tingling and she was basking in the afterglow of the most incredible lovemaking she'd ever indulged in. Sure, she'd told Keefe it was only sex. But she'd had sex and she knew the difference. She was more fulfilled than she ever thought she'd be. If only Keefe hadn't lied to her about who he was.

The ringing phone gave her a start. Then her heart skipped a beat as she reached over to the nightstand to pick up the receiver. She hoped that it was Keefe. Maybe they'd fix things.

"Hello."

"Is he gone?"

"Yes, he's gone," Ashleigh answered, trying hard not to let her disappointment show.

"Did he like everything you gave him to eat?"

The coarse laughter told Ashleigh that her friend had not been asking about her lasagna. "God, Nicki, get your mind out of the gutter."

"Come on, it's been a month now that the two of you have been playing this little cat and mouse game. I know you didn't let that brother go without getting a little. I wouldn't have."

"Yeah, we know. I don't think any man that's walked into your apartment has ever walked out without your getting a little."

"Ouch."

For a moment the line was silent. Ashleigh was angry but she had no right to take her anger out on her friend. She was angry only with herself.

"Nicki, look, I'm sorry—

"Don't be. I don't try to hide what I do. I like sex. That's why I'm getting it. And if you really don't like Cole, move over and let me have a shot at him. I don't give a damn what he does for a living if he can get the job done. Can he get the job done?" she purred.

"You're hopeless, and might I add, nasty."

Nicki laughed. "Thanks. I try. Oh come on. Stop trying to change the conversation. Did you get to know Cole a little better?"

"Oh yeah, I got to know him better. For starters his name's not Cole. It's Keefe. Keefe Black."

"The woman who bought your gown, wasn't her name Black? Is he related?"

"Bingo. He's Mia Black's, brother. The woman who has my wedding gown. I saw the resemblances but I let it go.

Ashleigh was fuming again. She had every reason to be upset. She'd been lied to for over a month. Then it struck her that Nicki had not said one word. That wasn't like her. She should be trashing both Keefe and Mia. "What's up?" she asked.

"I was just wondering why you're so angry. And don't lie and say you're not," Nicki said. "Are you upset that a janitor's sister bought your gown?"

Surprised, Ashleigh sputtered, "What are you talking about? Why would that matter?"

"Girl, I love you. But we both know you are a bit of a snob, like I'm a bit of a 'ho. I know that and I embrace it. You're a snob.

THE WEDDING GOWN

Admit it and get on with it. So tell me, did you lose it because the janitor's sister is going to be wearing your dream gown?"

Ashleigh was livid. She'd been called a snob twice in the last half hour and she was getting a bit tired of it. "Look, first for your information, Keefe Black isn't a janitor. He owns the whole damn building."

Nicki's laughter followed her admission and Ashleigh groaned. She didn't need her friend to tell her she'd made a horrible mistake. She was aware of it. Her heart had been trying to tell her that Keefe could be Mister Right, but she hadn't wanted to hear that. She'd thought he was a janitor. She groaned again. She *was* a snob.

"My God, you did something stupid, didn't you? Please, Ashleigh, tell me you didn't do anything stupid."

Ashleigh groaned for the third time. "I wish I could tell you I didn't, but I did." She shut her eyes and hugged the pillow tighter to her body, inhaling Keefe's masculine scent mixed with the lingering smells from their lovemaking.

"It wasn't all my fault," Ashleigh said, defending her actions. "I felt like a fool when he told me he was Mia's brother. It was like he'd...like he'd deliberately set me up. I may have gone overboard with the things I told him."

"What did you tell him?"

The excitement bubbling from Nicki's voice annoyed Ashleigh. Her friend was getting some sick pleasure from her pain. "You don't have to sound so happy," she snapped.

"Just tell me what you said to him."

"I told him he could drop by ever so often for sex. I said that we could never have anything more between us."

"Because?"

"Because he was a janitor. Alright. Are you happy now that I've said it? Yes, kill me. I told him I wouldn't date him because he had no money. And because he was a janitor."

"And?"

"And he called me a gold digger and a snob. He told me that he wouldn't date me. Then he threw his business card in my face and told me that he owned the whole damn building."

"Wow!" Nicki whispered.

"Is that all you have to say?" Ashleigh asked.

"How was the sex?"

Ashleigh laughed. She should have known. In the end Nicki cared about one thing and one thing only. Sex. She closed her eyes in memory, touching her finger to her breasts, then her lips, retracing Keefe's touches on her body. "It was unbelievable," she said at last. "He made love to me. Do you understand what I'm talking about?" She sighed. "He made love to me. I've never felt anything like it."

"You sound like he got to you."

"He did. I could see myself falling for him. I couldn't let it happen. I couldn't go through that again, Nicki."

For a long moment both friends were quiet before Nicki broke the silence. "Talk to him, Ashleigh. Call him and explain it to him. I know he has a crush on you. Just give it time."

"How can I explain now? Would you want to hear anything I had to say after I told you that I couldn't date you because you didn't have enough money? If I call him now, he'll think that I want him for his money. He'll really think I'm a gold digger. You have to admit that it looks bad."

"It doesn't look good. Even I'll have to say that. You really messed up this time. Too bad you picked the first good man you've run across to implement your take-no-brother's-bullshit plans. It should have been that no good ass Damien. By the way, where do you think he has his sorry ass?"

Ashleigh shuddered. "I could care less where Damien is or who he's with. More than likely he's in bed with some skank."

Nicki laughed and Ashleigh joined in before saying quietly, "What am I going to do, Nicki? How can I fix this? I knew he was something special. I knew it but I..."

"You were just trying to protect yourself. That's all. You didn't want to go through what Damien put you through. Don't beat yourself up about that."

"I thought you said I was a snob."

Nicki laughed. "You are. But you're my girl and I have your back. You're feeling bad. I'm not going to kick you when you're down. Damn that sorry ass Damien."

"Yeah, damn him," Ashleigh answered. "I hope to God whoever he's with won't get sucked in by him. Bye Nicki," she said and hung up the phone, not waiting to hear her friend's response.

Too bad that she'd involved herself so long with losers that when a real man came along, a man that she could see a future with, she ruined it. She lay down on the pillows holding them close, remembering Keefe's eyes as he'd looked at her. The tears slid down her face. "I'm sorry," she muttered to the air. "I just didn't want to get hurt." Again she thought, *damn Damien*.

"Mia, you're driving me crazy. I want you, you want me. What's the big deal?"

"The big deal, Damien, is that I have other things to consider. If you don't like the way things are going, leave." Mia moved away from Damien, from his hands and his lips that would, if she allowed them to, make her lose her focus.

"Mia, I've done everything that you've asked."

"Not everything, Damien." She cocked her head to the side, lifting her brow as she did so, knowing he knew what she meant.

He was annoyed. She could tell it by the very way he refused to meet her glance. Then she watched as he walked over to his leather jacket, reached into the inside pocket and pulled out several stapled papers. "Here." He threw the papers down on the couch beside her. She glanced at the papers and refused to pick them up.

"Damn, Mia, you're working my nerves," Damien said as he reached for the papers he'd carelessly tossed beside her. This time he held the papers out to her and she accepted them.

With a quizzical expression she eyed each and every paper carefully before turning and giving Damien a smile.

"Now can we?" he asked.

The look on his face made her laugh out loud. "Damien, grow up. You're not a little kid and I'm not a piece of candy, nor am I a convenient piece of tail for you."

"But…but…I got the tests, everything. I'm clean."

"I'm glad. But that's for your sake, Damien. I'm glad for you that with your history and all your whoring around you're okay." She gave him a meaningful glance, "For now. And you're darn lucky," she lectured, but before she could continue he was kissing her again, stopping her tirade. She gave in to the kiss, not really wanting to scold him, wanting the same thing that he did, to make love to him. But the time wasn't right. She knew it even if he didn't. They would have to wait a bit longer.

The kiss ended and Mia found herself struggling to regain control. Damien was a master all right, a master at manipulation. She had to be sure. She had too much riding on her future to throw it all away for a roll in the hay.

"Let me stay the night, Mia. Just let me sleep in the bed next to you. I just want to hold you," his sexy voice whispered to her and she backed away, glancing at the bulge that was straining to be released.

"Do I look like a fool? I mean, how dumb do you think I am? You no more want to just hold me than I want to just let you. And I've told you before, you can't stay here. My brother would kill you if he found you here."

She saw the look that came over his face and wished she'd not mentioned Keefe. The thought of her caring what her brother thought never failed to make Damien bristle with anger.

"I'm not in love with your brother. You're so ashamed of me that you can't even tell him that you're seeing me."

Mia felt a twinge of sadness. "You're wrong, Damien, he knows, but you forget I'm not free to just act on my feelings. I'm engaged, remember? Would you want me sleeping around if I were engaged to you? Oh never mind," she glared, "you're the one person who would have no idea how to be true. You were engaged to Ashleigh; you told her you loved her. Even the day I met her, I heard you tell her. Now I'm supposed to believe you so easily when you say you love me?"

She was getting angry also. The mention of her brother reminded her that he was avoiding her. She'd not seen or talked to him for over two weeks. He would not return a single call and when she'd gone to his home he wasn't there. She'd even left him a note on the table, a note she knew for a fact he'd gotten, because when she went again she found her note wadded up and thrown in the wastebasket.

"What am I supposed to do to make you believe me, Mia?

You've got me jumping through hoops, doing things I never thought I would do and still you refuse to give it up."

"Give it up!" she screamed. "That, my friend, is why you're not sharing my bed. I don't respond to things like that."

"You think you're better than me, Mia. If your relationship with your fiancé is so damn important, why are you with me? You may not be sleeping with me, but, baby girl, you want to, and we both know it. So I think whatever you think of my character, you'd better save a little of that sanctimonious lecture for yourself."

A shiver went through Mia, and she felt the tears well up in her eyes. Damien was right. She felt his arms envelope her, and he kissed her face.

"I'm sorry, Mia, forgive me. I'm just…I want you… and, oh hell, you…," he stammered. "I don't blame you, Mia, for making me wait, for wanting to be sure. I'm a man. It's my job to try."

As Damien held Mia in his arms, he knew without a doubt he was telling her the truth. He was utterly in love with her. And she was right, his past should give her reason to pause. Hell, the entire way they met was under suspicion. But never in his life had he ever begged a woman for anything, and never had he wanted to. He felt Mia's pain as she shivered, and he wanted to kick himself.

"Mia, you're not like me. I'm an asshole for saying that to you."

She brought her head around to look in his eyes. "No, you're not. I am the one who should be apologizing. I'm the one with the fiancé; I'm the one who should have used discretion. I should have told James the moment I knew I had feelings for you. But I don't know how to write him and tell him. I don't know which way seems crueler. For me to tell him when he gets home or…

"Damien, this is the last thing in the world I ever expected to happen. I went to Ashleigh's to buy a wedding gown and look at me now; I'm here with the man that broke her heart. I'm worse than you." She cried harder.

Mia's heart was breaking and Damien's heart was breaking for her. He led her over to the sofa and sat beside her. "Mia, look at me," he pleaded. "Everything's going to work out. I promise. I'm paying Ashleigh back just like you asked me to do. I can't make it up to her for hurting her, but I can give her back the money I've taken from her."

"What about Keefe?"

"Keefe's your problem, Mia. He's never going to believe that I love you no matter what, and I don't blame him. If you were my sister, I'd be having a fit."

"He hasn't talked to me in two weeks."

"Do you blame me for that, Mia?"

"No, Damien. I don't know if he's angry with me that I lied to him or just because I'm with you. It's a long story. My brother has issues with our mother."

"What happened with your mother?"

"For starters, my mother, our mother, has been married seven times. She's always on the lookout for a man with more money. She says it's love she's looking for, but Keefe says it's the money. It does appear that he's right. Now she's living in Phoenix."

"So how does that make a problem for you and your brother?"

Mia closed her eyes tightly; she didn't want to cry. "Keefe thinks she's a tramp, a slut. Now he thinks I'm just like her. I love him, Damien. Keefe's all I have. I don't like hurting him."

Damien held Mia tightly against his chest. "He's not all you have, Mia. Not anymore."

She didn't answer so he brought her head around to face him so that he could look into her eyes. "Mia, you can count on me." He saw a wary look come into her eyes. "Mia, I'm going to prove to you that you can count on me." "It's not just you. We're hurting so many people. Keefe, James, even Ashleigh. I'm just afraid of the payback." Mia shivered again. "I wish I'd never bought Ashleigh's gown. I wish I'd never met her."

"If you'd never met Ashleigh, we would have never met."

"I know," she whispered as she caressed his cheek. She started crying again. "I wish I could let this go. I know how upset you get when I mention Keefe. But, Damien, you have to understand, I can't forget that I've hurt my brother. I've really disappointed him. It's killing me knowing that he thinks I'm like my mother. He hates her and now I'm afraid that he hates me also."

"Mia, if you have to make a choice between us, your brother or me, do I even stand a chance?"

For an answer he only got more tears. He knew what he had to do. He had to win her brother over. An impossibility.

Ashleigh couldn't believe it. For two weeks her emotions had been on a constant roller coaster. She'd dialed Keefe's cell phone more than a dozen times. True, she'd always hung up before it rang. She was thankful for that at least. Keefe would never know that she'd called.

Wanting to blame someone else for the mess, she'd alternated between Mia Black and Damien. It had taken the last bit of restraint she possessed not to call the woman up and tell her to return her dress. As much as she wanted to, she needed the money from the gown. Her bank was going crazy, bouncing her checks. And until things were straightened out, she couldn't afford to be picky about who had her dream gown.

As for Damien, she couldn't even be mad at him. He was sending her a little money each week, not much, but considering the financial troubles she'd found herself in lately, every little bit helped.

Ashleigh glanced toward the silent bell over the door of her shop. Business was slow but she wasn't worried. She'd straighten things out. She always had.

No, what worried her was the knowledge that she couldn't stop thinking of Keefe Black. Her body craved his touches and her heart craved his love.

Keefe picked the phone up, the loneliness of the past two weeks overriding his anger and disappointment. He wished like hell he'd not been such a cheap bastard. It was all his fault. If he'd never read the damn notice about the wedding gown, he'd never have gotten into a fight with Mia. Mia would have never met Damien and in all probability he would have never met Ashleigh.

Thinking of Ashleigh hurt in a place he'd buried so deeply that the intensity of it caught him by surprise. He'd sworn he would never be so affected by a woman again. But he was wrong. He'd fallen in love with Ashleigh. And he'd made love to her. His eyes closed in pain as he remembered how sweet their lovemaking had been. He had been a fool to open his heart. He'd thought she had feelings for him. But she was only a gold digger. Damn.

And Mia. He'd put his sister in a position to meet the scum of the earth. She was too naive to defend herself against someone like

Damien and for the past two weeks he'd left her with no one else to turn to.

Damn, if he'd not been so hurt over her lying to him and Ashleigh's rejection, he would have thought about that.

He dialed and listened to her phone ring. He hung up and dialed again. This time her machine came on. He cursed under his breath, knowing she was home, knowing that she wasn't answering her phone because she was with that…that—God, how he hated to even think about that. His little baby sister might at this very moment be sharing her bed with a man who'd had more women than their mother had had men. No, he wouldn't think about that.

"Mia, pick up the damn phone," he shouted at her recorder. "Pick it up," he demanded in an even sterner voice. When she didn't he continued, "Mia, I'm on my way over there. You've got one hour. If you don't want a scene, your company will be gone by the time I get there."

With that Keefe hung up the phone. He hoped like hell that he found Damien there in his sister's apartment. He needed someone to take his anger out on and Damien would do just fine.

"So I suppose you want me to leave?"

Mia looked at the phone, her brother's shouting still ringing in her ears, and then she looked at Damien. "No, I don't want you to leave."

"Thanks for that, baby." He pulled her up from the sofa and kissed her. "I know you need to straighten things out with your brother. I'll go, okay? Call me if you need me."

"Damien," Mia called to him as he headed for the door. He turned back. "I'm sorry for the things I said to you tonight. I wouldn't be with you now if I didn't care about you. I'm not ashamed of you, Damien."

He smiled at her and walked out the door, wanting to believe her but unable to. In the end it didn't matter. Even if she weren't ashamed of him, he knew she had every right to be.

For the first time in his life, Damien wished that he were successful, that he'd made something of his life; that he deserved to be in love with an angel. And for the first time in his life he was ashamed.

CHAPTER EIGHT

From where she sat on the couch, Mia heard her brother's key in the lock. For weeks he'd avoided her. Now that he was ready to talk, scratch that, now that he was ready to lecture her or fight, he was willing to come over.

"Is he here, Mia?"

"What do you think?"

"I think you've changed, Mia, and I don't like it." He looked at her and felt the pain of his heart breaking. For the first time in his entire life Keefe felt totally lost. Mia's lie hurt a thousand times more than their mother's lies, all the times she'd promised to be a mother, all the times she hadn't, all the men he'd walked in and found her with. Marriage and commitment had never meant a damn thing to her. He thought he'd taught Mia to be true. To even think that their mother's genes ran in her blood was a cruel blow.

"I know what you're thinking, Kee. I can see it in your eyes."

"Can you, Mia? Can you really see what I'm thinking right now?"

"Yes. You're thinking that I'm like her, that I'm my mother's daughter."

He swallowed. "Is there a reason I shouldn't be thinking that?" He saw the sadness that pinched her face. "Mia, why, why would you even give a guy like that the time of day?" He saw the tears in her eyes and turned away, Mia's tears were his kryptonite, and he needed to get his words out.

"What about James? How can you sleep with that guy when you're engaged to be married in a few short months to another man?"

"I haven't slept with him." She saw her brother's raised brows. "I haven't slept with him," she repeated. "You don't believe me?"

"You've picked up a new skill, Mia. You've learned to lie."

That hurt, as she knew her brother had meant for it to do. "I'm not lying to you, Kee. I haven't." She could have eased his mind and told him then that she'd never slept with anyone but she didn't.

"What about James? Do you think that would make a difference to him? Do you think he would approve of your relationship?"

"What do you want me to do, write him a Dear John letter? I'm hoping he'll be home soon; then I'll tell him."

"Then do me a favor. Don't sleep with Damien until you tell James. Don't go behind his back. Don't cheat on him, Mia."

"I love Damien."

"Mia, he's just looking for a woman to take care of him. I'm surprised he hasn't asked to move in here."

"He moved back home with his mother." She looked hopefully at her brother but from the sneer on his face she knew that didn't impress him. She grabbed the medical papers Damien had given her earlier in the evening.

"Look what he did. He went to the doctor to get tested for me, because he loves me. He's even gotten a part-time job."

Keefe barely glanced at the papers. Seeing the negative HIV test only fueled his foul mood. Did his sister really think he wanted to know she was seriously contemplating having sex with that loser?

Before he knew what he was doing, he was shaking his sister by the shoulders. Her look of astonishment, then pain, stopped him. He knew he'd not hurt her physically but he'd hurt her. Never once in her entire life had he ever before put a hand on her in anger. That was Damien's fault. God, how he hated Damien and everything about him.

"Mia, don't look at me like that, please," he begged and took her again in his arms, this time to hold her. "Stop seeing him, Mia, please. Promise me."

"I don't know if I can, Kee. I told you, I love him. I don't want to hurt him. He thinks I'm ashamed of him. He's trying so hard to change, and he has. He loves me, Keefe."

Keefe's eyes closed in agony. His sister was behaving as foolishly as Ashleigh. "He told Ashleigh that he loved her too. How much money have you given him, Mia? You've always been a soft touch."

"But I'm not a fool. I haven't given him a cent and he hasn't asked me for money."

"I don't know that I believe you. But you are a fool if you believe him. And sooner or later he's going to want something from you. I'm not going to support him, Mia."

Mia pulled away from her brother, getting his meaning. Her own anger now flared up. "Just what are you saying, Kee?"

"I think I made it plain. I'm not taking care of him. I'm not putting out a dime of my money for him." He held out his palm, ignoring the look of hurt in his sister's eyes.

She stomped away and he watched her, watched as she went into her bedroom, then watched as she came back and handed over their joint checkbook and joint savings account. He took the books and shoved them in his pocket.

"It's always money with you, isn't it, Keefe? You're so scared of love that you don't give anyone a chance to love you because they may want your precious money. Well, dear brother, you no longer have to worry as far as I'm concerned. You have your money. So now what? Are you going to throw me on the junk heap? What?"

It was killing her, fighting with Keefe. She couldn't believe it. She'd known he would be angry, but for him to believe she'd ever use his money to fund Damien was an out and out insult. If it had not been for his tactless insult, she would have never spoken her next words.

"Is that the reason Ashleigh doesn't want you, big brother? Did you accuse her of wanting your money?"

He was glaring openly at her and she didn't give a darn.

"How do you know what happened with Ashleigh?"

"She called. She wanted to know if you were really my brother and she wanted to know why we both lied to her. You big hypocrite," Mia screamed. "You accuse me of lying and you did the same thing."

"It was not the same thing and you know it," Keefe defended his action. "It was only a joke."

"Why don't you try telling Ashleigh that you went to bed with her under an assumed name because it was all a joke. I don't think she looked at it as a joke. Liar, liar!" she screamed at him again.

"I told her my name."

"Yeah, after the fact. Do you think she appreciated that, big brother? Then you called her a gold digger?"

"I called it like I saw it. She said she couldn't date me because I was a janitor. That makes her a gold digger."

"Did you ever stop to think that she'd just gotten out of a bad relationship, that she was just trying to protect herself?" *Oh darn*, Mia thought, *why didn't I shut up when I made my point?* She'd now brought the conversation back around to the subject of Damien. Darn, darn, darn. When would she ever learn?

"I don't believe you said that." Keefe laughed at his sister.

"You're right, Ashleigh had just dumped a low life, two-timing wom-anizing mooch, a slime ball who hit on another woman in her face, in the very wedding gown she'd planned to marry him in. And what did you do, little sister? You picked up the trash that she threw out. And you want what for that? My praise, my support? Dream on."

He stood there glaring at her. "Tell me something, Mia. Does he mean more to you than I do, a man you've known for what, a cou-ple of months?"

"Keefe, it sounds like you're giving me an ultimatum. Are you telling me that if I continue to see Damien you're not going to be my brother any more?"

He closed his eyes halfway, tightening the muscles in his jaws, trying to control himself before he answered her. "Yes, Mia, that's exactly what I'm doing. Make a choice here and now, Damien or me."

"I thought it was Damien or James."

"You're playing games, Mia, and I'm not. I mean it. I don't want you acting like a tramp."

"Like Mom?" Mia interrupted.

"Yeah, like Mom." He didn't hesitate. "At least have the decency to tell James your feelings."

"Keefe, what do you really want me to do?"

"I want you to marry James. I want you to honor your commit-ment. I want you to stop behaving like...like her."

"Like Mom." Mia shook her head. "You've got it, Kee. I won't see Damien again, at least until after I've had a chance to tell James."

"That wasn't all that I asked. I want you to continue with your wedding plans. I want you married and safe."

"So you can stop worrying about me? Is that it? You're tired of worrying about me so you want me married? Well, Keefe, you can forget about Damien. I doubt that he's going to sit around waiting months for me, and he's definitely not going to like knowing that I stopped seeing him because my big brother demanded it. So you're probably going to get your wish. I hope that makes you happy, Kee."

He should have stopped there but he didn't. "Promise me, Mia, promise me that you're not going to see him, promise me that I can trust your word, that I can believe you."

"Why don't you move back in, monitor me, make sure to tuck me in every night, check under my covers for a man, look in my closets and under my bed. Don't take my word for it. Put me under house arrest."

He knew she was being sarcastic. It didn't matter; he wanted to know that she was keeping her promise and besides that, he was lonely, he needed to be around someone who gave a damn about him. *Well, someone who used to give a damn about him.* He looked at his sister, at the dullness of her eyes. Their sparkle was gone and he was responsible.

"That sounds like a good idea. Since I'm already here I might as well stay." He ignored the daggers her eyes were throwing at him, glad that it was only a look and not actual weapons. He also ignored her slammed bedroom door. She had no way of knowing just how much he needed to be around her, even with her hating him. That was better than the loneliness he'd endured for the past two weeks.

Mia slammed the door on her brother, wishing it hadn't come to this, him demanding that she choose. He knew good and well she'd never choose anyone over him, not even the man she loved. She owed her brother everything. That thought drove her to call Damien.

"Damien," she said when she heard his voice on the line.

"Do you want me to make it easy for you?" he asked.

"I wish you would."

"I'm in love with you, Mia."

"I know, but Keefe is right. I have to tell James."

"When are you telling him?"

"Not until he returns home."

"And what do you expect me to do, wait until God knows when for him to come home? Then maybe you'll call me or maybe when you see him you'll wonder why you ever bothered with someone like me."

"Damien, just give me a chance to end my engagement the right way. After that we'll work on making my brother approve of you. We have to believe it will all work out. If you really love me, if our love is real, then you'll wait. I can't promise you anything but I did promise my brother and I'm going to keep my promise to him."

"And while you're keeping your promise to your brother what am I supposed to do? I mean, let's make sure this is spelled out. Do I get to date other women while you wait for Uncle Sam to let your fiancé come home?"

"No, Damien, you don't get to date."

"You expect me to remain celibate for something that may or may not happen?"

"I don't expect anything from you, Damien. It's your life, but if you go back to whoring around, don't expect me to ever sleep with you."

"Then you do expect me to just sit around waiting for you."

"You're right. I guess I do expect certain things. I expect you to behave like a man in love. I expect you to do whatever it takes to make my brother approve of you. I expect you to understand that I shouldn't have ever started this relationship with you in the midst of planning a wedding. And I expect you to know how hard this has been for me. I love you, Damien, or I wouldn't be in this predicament. I wouldn't have lied to James, and I definitely would never have lied to my brother."

"You're not fooling me, Mia. This isn't really about James. It's about your brother. If you were truly in love with James you would have never walked away with me that first day. Hell, you fell for me the same instant I fell for you, right there in Ashleigh's living room wearing her gown. I saw it in your eyes. Why do you think I waited for you to come out?"

"Just because it happened doesn't make it right. James isn't with me. Do you think he's found someone else simply because I'm not there? I'll answer that for you. No. He's not that kind of man. And…"

"And until me, you weren't that kind of woman, right?"

"I'm doing the right thing, Damien, just trust me, and trust that things will work out."

"Go to hell, Mia. You, your precious brother and your fiancé, you can all just go to hell."

Damien slammed the phone down and caught his mother staring at him. "She doesn't think I'm good enough for her. Her brother told her to stop seeing me and she's acting like a little kid. She agreed."

"So what are you going to do?" his mother asked.

Damien swallowed his anger and his hurt. "I'm going to prove to her that I love her, that I'm good enough for her. I'm going to wait for her." He watched his mother smile. She didn't believe him. Okay, she would be another person he'd have to prove himself to.

CHAPTER NINE

"Ashleigh, I still can't believe he owns the building and you let him get away."

Nicki was laughing and frankly Ashleigh was getting a little tired of it. She'd expected her friend to do some laughing but it had been two weeks already. Enough was enough.

"What made you just blurt it out that you couldn't date him?"

"I told you he wanted more than a good time in bed."

"Did he say that?"

"He didn't have to. The look in his eyes said he was looking for more than sex."

"You haven't told me everything. There has to be something you're holding back. Were you starting to have feelings for him? I mean real feelings. Were you falling in love with him?"

Ashleigh looked away, not wanting her friend to see the secret she'd kept hidden from her. It did no good. She knew anyway.

"That's it, you felt something for him. That's why you've been in such a foul mood. You've been mooning over Keefe. Oh man, did you blow it. Why didn't you at least give it some time?"

She was wondering the same thing, but she knew why she'd told him immediately after the most fulfilling night she'd had in her entire life. "Nicki, I was determined not to hook up with another loser."

"Did you think he was a loser? I mean, really?"

"I wish I could say no without it making me seem like I was

money hungry, but come on. How much money could he have been making if he were the janitor?"

"I bet you feel like a fool now, don't you?"

"If he hadn't called me a gold digger maybe I would, but I think that wipes the slate clean."

"You can't blame him. I mean, you were sort of acting like one."

Ashleigh's mouth fell open and she stared at her friend with wide-eyed wonder. "Excuse me, but didn't we talk about this? You said you had my back. Remember? Besides, aren't you the one who said enough of feeding strays?"

"I also told you you were being a snob but you didn't listen to that. Why the heck would you listen to anything I said anyway? At least you got some before he kicked your ass to the curb."

"He didn't kick me to the curb, I dumped him."

"Yeah, that's what you want to believe. Honey, I bet when you found out the brother owned the building you were drooling. Then he hit you with a one-two punch, called you a gold digger, and now to salvage your pride you think you dumped him. Go ahead, keep up the illusion if it helps you but I don't think he'd bother with you again in this lifetime, no matter what you had to offer."

Ashleigh was taken aback. "I didn't say I had any plans to try to get him back." The way Nicki was behaving, Ashleigh was glad she'd not told her friend that she'd tried calling Keefe. A sense of regret washed over her and she wished she'd waited for him to confess.

"None of this would have ever happened if he'd told me the truth in the first place. He lied, let's not forget that."

"Ashleigh, you were so angry about Damien when you met the man that you wouldn't have listened to anything he had to say. Anyway, you're the one who assumed he was the janitor. I can't say I blame him for going along with it to teach you a lesson."

For an answer Ashleigh frowned. "I told him I hate liars."

"Yeah, and the truth keeps your bed warm, right?"

"Don't you ever think of anything except sex?"

As expected, Nicki grinned at her and made an obscene gesture with her finger.

"You're disgusting."

"So what? I have a man."

"One week, Nicki, he's not *your man* after only one week."

"He's still more than you have."

Ashleigh smiled, pretending that her friend's remark didn't hurt. She hated admitting it to herself, but that was one of the reasons she'd stuck with Damien long after she'd known it was over. She didn't want to be alone. She wasn't a fool. She'd known long before he'd stopped making love to her that the fire was gone. Still, she'd held on. He'd needed her, needed her help, and that she wasn't so quick to let go of.

"Damien's been sending me money," Ashleigh said, changing the subject.

"You're kidding." Nicki nearly choked on the beer she was drinking. "Where the hell did he get money? Oh let me guess. He has a new woman taking care of his sorry ass?"

"Sort of," Ashleigh smiled, "he moved back home with his mother, but he has a job. He called me, told me he wasn't making much money but that he would send me whatever he could each week."

"What do you want to bet if he sent you money it was nowhere near what he was making?"

"You're wrong there. He also sends me a copy of his pay stub."

"You're kidding. Why?"

"He said he's sorry. He also told me that he'd met a woman."

"Are you sure it's not that woman's money that he's sending you? You're not feeling sorry for him, are you? Maybe this is his latest trick to wear you down, make you take him back, have you paying his bills again."

"Isn't this where we started this conversation? Look, I'll admit the whole thing with Damien had me a little freaked out. I don't want to worry about him or about Cole. You know, even now it's hard for me to think of him being named Keefe."

"Listen, aren't you even a little angry with Mia that she lied to us? I mean, we did bring her into our sister circle."

"I thought about it and I called her on it. You can't really blame her. I mean, he is her brother and she didn't know any of us. She didn't owe us any loyalties. Besides, I think she felt bad about doing it. Don't you remember she gave me twice what I was asking?"

"Yeah, and she did say her brother was paying for it." Nicki grinned. "You know the clues were there staring us in the face. Keefe was way too interested in the dress. He was stunned and tried to tell Mia not to pay that much. Remember, Ashleigh?"

"Yeah, I remember. That's why I don't blame her."

"There's a concert over at Dunley Hall tonight. I got us tickets. Want to go?"

Mia barely glanced at her brother. "Why not? I don't have anything else to do."

Keefe worried his lip with the tip of his tongue. He had thought it would get easier but it hadn't. It had been over a month and Mia was still angry with him, but at least she was keeping her promise.

She wasn't seeing Damien.

"Mia, how long do you plan on treating me like the enemy? The way you're acting, someone would think I'm out to ruin your happiness." He ignored her raised brows. "Have you heard anything from James?"

"I got a couple of letters from him today," Mia answered matter-of-factly.

"So what does he have to say? Does he have any idea when he's going to return home?"

Mia forgot that she was supposed to be angry with her brother. She wanted to discuss the last few letters she'd gotten from James. James had not mentioned the wedding, and not even said in a single one that he missed or loved her.

"I think something's going on with James." Keefe raised his brows. She knew he thought she was pulling at straws, so she got up and got the letters for him and stood at his shoulder watching as he read them.

Keefe shrugged his shoulder. "I don't see a problem."

"No problem? Do you think these letters are from a man missing the woman he loves?"

"I don't know. Maybe his letters are in response to yours. Do you tell him that you miss him, that you love him? Are you mentioning the wedding plans?"

Mia looked away. "I do tell him that I can't wait for him to come home and to be safe and take care of himself."

"Mia, I don't see anything wrong with the letters. I think you want to find something wrong here. So how's Damien doing?" he asked.

Mia shook her head and looked sadly at her brother. "Do you really think that if I were seeing him I would fall for that? Keefe, I promised you that I wouldn't see or talk to him and I haven't."

"He hasn't tried to call you?"

"No, Keefe."

"And you think he loves you. Hell, if someone told me that she couldn't see me because her brother hated my guts I'd tell her to go to hell."

"He did."

"He did?"

"Yes, he did."

"He told you to go to hell?"

Mia took a moment to stare at her brother. "Yes, he told me to go to hell and he told me to tell you and James to join me." She smiled then, the first real smile that had touched her lips in over a month. "Seems like you have something in common after all."

Keefe decided not to glare at his sister. He was tired of fighting. He had nothing in common with Damien. "Mia, let's just go have a good time, okay?"

Keefe had spent almost the entire first half of the concert looking at his sister. She was laughing, talking to him, singing along with the artist and having a good time. When she leaned over to him and whispered in his ear that she was sorry for the way she'd been behaving, it made it all worthwhile. They would be okay.

"Mia, I'm going to go out and get something to drink. You want to come with me or do you want me to bring you something back?"

"I'm fine." Mia smiled at her brother. "I'm having a good time."

"Are you really?"

"Yes, really. And I love you for thinking of this. It was just what we needed. Now if you want something to drink you'd better hurry. Intermission is only fifteen minutes.

Keefe stood in line, not noticing the woman in front of him. His mind was on Mia, grateful that she'd come around. Then he heard the woman's voice and the blood chilled in his veins.

He waited behind her, not moving as she turned from the counter with her drink in her hand. She bumped into him, spilling a little of the icy liquid on his chest. She gave a breathy "Excuse me," and moved backwards. He stood still.

Her eyes slowly found his and recognition caused her to smile in hesitation. "Cole, I'm sorry."

"It's Keefe, Ashleigh."

"I keep forgetting. How are you?"

"I'm fine. And you?" *So civilized*, he thought. He should get his drink and go and he was about to do just that before she licked her lips with her tongue. He knew she wasn't aware of what that simple motion was doing to him but his body was definitely aware of it.

His eyes slid over her body and he remembered how right she'd felt in his arms, how much he'd enjoyed making love to her. He could feel the blood that should have been going to his brain being rerouted south.

Ashleigh was everything that he'd sworn not to want, not to ever become involved with. The blood reached its destination and he swallowed, his arousal evident. He only prayed she wouldn't look down.

She was staring at the man who'd given her back a sense of her own needs and regardless of everything that had happened, she had that. Ashleigh was trying everything in her power to keep from remembering how he looked naked, his body glistening with sweat, his muscles bunched as he plunged into her over and over.

She had to stop remembering. She licked her lips, trying to curtail the warmth now invading her body. There was a tightening in her groin, a kind of flicker and she was filling quickly with desire.

Her eyes fastened on Keefe's lips and she remembered the taste of him. He had wonderful full lips. She stood a moment appraising him. What the hell, it wasn't like he cared. She looked at his broad shoulders covered with a form-fitting pale green sweater. She smiled. Only a man secure in his masculinity would dare wear that color. She continued smiling as her eyes traveled downward. Then she saw it, that beautiful bulge that let her know that he wasn't immune to her.

She caught a couple of women looking his way and whispering and a tinge of jealousy cascaded through her. For one brief moment she almost wished he were wearing the uniform of a janitor. Then maybe the women wouldn't give him a second look. She turned slightly to glare at the women. *Or a third look*, she thought.

"I have to get back in. Mia's waiting for me."

"Oh, you came here with your sister? How is she? Is the dress okay?"

"I haven't asked about it, but I don't see why not. As for my sister, she's a woman, what can I say? She has her good days and her bad ones and like most women, lately there've been more bad days."

"Are you blaming me for that also?" Ashleigh detected something that Keefe wasn't saying and there had been just a slight undercurrent of blame. She wasn't being paranoid.

"Would you mind if I said hello?" Ashleigh asked.

"You're not friends, why do you want to see her?"

Now he was pissing her off. He was being just plain rude. "Grow up," she muttered and moved away. "You're not your sister's keeper. If she doesn't want to talk to me, she's a big girl. She can tell me herself."

There was a buzzing in his head, the beginning of a great headache. He could feel it coming on. He closed his eyes. He was tired of everyone telling him that Mia was not a kid; that she could take care of herself. Taking care of his sister was his job. It had been his job ever since their mother left them and it was still his job. He didn't care what anyone thought.

One would have thought with all the pressure in his head there would have been little room in his body for an erection, but there it remained just the same. He glared at Ashleigh, knowing that the reason he didn't want her coming back to where they were sitting had as much to do with his own feelings on seeing her as with Mia.

He didn't know if Mia would feel guilty or not about being with Ashleigh's ex. He didn't know if he believed her about not having gone to bed with Damien and it didn't much matter. She was in love with the man who'd caused Ashleigh so much heartache and he did- n't know if Mia was ready to deal with that.

"Suit yourself." Keefe walked away, not waiting for Ashleigh but knowing that she was following him. His entire body was tingling with knowing and he wanted her. He thought he'd gotten over the infatuation he'd had with her but seeing her again was making him know he'd only shoved those feelings aside.

He felt her touch his arms. "We don't have to be enemies, Keefe."

He whirled around to face her. "What do you propose we be?"

"Friends, for a start."

"Now that you know I have money you want to be my friend? No thanks." He turned forward and increased his pace. He spotted Mia's smiling face looking for him, probably wondering what was taking him so long. Then he saw the slight pause as she spotted Ashleigh behind him. He'd known this wasn't a good idea.

"Ashleigh, hi, how are you?" Mia stuck out her hand but Ashleigh ignored it and gave her a warm hug instead.

"Listen, I think with all the things we've shared a hug is more in order."

Keefe turned and stared at Ashleigh, wondering what the hell she was talking about.

Ashleigh observed the confused looks of the brother and sister. So much alike. She had seen the resemblance the first day, their tawny skin, the light brown eyes with golden flecks and their smiles lazy and sweet. She glanced at Keefe. *And sexy as hell*, she thought.

"Mia, I'm talking about our sister circle, the cleansing, remember? And of course the wedding gown."

"Of course," Mia stammered. Her eyes slid over to her brother. She noticed he wasn't looking at either of them. He was clearly uncomfortable.

"Ashleigh, it's so good to see you. Are you enjoying the concert?" There, she'd said the right words, asked the right question, and she was sure her face held a smile. It had to; she was stretching her lips into something and her jaw ached with the effort. She could feel the tiny tremors as the muscles fought back, resisting her efforts.

The flashing lights warned them the show was about to resume, so Ashleigh moved back into the aisle. She bit her lips and looked directly at Keefe. "I'd like to explain things to you. Please, would you come by my apartment so we can talk?"

She was so afraid that he was going to call her some awful name that everyone would hear. She ran her tongue over her lips, her heart pounding, and she held her hand out for Keefe to shake. For a long moment she didn't know if he would but he did and her heart lurched in her chest. The tips of her fingers burned from the contact. She brought her eyes upward to look into his. She smiled but he didn't smile in return, so she walked away.

Keefe took his seat beside his sister. The concert was ruined for him. All he could think of was the way he'd felt with Ashleigh lying beneath him, on top of him, him in her mouth, her in his, and he wanted the sweetness again. She was a gold digger, he reminded himself, forget about her.

He glanced at Mia. She was no longer smiling; in fact, there appeared to be a permanent grimace of pain stretching her features. He wondered if it was her guilt over falling for Ashleigh's man or buying her dress. He watched her fingers twitching nervously in her lap and avoided the sidelong glances she was giving him.

They stayed like that until the show was nearly over and Keefe made a decision. He reached over for his sister's hand and held it in his own. "I'm not going to see her," he whispered to her but instead of the relief he'd expected to see, the guilt only intensified.

Mia had watched the way her brother had tried to pretend that he was unaffected by Ashleigh's presence, but she knew him well. Keefe didn't give his heart easily to people. He kept himself insulated so nothing and no one could hurt him. With Ashleigh he'd allowed himself to become vulnerable and he was hurting.

She'd seen that Ashleigh was attracted to him and she truly didn't believe she was after her brother's money, but she didn't know if she would have any luck convincing him of that. Then out of the blue the thought came to her: why try?

She did her best to let go of the thought but it hung in there festering, telling her she would never have to see Ashleigh's face again or admit to her what she'd done if Keefe didn't see her.

Then she happened to glimpse the sadness that was in her

brother's eyes and she felt like the selfish brat that she was. She'd betrayed her brother twice, first by lying to him, now by wanting to take away his shot at happiness to protect her own guilty secret. With that knowledge the unadulterated guilt rolled over her in waves, crushing her. She wanted to run screaming from the theater, but she sat next to the man who'd given up his own childhood in order for her to have one. And how did she repay him? With treachery.

She thought of Treece, beautiful long-legged Treece, with warm brown skin and laughing brown eyes. A perfect complement to her brother's coloring and somber behavior. She had been his first chance at love, and she was the first woman to break his heart. No, Mia winced, the first woman to break Keefe's heart was their mother.

Treece had even fooled Mia with the playful manner in which she spoke of her love for Keefe. Then the day came when she'd come to Keefe crying that she was in trouble and needed money, twenty-five thousand dollars to be exact. Keefe had come to her and she'd told him to give it to Treece, that he loved her and she loved him. Mia had promised him it would be okay.

But it wasn't. Treece had purposefully sought Keefe out, making him fall in love with her. Her plan all along had been to con him out of money. In the end they'd found out Treece was sleeping with several men and had taken each of them for a bundle and given it all to her boyfriend who was in prison for pushing dope.

None of the men had seen it coming. Keefe felt like a fool, as did the rest of the men when the whole sordid story came out in the papers. Mia blamed herself for not seeing through Treece. Keefe's heart was broken, but he'd not taken it out on her.

Now after almost five years he'd opened his heart up again and it was all her fault in a way that he'd once again gotten hurt. She'd pushed him to pursue Ashleigh. Yes, she felt guilty, guilty for constantly hurting her brother, guilty for wanting Damien, knowing that having him would surely wreck any possibility of a relationship Keefe might have with Ashleigh.

When he reached for her hand she'd turned to face him and he'd whispered to her, "I'm not going to see her." As always, he wanted to protect her. He'd thought her silence was her guilt over Ashleigh and he was partially right, only he didn't know the extent of it. She was exactly like their mother.

CHAPTER TEN

Several torturous weeks had passed since running into Ashleigh at the concert, but Keefe still couldn't get her off his mind. Every night he dreamed of her, dreamed of making love to her, and every night the script had the same revision: Ashleigh did not tell him that she wanted a man with money.

Keefe corrected himself. Even in the actual version that was not what she had actually done. She had said she couldn't date a man with no money, which in his book spelled the same thing.

His relationship with his sister had returned to being strained. He had tried everything to remedy it and he cursed daily that he had taken her to that concert, even though she'd been having a good time before she saw Ashleigh.

It appeared that demons were chasing both of them. Mia had stopped mentioning the cryptic messages she was getting from James. Instead, she silently laid the letters out on the table for him to see, along with a copy of the letters she'd written to him.

Even Keefe had to admit in his heart that something was wrong. He'd never been in the service but James sure as hell didn't sound like a man missing the woman he loved. His letters were indifferent. They could have been written to a buddy of his. Not once had he signed them "With love." He simply scrawled his name at the bottom.

With each letter that Mia left on the table he knew she was longing to be with Damien, but she'd promised him not to. The pain of her promise was evident in the sadness that permeated Mia's soul and invaded their home. He thought of just moving back to his own home, leaving Mia to her own devices, but the thought of Damien coming back into her life made him stay. She was miserable and he was miserable for making her that way. Still, he could think of nothing else to do. So they ate together, went out together and were lonely together, something they'd never been before. He missed his sister enjoying his company, him enjoying hers. With great sadness he convinced himself that it was more important that he protect her than have her friendship. The lie hurt like hell.

Keefe found himself at Ashleigh's door one Sunday afternoon. He knocked before he could talk himself out of it. When she opened the door, he stepped into the apartment, looked around and shrugged his shoulders. He couldn't speak, didn't want to say out loud why he was there. The truth was that he wanted her. He'd wanted her every day since they'd made love and the wanting had only gotten stronger.

She was staring at him with a small, frightened smile, her head tilted to the side. Closing her eyes, she fell into his arms and the battle was over. His lips found hers and he kissed them, relishing the taste he'd been denied because of his lies and her greed. He wouldn't think about that now.

Ashleigh couldn't believe that she was in Keefe's arms, that she was kissing him. She'd been missing him for so long she'd almost given up hope of ever touching him again.

As much as she wanted to continue kissing him, she wanted to look at him, maybe ask why it had taken him so long to come to her. She attempted to pull away but he pulled her back. His hand found its way under her blouse, the process apparently slower than he wanted. When he pulled the blouse from her shoulders, the buttons popped in his haste.

"I'll buy you another one," he said.

A stab of pain pierced her and she closed her eyes, unable to prevent the hurt that tugged at her from coming through.

"I don't want your money."

She pulled away and he pulled her back. "I'll buy you another one," he repeated, "because I ruined it."

Before she could pull away again, he gazed hungrily at her upper torso. His look seared her with desire. Lust blazed from his eyes and he ripped the lacy bra from her body as easily as if it had been made of tissue paper. A look came into his eyes and she shook her head. "Don't say it," she whispered. "You don't need to replace it."

"Ashleigh," he moaned, sucking one nipple into his mouth. She shuddered. This time she would ignore the voices telling her to stop. She didn't want to resist Keefe's ardent touches. She hungered for them.

His touches were quickly driving any lingering thoughts of resistance far from her. In fact, what she did was lower her hand and touch him. Tremors of desire inflamed her body. Keefe's moan, low and guttural, filled the room, fueling both of their needs. She wrapped her arms around him as he lifted her in his arms and carried her to the bedroom.

Within seconds their clothing was scattered about the room and Keefe was ripping open the condom. They had no time for gentle caresses. Ashleigh acknowledged his urgency, her need as great as his. She wanted him to be buried deep inside her.

With each thrust the passion mounted between them. She was clawing his back, begging him to hurry. She knew that he'd missed the magic they'd found as much as she had. His need matched her own.

"Keefe," Ashleigh moaned. "I missed you," she admitted. There was no need to be coy and pretend otherwise. She'd blown her chance at coyness when she'd opened the door to him. A shiver claimed Ashleigh's heart as surely as Keefe was claiming her body. No, there was no time for pretense. On her first sight of him standing at her door, she'd thanked God and fallen into Keefe's arms, knowing why he was there. He wanted her. That thought didn't bother her. She wanted him too.

And now that he was inside her, she knew it was where he belonged. Their coupling had been fast, just what she needed. She'd wanted him so badly that the moment he entered her, she had to fight to hold back the climax. Now she was lying beneath him, once again moaning like a whore, begging him to give her more. Desire made her wanton. She'd never experienced anything like what she was experiencing now and she wouldn't regret it, no matter what happened after. No, she wouldn't regret it.

Her entire body was trembling. Her abdominal muscles tensed and when she felt Keefe shudder and hold her even tighter, she knew he was about to come. She gave in to the demands of her body and joined him. His growling sent her spiraling over the edge. She found herself biting his shoulder as she screamed out his name. She heard him growl again. The force of their combined climax took her by surprise. It lasted for several minutes and when it was over, Keefe fell against her body and lay there speechless. His arms circled her and she held him to her.

After a few moments, he raised up and looked down at her,

touched a hand gently to her brow to push back a stray strand of hair so gently that if he didn't hate her she would have thought he cared. He rolled off her and pulled her head to rest on his chest.

They didn't talk for a while and Ashleigh wondered if it was because they both knew that their words held the power to kill what had just happened.

She didn't like the silence, it fed her doubts. Ashleigh had a momentary thought that now that it was over Keefe was regretting it. Her memory of him calling her a gold digger fed her insecurities, making her wonder why she'd given in so easily to the look in Keefe's eyes. But when she'd opened the door and saw him standing there, his reasons for being there hadn't mattered, just the fact that he was. And she'd wanted him, wanted him in her bed. Her entire being had trembled with wanting.

Finally she could take it no longer; she had to know. "So what was I, Keefe? I mean, what just happened between us? Was that a booty call?"

Again his fingers caressed her before he answered, "What do you want it to be?"

"Not a booty call," she answered.

"Then it wasn't."

"Keefe, do you think it would be possible for us to start over?"

"I don't know. Our beginning wasn't promising. You think of me as a liar and I think of you as…"

"But I'm not." Ashleigh looked into his eyes. "I'm not. I don't want anything from you, Keefe. I make my own money. What I said to you before, maybe I didn't say it in the right way, but all I meant was that I couldn't be with a man who didn't have his own money. Not for me. I don't want a man's money. I just don't want him to want mine."

Keefe didn't answer; he just lay there with his fingers entwined with hers. All Ashleigh knew for sure was that he wanted to make love to her again. They'd only taken the edge off.

"Are you listening to me?"

"Yes, I'm listening," he answered.

She knew he wasn't, not really. She ran a finger down the side of his arm and he turned so that he was over her a few inches and looking down into her face.

"Tell me again," he said.

"I don't want you for your money, Keefe. That's one thing you won't have to worry about. I'll never ask you for money. I have my own."

"So you want to start over, pretend we're meeting for the first time, no lies between us?"

"No lies, Keefe. If there's something else about yourself that you haven't told me, do so now. I don't want to start caring about you and find out that Mia is not really your sister but an old girlfriend." She looked into his eyes. "Is there anything about either you or your sister that I should know?"

Damien flashed across Keefe's mind but it had been months since Mia had seen or talked to him. The man was no longer a problem for them. So in all honesty he answered, "From this moment on we're starting over. There is nothing that I'm going to keep from you, no secrets that you need to know about."

"That I need to know about?"

"Okay, no more secrets."

Ashleigh smiled at him and as he leaned into her to kiss her, he said a silent thank you that Mia wasn't seeing Damien. In a few short months James would return home, they would be happy and Mia would be happy for him that he'd found someone. His lips captured Ashleigh's. *Yes, his sister would be happy for him,* he thought as he held the woman he was falling for, tasting her and knowing that surely nothing in all of heaven could taste as sweet.

"What about you, Ashleigh, any secrets?"

"I think you've discovered all my secrets," Ashleigh answered. She ran her tongue across his lips, needing to taste what she'd longed for. "Just make love to me, Keefe, as if this were our last time. And I'll make love to you in the same manner."

And she did.

Ashleigh stood facing her front door. She was laughing and hugging herself and had been since Keefe had kissed her and said goodbye.

She was happy. She couldn't remember when she had ever been filled with such joy. She'd spent the entire afternoon making love with Keefe. Her body still tingled with sated contentment. They had not done much talking. They'd been too busy fulfilling the needs of their bodies. They'd spoken with their hands, their lips and their eyes.

The most important words, though, had somehow managed to be said. They were going to try again. Ashleigh couldn't believe it. In spite of all she'd done, she'd been given another chance. Laughing out loud, she left the door and began dancing around the room, screaming at the top of her lungs. "Yes, yes, thank you, God." After all the losers in her life, she was finally having a chance to start a relationship with a man who didn't need her to take care of him. She raced for the phone. She couldn't wait to tell Nicki.

Keefe walked into Mia's apartment on top of the world. He couldn't wipe the grin from his face. He'd spent the entire afternoon making love to Ashleigh, in the shower, in her bed and once with her standing, her back braced against the wall.

The house was quiet. He couldn't wait to find Mia and tell her, hear her 'I told you so.' He wouldn't mind hearing it. This was too wonderful. Besides that, his sister had been right. Ashleigh was the perfect woman for him.

"Mia," Keefe called as he walked around looking for his sister. He spotted paper on the table and knew it had to be a letter from James. He walked over to examine it.

Mia, sorry I'm taking so long to tell you this, but I just couldn't think of a way to do it. I know I'm hurting you but I can't let you go on planning a wedding that's not going to happen. I found someone, Mia. I've been married for almost four months. I tried to tell you in the other letters but I couldn't. Maybe in time you'll stop hating me and realize that love happens in the oddest of ways. I'll always remain your friend.

Damn, Keefe dropped the letter and ran for his sister's bedroom. He barely knocked before bursting through the door. "Mia, I read it. Are you okay?" Mia was watching him but didn't seem to see him. "Mia, have you taken something? You're scaring me."

Her eyes turned toward him and finally the dead look went away. But what came next was even worse. She began weeping uncontrollably, breaking his heart. He wished like hell James was somewhere around right now. He would break his neck.

"Mia, don't cry, baby. It's going to be all right. I'll help you through it."

Mia glanced up at her brother through her tears. "I'm not crying because of the letter, or about James." She saw the shock come into her brother's eyes. "I don't love him, Kee. I'm crying because these last few months have all been wasted. For what? James didn't love me either; for four months he's been married. I knew something was going on. I tried to tell you." Her voice had turned accusing. She recognized it and hated herself for using that against him.

Keefe swallowed. He knew what was coming and wished he could stop it. Mia was crying because she wanted something he didn't want her to have, something that in his opinion would be bad for her, hurt her in the end.

"I want to call Damien," Mia said at last, putting it out there. "I've done as you asked, Kee." She cried harder. "I've kept my promise. I haven't seen or talked to Damien. I love him, I want to call him."

"You haven't called him already?" he asked.

"No, I wouldn't do that until I talked to you."

"Mia, he's bad news. I don't want you with him."

"Don't you want me to be happy?" she asked, tears streaming down her face. She fell against his chest, clinging to his neck, "Keefe, please."

"What about Ashleigh?" he whispered to her over the lump in his throat. "What about her feelings?"

She wiped at the tears and almost smiled. "You don't even like Ashleigh. You haven't seen her. How is she ever going to know? It not like we're lying to her, Kee. She's not in our lives."

He couldn't answer. His sister was miserable and God, how he wanted to make her happy, make her smile. Visions of his lips on Ashleigh's breasts flashed before him, and he shuddered at the stab of pain. He'd promised not to lie to her anymore. What the hell was he going to do? The answer was obvious: what he'd done their entire life. Mia came first. She had to come first. He had to make sure she was happy before he could worry about his own happiness.

"Go ahead, call him, Mia." He picked up the phone and handed it to her, feeling as if he'd just handed her a dagger with which to cut out his heart. How the hell was he supposed to choose his happiness over his sister's? He couldn't—not in a million years. "I'll see you a little later," Keefe said as he leaned down to place a kiss on his sister's forehead. "I have to take care of something."

"Ashleigh, would it be okay if I come by? I need to see you." Keefe tried to keep his voice normal, not alert her that the bottom had just dropped out of his world.

"Give me fifteen minutes," Ashleigh answered. "I want to take a quick shower. Hurry," she whispered and disconnected before he could say another word. *How the hell am I going to do th*is? Keefe groaned.

Ashleigh dashed into the shower, pushing aside her worries about the call from the bank and the official letter from the IRS threatening to seize her shop for back taxes. She'd called her accountant. He'd handle things. Right now, her thoughts were on Keefe. She couldn't wait to see him, to make love to him. Maybe she'd even tell him how she felt. Maybe.

In record time her shower was done, she'd brushed and gargled and now stood in her bedroom spraying on the cologne she'd bought during her lunch hour. A purchase she couldn't afford, according to the bank. But she was confident there'd been a mistake. Besides, she wanted to smell delicious for Keefe. She imagined his reaction when he got his first tantalizing whiff of her cologne. That alone would be worth the money.

A knock sounded on her door and Ashleigh rushed to open it, pausing only long enough to peep through the keyhole. She smiled at the sight of Keefe.

"Get in here," she said and pulled Keefe into the apartment, immediately falling into his arms.

"Ash," he moaned as he held her tight, so tight that it alarmed her. He was trembling and when she attempted to pull away he held her even closer.

"Keefe, is there something wrong?"

He lifted his face and she saw the haunted look in his eyes. "Keefe?" she repeated. There was something going on. If she didn't know it from the tightening in her limbs and her suddenly dry throat, she would have known from Keefe's reaction. He was biting his lips, trembling visibly. And then he shut his eyes.

An icy coldness snaked its way up her spine. Whatever it was, was bad. She managed to pull away and began rocking unconsciously with her arms folded across her chest. "Keefe?" she asked again. She almost wished she hadn't because when he opened his eyes, her fears were mirrored there.

"What is it," she asked, backing farther away. "Just tell me, get it over with." He reached out a hand to touch her and she moaned. "No, tell it to me straight."

"It's my sister. Mia." He stopped.

She took a tentative step back toward him, a tinge of hope propelling her, followed immediately by guilt that she'd momentarily found comfort in the idea that something horrible had happened to Keefe's sister. She knew it was only because it would mean the look she'd seen in his eyes didn't concern her. He hadn't come to break up with her. She shuddered at her selfish thought and moved even closer to comfort the man she was sure she was falling in love with.

"Is she...was she...in an accident?"

Until that moment Keefe had been unaware of what his actions, his words, had conveyed to Ashleigh. He shook his head. "No accident." He blinked, trying to clear his head. He licked his lips repeatedly, finding the words hard to say. Ashleigh was standing so close to him and she smelled so good. God, how he wanted to hold her, bury himself in her, love her. A shudder claimed him and he reached out for her. She didn't resist but allowed him to draw her into his arms.

"Ashleigh, I'm sorry, he moaned into her neck, inhaling the scent of her to carry away with him. He pulled her in closer as she attempted to pull away.

"What are you sorry about? What happened to Mia?" Ashleigh asked, now worrying for a different reason. Keefe was behaving irrationally.

"Her fiancé, he married someone else," Keefe said at last.

"Did Mia...do something to herself? Did she take something? Keefe, is your sister..."

This time when he pulled away the look Ashleigh witnessed was far different. There was so much pain there. But there was also a hint of anger. "What's going on?" she asked hesitantly. "You're scaring me. Just tell me what's wrong with your sister. Come sit down." She held his hand and led him to the sofa. "Okay, tell me."

"I can't see you anymore."

Boom. Her mind slammed shut, white noise filling it. Then she heard her heart breaking into a zillion pieces. "Why?" she asked at last.

"Mia. Mia needs me."

"I can understand that," Ashleigh rushed out, trying for any solution to make the situation better. She didn't want to lose Keefe. Not now. *Please, dear God, help me find a way. Don't let this be happening.*

"You want to spend some time with your sister, help her get over this. I won't go crazy if you're not around for a couple of weeks. Is that what you thought?"

She attempted to smile. Her fingers found his and held on tight. "I understand about family, really I do, Keefe. I know you want to help your sister. I want to help her too. Let me talk with her. She probably needs a woman. I'll get my friends together. We'll do a sister circle for her. We'll help her get over the pain."

"No," he said and stood. "The timing isn't right. Mia needs me. I'm sorry, but I have to be there for her."

"I could help."

"No, it's not that easy."

"Why isn't it?"

"It's complicated. Look, I can't worry about myself. I have to think about my sister. Her happiness is all that matters to me."

"What about you, Keefe? Don't you deserve to be happy? What about me? I thought you said I wasn't just a booty call."

He groaned out loud. "God, Ashleigh you're not." He walked

toward her, but she got up from the sofa and moved away.

"No? Then why don't you tell me what I am to you."

She watched as he shook his head, seeming to be in a battle. She thought for a moment he was going to tell her that he loved her, ask her to wait until his sister was healed, that she was beginning to be important to him, if only a little. But then he looked into her eyes. She knew. It was over. Ashleigh went cold all over.

"Mia is all the family I have. She's my first priority. I'm the one who raised her. I love her, Ashleigh. I would give my life to protect her. You have to understand that. I won't hurt her. And I won't allow anyone else to hurt her."

There'd been a warning in there somewhere. She was sure of it. But why? "I haven't hurt your sister, Keefe. I only met her one time…and I liked her. I only wanted to help you and Mia, not hurt her." As she watched, his eyes glazed over, then closed.

"I wish you could help." He opened his eyes and smiled at her. "You have no idea how much I wish you could help. I'm sorry about this. I didn't want to hurt you." Keefe shook his head. "I didn't want to come over. I didn't want to see the look that I'm seeing now on your face. I almost took the coward's way out and called you. But you deserve so much better than that, Ashleigh. You deserve so much more than I can give you."

"Apparently not. You're dumping me for your sister." She snorted. "I can't believe it."

"I'm all she has, Ashleigh. I'm sorry but I have to protect her."

"From me?"

"From everyone."

With that he headed for the door. Ashleigh stared after him in shocked disbelief. This didn't just happen. But then again, what had made her think that finally things would go right for her? That she'd have a good man and a stable relationship.

No, she hadn't hooked up with another loser. She'd fallen for someone much worse. A man who would never put her first. A man committed to making one person happy. His sister. *Damn. What a joke,* she thought and fell where she was, sobbing her heart out.

Keefe practically ran for the elevator. He had to get away from Ashleigh. Leaving her was hard, possibly the hardest thing he'd ever done in his life. He walked into the elevator. And to think he was giving her up so that his sister could be with a man who would break her heart. Ironic when he thought of it. He'd just done the same thing to Ashleigh.

Jealousy claimed Ashleigh. Mia had everything Ashleigh wanted: Ashleigh's dream gown and Keefe's love. Ashleigh wished she'd never put that blasted notice in the laundry room. She didn't want to hate the young woman who'd bought her gown. It was irrational.

Yet she couldn't help feeling the anger as pain twisted her insides. She could forgive the young woman for the gown. After all, the money had come in handy. But for the first time in her life, Ashleigh had met a decent man. A man that she'd just begun to love and Mia had taken that also. How was she supposed to compete with a lifetime of love Keefe had invested in his sister?

133

CHAPTER ELEVEN

For the second time in one week, Keefe walked into the apartment and found it dark. Mia was nowhere in sight, but something alerted him that she was home. He sighed loudly. Neither of them was happy. It had been five days since he'd gone to Ashleigh and told her that he was sorry, that the timing wasn't right for them, that his sister wasn't going to be getting married after all and that she needed him.

He'd brushed aside Ashleigh's offers of help, wishing he could tell her all of it, but he couldn't. Mia wasn't ready to deal with her guilt over falling in love with Damien and having Ashleigh's gown. His sister's happiness had to be all that mattered to him.

He sighed again and sank into a chair, needing a moment before going in to check on her. She'd called Damien, fully expecting he would be happy to hear from her; instead, he'd told her to go to hell. Again.

After sitting in the darkened room for a few minutes, Keefe knocked on Mia's bedroom door. He heard her softly murmured, "Come in," pasted a smile on his face, then opened the door.

"Mia, you didn't go to work today?" Keefe asked carefully so that his tone did not imply scolding.

"No. I…I didn't feel up to it… I thought, well, I thought Damien might call me."

"Mia, it's been five days. How long are you going to wait?"

"I know he loves me, he's just angry."

Keefe sighed again, then saw the quick flash of pain on his sister's face and wished he could keep his feelings about Damien to himself.

"Is he even talking to you, Mia?"

"No, his mother tells me he's working when I call her home, and he won't answer his cell when I call. He knows my number."

"Didn't you try blocking it?"

"Of course I did," Mia answered, her tone a bit annoyed that he was treating her like a child. "He must have figured that was me also."

He saw the gleam in her eyes a moment before her mouth opened and he screamed, "Hell no, Mia. I'm not calling him."

"Please." She was on her feet with a pleading smile on her face, a sign of hope in her voice. "Oh, Keefe, please, he'll answer. Then you can ask him to talk to me."

He closed his eyes and turned away, not wanting to fall prey to her demands. She was manipulating him, using his love for her, just as she always had. In a flash her arms were nearly strangling him. She pressed her head close to his, kissed his cheeks and forehead as she pleaded with him. "Pleasseee, please," she continued until simply wanting to shut her up, he threw up his hands and screamed, "Okay, okay, once, Mia, once."

He stalked out to the kitchen, snatched up his phone and returned to Mia's bedroom. "What's his number?" He punched the numbers in with more force than was necessary, half of him praying the bastard wouldn't pick up, the other half, seeing the look on Mia's face, praying that he would.

"Hello." The voice was hesitant, no doubt wondering who was calling him.

"This is Keefe Black, Mia's brother." Keefe waited. "She asked me to call you; she just wants to talk with you."

"Why? Have you now given her permission to date the low-life, now that Mr. Perfect has dumped her?"

God, how he hated the man. He wanted to tell the jerk off, tell him where to go, what to do. Then he glanced at his sister and tempered his response. "No, I didn't give her my permission. I told her the truth, that you're a womanizing, two-timing loser and that she should be grateful that you weren't returning her calls."

Mia's face fell. Though she tried to reach for the phone, Keefe held it out of her reach. She'd asked him to make the call, and now she'd just have to let him deal with it in his own way.

Still holding the phone away from his sister, Keefe waited for a reply from Damien. After a moment of silence, there was laughter, not malicious but as though responding to a joke, pleasant laughter.

"Then you're telling me that despite your feelings on this, Mia wants to see me?"

"That's what I'm saying."

"Then do you mind if I talk to her?"

"Yes, I mind, but I'll give her the phone." Keefe looked at Mia before passing the phone over and walking out of her room, closing the door firmly behind him.

Keefe sat nursing a beer, trying not to listen to the muffled voices from his sister's bedroom, trying not to allow himself to give in to the desire to call Ashleigh, trying not to allow the pain to overcome him. All this pain, for what?

He glanced around at the sound of Mia's footsteps. She gave her head a shake in answer to his look, then held out his cell phone.

"It didn't help?"

"No," Mia answered. "It didn't help."

"He's no longer in love with you?"

"He said he loves me but he's going to try and forget that. I guess I waited too long."

"What are you going to do?"

"Nothing. I took my chance when I asked him to wait."

"I'm sorry, Mia"

"No you're not."

He smiled. "I am sorry that you're hurting. That much is true." He smiled again. "Don't worry, baby, you're going to be okay. We both are."

"Do you really believe that?"

"Mia, why don't we just forget everything for now. I'll go rent us a couple of movies and pick up some food, and then we'll just have a fun night together. How about it," he urged. "We always have fun together."

"Yes, you're right," she agreed, knowing her brother was trying to keep her mind off Damien. "Okay, go get the movies. We'll make a night of it."

Keefe couldn't prevent the smile from curving his lips as he returned home, his arms filled with a bag of the newest DVD releases and enough food for an army. He'd bought pizza, then remembered how much Mia liked egg rolls and had gone to get some and ended up with an entire takeout order, everything from egg foo young to fried rice.

Tonight he would comfort his baby sister. Tomorrow he would comfort himself. The thought of holding Ashleigh in his arms filled him with joy. And he would tell her all of it; he would tell her about Mia and Damien. They'd work through it. He was sure of it.

He'd done everything his sister had asked, even called the guy. Now when he returned to Ashleigh there would be nothing standing in their way, nothing to mar their future happiness.

"Mia," he called, "I'm back." He stopped. His sister was cuddled up on the sofa with a man. Anger surged through him as he stopped short. "Mia," he said sternly.

"Kee, I'm sorry, I didn't hear you come in."

"I'm sure you didn't," he answered. He ignored Damien, his stomach churning as the man stood to face him. He'd had only a glimmer of hope that it would be anyone else his sister was kissing but had known it wouldn't be.

"Here's the stuff." He tossed the bags on the coffee table, anger infusing his body.

Damien's hand was out there in the air. He was smiling at Keefe while his arm was wrapped protectively around Mia.

Keefe glanced from Damien's outstretched hand to Mia's pleading face and still he couldn't bring himself to accept the man's hand. Finally Damien dropped his hand.

"I know you don't like me," Damien said at last, and Keefe could feel his lips curling into a sneer. That was an understatement if ever there was one.

"I haven't done anything to you or to your sister." Damien's head tilted to the side. "But this feeling you have for me, this dislike, it seems personal. You don't know me, do you?" He smiled again. "I only remember meeting you that one time at Ashleigh's apartment."

He was studying Keefe, making it obvious. Keefe didn't like it but he'd be damned if he'd turn away.

"I know enough," Keefe muttered at last, "and you're right. What I know I don't like. Since you brought Ashleigh's name up, what about her?"

The tension mounted in the room. Damien released Mia and thoughtfully studied Keefe.

"Is there something going on between you and Ashleigh?" Damien asked at last. "Is that the reason for your level of hostility?"

Keefe glared at Damien. How was it possible that a man he didn't know, a man he detested, could read him more easily than the sister he adored?

At a loss for words, Keefe just stood there. As Damien continued to study him, Keefe saw the recognition that'd he'd been right dawn in Damien's eyes and then, of all things, compassion. It was the compassion that freed Keefe's tongue.

"Even if that were true, do you really think any woman would want to have a relationship with the brother of the woman who's...," he paused, hesitant to utter the words, "involved with the man who used her, then dumped her, the same woman who bought her wedding gown, the gown she was going to use to marry said boyfriend?"

He was aware of the quick flash of guilt that darted into his sister's eyes, the flush that stained her cheeks. He'd not intended to say anything to hurt her but...

"Kee, do you still have feelings for her?" Mia interjected.

Keefe walked toward the kitchen. "Eat your food, Mia. You've got what you wanted. Just remember that you're the one who wanted him. He was with Ashleigh for years, and look how he treated her. Do you think he's really going to treat you any better?"

Keefe turned on the kitchen faucet full force, scooped up several handfuls of icy water and washed his face. He was shaking. Damn. Every time it seemed it would be okay, that maybe he could go after what he wanted, something happened. Seeing Damien in the apartment when he got back was like a kick to the gut.

When he at last thought he'd regained some semblance of control, he reached for a paper towel to dry his face and found Damien standing there holding out several towels. He ignored them and got his own.

"Where's Mia?" Keefe asked Damien.

"She's giving us a couple of minutes to talk. Alone. She said she'd going to visit a neighbor for a few minutes."

"I don't think we have anything to talk about," Keefe retorted. "Everything I had to say to you I've already said."

Damien smiled. "I doubt that, but I have something to say to you. Man, it's there in your eyes. Why haven't you told Mia?"

When Keefe only stared, understanding again dawned in Damien's eyes. "It's because of Mia, isn't it? You don't want her feeling guilty, so you're not going after a woman that you want. I'm impressed."

"I didn't intend to try to impress you. It doesn't matter what you think about me."

"But I'm right," Damien insisted, "you're giving her up for Mia. Why? I don't understand. You had nothing to do with my falling in love with your sister. Why don't you tell Mia how you feel?"

"That's my business. And if nothing else, I expect you to be man enough not to tell my sister."

"Ashleigh won't hold this against you."

Keefe rolled his eyes. "Get real."

Damien worried his lips. "You're probably right. I don't know what to think. Thanks, man."

"I'm not doing this for you," Keefe all but growled.

"Believe me, I'm well aware of that fact, but I care about Mia. I don't want her worrying either, so that's why I'm saying thanks."

"You care about her?" Keefe laughed. "You care about her?" he repeated. "I love her, I've loved her her entire life. And you're right, Damien, I do have something else to say to you. You hurt my sister in any way I'll make you pay."

"You're threatening me?" Damien leaned against the doorjamb. "Why?"

"Believe me, this is no idle threat. You hurt Mia and you're going to wish you'd never heard of her or me. I can guarantee that."

Only inches separated the two men, both angry at this point. Then Damien sighed and took several steps back. He smiled. "I'm not stupid. Don't you think I know that if I took a swing at you your sister would dump me in a heartbeat?"

Keefe was still glaring. He was not so sure that the words Damien spoke were correct. Until Mia met Damien he would have agreed about her reaction. Now he didn't know, but he wasn't going to let Damien know that.

"I'm not going to hurt her," Damien said at last. "I'm in love with Mia."

"You said you were in love with Ashleigh, too, didn't you?"

"I did love Ashleigh. Matter of fact, I always will, but I was never *in love* with her. And I doubt that she was ever in love with me."

"Then why in hell was she planning on marrying you? Why did you even bother asking her?"

"I never did. She said she was ready to get married, that she wasn't getting any younger and she was ready to have babies. I said okay."

"Are you saying she asked you?"

"Not exactly. It just sort of happened like I said. That was all there was to it."

Keefe clicked his teeth against his gums. "That still doesn't excuse what you did to her. You're still a bum in my book."

Damien smiled, "Bum I can take. I've been called worse. You're right. I took advantage of Ashleigh."

"You used her."

"No, I took advantage of her."

"What the hell is the difference?"

"One sounds better."

"Are you trying to be a wise ass?"

"No, I'm attempting to be truthful, man-to-man." Keefe's brows lifted but Damien continued. "I'm not out to prove myself to you, but to Mia. I love her and she's the only one who has to believe that."

They heard the door open and both turned toward the sound. "Don't hurt her," Keefe growled again.

"I don't intend to," Damien answered and walked back through the door to embrace Mia.

Keefe watched them for a moment, the way they looked into each other's eyes, smiling before finally kissing. He could almost believe the man loved his sister. He closed his eyes and turned away.

Now what the hell was he supposed to do? Keefe lay on his bed in the second bedroom of Mia's apartment, knowing that it was high time he left his sister's home and returned to his own. Sounds of muffled laughter floated to him.

With a groan, he reached for the phone and dialed it, holding his breath.

"Ashleigh," he whispered, the sound of her voice taking his breath away. "How are you?"

"What do you want?" she asked.

"Just to see how you are."

"Go to hell," she said and slammed the phone in his ear.

He deserved that. He knew it. But still it hurt. He stretched out on the bed too tired to even undress. Yes, tomorrow he would return to his own home.

"Was that him?"

"Yes."

"Want me to get a couple of brothers I know to kick his ass?"

For the first time in nearly a week, Ashleigh smiled. "Let me think about it."

"You okay?" Nicki asked.

"You'd think I'd be used to this by now, wouldn't you? I mean, it seems to be a habit, me getting the shaft."

"Don't, Ash."

"Don't worry," Ashleigh answered. "Amazingly, I'm not bitter. I mean, think about it. At least what happened was original. I'd never been dumped for a guy's sister before."

"You ask, me that's pretty weird, if not out and out freaky. You sho there's nothing going on there?"

Ashleigh shook her head. "Not this time, Nicki. I appreciate your wanting to trash Keefe for me. But that's not what this was about. There is something with his sister, some obligation he feels, but it's not what you think."

"I know, girl. I was just trying to make you feel better."

"I know."

"You want to do a sister circle?"

"No."

"Well, what do you want?"

"I want Keefe."

"I can't help you with that."

"I know," Ashleigh said. "Just help me with the books. I have to find out where the hell my money has disappeared to."

"What did your accountant have to say about it?"

"He told me not to worry, that it was all a mistake."

"But?"

"I'm worried."

Keefe threw the last of his things into a bag. "Mia, I'm not angry with you," he told her for perhaps the hundredth time. "I have my own place and right now we both need our own space."

"You're saying the right words, big brother, but your eyes are saying something entirely different. You're disappointed in me, aren't you?"

Keefe couldn't help sighing. "It's not that I'm disappointed in you. I just wanted better for you, that's all. I thought I'd taught you to want better for yourself." He stopped what he was doing and turned to her. "You're just not the sort I ever thought would want leftovers. He's…" Keefe shook his head. What was the use? He'd told Mia often enough that Damien wasn't good enough for her. Did she even care? "Mia, he doesn't even have a decent job."

"But he's working; he's working every day."

"Through a temp agency. Why doesn't he find a permanent job? I don't care if it's at a fast food place slinging burgers. At least that would be a start."

"Jobs are hard to find right now."

Keefe snorted. "That's not true. There are plenty of good jobs out there right now for people who want them. I have several friends who tell me how hard it is for them to get good, reliable help."

Almost before the words were out of his mouth Keefe realized he'd made another mistake. Mia was pulling on his arms instantly, pleading with him, "Keefe, oh my God, I didn't think about it before. Help Damien find a job. Please!"

He couldn't believe it. Sure he'd raised her, but even he didn't believe the gall. "Mia, you can't be serious, you're not asking me to get the guy a job. I can't stand him."

"You don't have to like him to recommend him to a friend who's hiring."

"I wouldn't recommend him to be a dogcatcher. Besides, my friends are all looking for reliable workers and the one thing I know about Damien is that he's unreliable. In fact, the best thing I can say about him is that you can rely on him to be unreliable." He laughed, ignoring Mia's hurt look.

"Keefe, you have connections. You know how hard it is to get a job. Please help him."

"No."

"Why?"

"I don't like him."

"That's not a reason."

"I don't need a reason."

"Keefe, help him. I love him."

"Then you help him," Keefe answered.

"I've tried," she said. Keefe watched as a look of regret crossed her face. "I've tried everyone that I know."

"Are you giving him money, Mia?"

"No, Keefe. I'm only trying to help him find a job, polish up his résumé, help him look through the want ads."

"Are you sure you're not giving him any money?"

"If I were, Kee, that would be my business and my money. I gave you back our joint accounts. Remember?"

His eyes strayed toward the counter top and rested on her checkbook. Mia's gaze followed his own and she stormed over to the counter, picked the checkbook up and handed it over to her brother.

She gave him a sad look as she shook his head. "You have any idea how insulting this is? I'm not an idiot."

"You could have fooled me."

She flinched as though she'd been struck and Keefe clenched his teeth in anger, anger at himself. Here he'd been lecturing Damien on how to treat Mia and he was the one hurting her.

"I guess then that I did fool you," Mia said and sat back down. "Go ahead, Keefe, go over my checkbook, see if there's anything there that makes you suspicious. Tell you what, keep the damn thing. Then you can pretend I'm still ten years old."

Keefe ignored her swearing. He wanted not to open the thing but he couldn't help himself. He had to know if his sister was being taken for a ride. He reviewed each entry, going from the beginning, way before she ever met Damien, *just in case*, a voice whispered. He hated the thought that Mia would lie to him, but she had once and now… He kept looking and when he was done he glanced in her direction.

"What kind of job is it that you want me to get for him, a managerial position?"

"No, Kee, just a job with benefits and a decent salary." She stopped there. She didn't want to mention that Damien wouldn't have the job for long, that he would be discovered eventually, that he was talented and he could sing. No, her brother would probably have her committed for such words; she knew Ashleigh had thought the same thing, that she could help Damien fulfill his dream. No, she wouldn't let Keefe in on that little secret.

Keefe gritted his teeth and smiled, a plan forming in his head. "Are you so sure of that, Mia, that he will take any job that's offered to him?"

"I'm sure," Mia reaffirmed.

"You'd better be damn sure," Keefe answered. "I'm only going to do this once. Call him," he urged, "tell him what you've asked of me. Prove to me that his answer is the same as yours." He waited while Mia made the call, refusing to leave to give her privacy. When she was done, she glared at him.

"So what did lover boy have to say?"

"He said he could just imagine the kind of job you'll get for him."

"Yes, but is he willing to take it?" Keefe asked. "Is he man enough to do a real man's job and stick to it?"

"He is," Mia answered, wondering what her brother had in mind.

"Then consider it done. I have the perfect job for him." Keefe laughed, grabbed his bag and walked out.

CHAPTER TWELVE

Mia was practically walking on clouds. Only three weeks had passed and everything was different. Damien was working. Full time. And he'd had a couple of non-paying singing jobs. She could feel it in her veins, things were looking up for them.

She hadn't seen much of her brother but if he happened to come over when Damien was there, he'd laugh a lot, obviously laughing at Damien for some reason. Suspicious, she'd asked Damien several times what job her brother had gotten him and he'd smiled and said, "A job that I assume he thought went with my skills." Then he'd kiss her and she'd forget all about it until later.

Mia had tried several times to ask Keefe but he always laughed and told her, "Hey, you told me to get him a job. If he doesn't like it, let him quit." Then he'd laugh some more. It was getting so that Mia was afraid to ask either of them. She decided to leave well enough alone. When she heard her brother's key in the lock, she ran to give him a hug. Her eyes probed his face. Even though they had not spoken of it, she did realize what he'd done for her. He hadn't gone after Ashleigh. What she'd allowed her brother to sacrifice for her haunted her. She knew she'd been selfish. Mia was determined to make up for that. She'd already tried setting him up with dates with two of her friends. Unfortunately, neither had worked out. Keefe wasn't interested in either one. But Mia was still looking.

"Ready," Mia said, looking for her sweater. "The movie starts in an hour so we're not going to be able to stop and eat." She smiled at her brother. "Tell you what. I'll bring some candy bars and we can eat after."

She'd ignored it the first time her brother had winced. This time she couldn't. "What's wrong?" she asked as she forgot about her sweater.

"I'm not sure," Keefe lied, "I just don't feel much like going out." He knew damn well what was bothering him. He couldn't get Ashleigh out of his mind.

Mia looked away, then turned back. Her brother had given up far too much for her to be happy. "You're thinking about her, aren't you?"

He didn't answer, just stared at her with a wistful smile.

"Let me tell her, Keefe. I can't stand seeing you so miserable."

Keefe brought his gaze to rest on his sister. "For the past several months you've been off in your own little world. I didn't know that you were even aware that I still existed." He smiled to take away the sting.

"I have been pretty selfish. Tell me something, Kee. How have you managed to put up with me all of these years?"

"Who else would have you?" he teased. When he saw the look that crossed his sister's face, he realized what was intended to be a joke had hit too close to home.

"You've given up a lot for me, and how do I repay you?" Mia sat next to her brother. "Am I the biggest disappointment in your entire life?"

"Mia, you're not. You're my greatest joy." He wanted to change the subject; he didn't want to remember their childhood, not tonight.

"First Mom, then Treece, now me. My poor brother. Your life hasn't been easy, has it? A string of unappreciative, manipulative women."

Keefe sighed, then leaned into the cushions. "Mia, I don't like the way things have been with us lately. Despite the things I've said to you I never really meant them. You're not like Mom and you're definitely not like Treece."

"Keefe, I wish I had seen it coming with her. I really liked her, liked the way you were with her, so carefree, so young, so happy." She paused and looked at her brother. "You haven't had a lot of happiness, have you?"

"Mia, why are you doing this?"

"It's something that I should have done a long time ago. I've forced you to give up being happy so that I can be and every time I look at you I hurt. Keefe, I love you so much and most of the time I don't show it. I've done nothing but take and it's time I stop. It's time you held me accountable."

"If you're going to make me happy, you must be getting ready to dump Damien."

He laughed, wanting to take that look from her eyes, then swatted her playfully, on her leg. "You were a real handful, I'll admit that. Now can we please change the subject? I don't want to talk about this, Mia."

His sister leaned into him and his arm came around her protectively. He saw tears sliding down her cheeks and traced one with the tip of his finger. He held her close, wanting to cry himself. "What's wrong, Mia? What has you so sad?"

"I wasn't until I looked at you. I've been trying so hard to pretend that everything is fine. I mean, even Damien knows that you have feelings for Ashleigh."

"Did he say anything to you?"

"No, I'm talking about the night that he asked you. I've thought a lot about that and about our entire life, Mom, her leaving us. The different relatives that would let us stay for a few days, then would want us gone so badly that it was obvious. The foster homes—"

"Mia."

"No, Kee, I've never told you, but all the times you tried to make me think that Mom hadn't forgotten us, that she really did love us, I never thanked you for that. I know that it was you who bought the gifts and told me they were from her." She felt his hand grasping hers. "Of course I didn't know it at the time. I remember how I yelled at you that you were trying to keep her away from me. I'm so sorry for making everything even harder for you."

"It wasn't your fault, Mia. You should have had your mother with you; you were just a little girl. You deserved to be happy."

"So did you. You needed a mother also, you still do." She gave his fingers a gentle squeeze. "I wonder about it sometimes. How in the world were you able to stay in school and take care of us at the same time? I know it couldn't have been easy, but you always made it seem like fun. How did you do it?"

Keefe laughed, remembering along with Mia. "I tell you, sometimes I don't know. I just knew that I always needed to have a job that would provide us with food."

"Yeah, we ate good, didn't we? I think you worked at every kind of fast food place and restaurant that would hire you, and if they wouldn't let me stay in the building, you found another job." She kissed her brother's cheek and looked deep into his eyes, knowing what she had to do. "I love you, big brother, with all my heart and soul. You can stop worrying about me now; you've done a good job. I'm going to be okay. We both are," she whispered as she gave his hands a squeeze.

"Mia, yes, of course I remember you. How are you?" Ashleigh's voice was friendly but somewhat reserved. Mia didn't blame her. She'd probably had more than enough of her family.

"I was wondering if I could come over and visit you. I really need to talk to you."

"Is it about the gown? Is something wrong?"

Mia had almost forgotten the gown. "Ashleigh, I really need to talk to you in person. Maybe we could meet somewhere. I'll buy you lunch or dinner," she added, thinking it might be better to have the meeting in a public place just in case Ashleigh was inclined to kill her. Then maybe she'd at least have witnesses, if no help.

She made arrangements with Ashleigh to meet in a couple of days for lunch. She was doing the right thing, she knew it. For the first time in months she felt the burden she'd carried in her heart beginning to feel lighter. It wasn't gone but she could breathe. If she could fix things for her brother, she was sure as hell going to try.

"Nicki, I have a good feeling about this. I don't want to jinx it by saying too much, but I think Keefe put his sister up to call me."

"You don't know that for sure."

"If you're saying I don't have concrete proof, then no, I don't. But I'm going with my instincts. Why would his sister call me if it didn't have something to do with Keefe?"

Nicki laughed. "I hope it does. I'm sick of you mooning over the guy. It's time one of you made a move."

"Tell you what, if I'm right and he's sending his sister to feel me out, I won't do anything stupid. I'll welcome him back with open arms." Ashleigh closed her eyes. She replayed every kiss, every touch, every smile. Even his scent lingered in her senses. She couldn't wait to meet Keefe's sister.

Ashleigh scanned the restaurant, then spotted Mia. "Mia, how nice to see you again." Ashleigh smiled warmly at her and made a step to embrace her, give her a hug as she'd done the last times she'd seen her. But something in Mia's look stopped her. Maybe it was the way Mia's eyes darted around the room before landing on her and the sick look on her face. Ashleigh couldn't help staring as she watched Mia struggle to return her smile.

"Is there a problem, Mia?" Ashleigh looked down, biting her lip, grateful to whatever forces kept her from blurting out what she really wanted to ask: *Does Keefe want me back?*

"We need to talk," Mia all but whispered.

Once again Ashleigh was struck by the oddity of the situation. The young woman was behaving strangely. They were not friends, making her choice of words, 'we need to talk,' all the more glaring. Unless it concerned Keefe Ashleigh couldn't imagine what they *needed* to talk about. She didn't have any answer for Mia's statement so she kept quiet. They both sensed the strained atmosphere and made small talk while going to a table.

"Lunch is my treat," Mia said, picking up her water glass and taking a drink.

"Thanks. Now tell me what's so urgent." Ashleigh was determined not to let the hope that was in her heart come through in her words.

"Nothing's urgent; it's just something I need to tell you."

Ashleigh studied Mia. "I should have known you and Keefe are brother and sister. You look so much alike. I think I saw it that first day but so much was going on that I didn't dwell on it. If you wanted to apologize for not telling me, don't worry about it."

The waitress chose that moment to come and take their orders. Ashleigh watched Mia, wondering what she would do if the woman had not come to tell her that Keefe wanted her back. She smiled, trying to put Mia at ease. "You look so scared. Whatever it is, it can't be that bad. What made you call me?"

"I have to tell you why my brother stopped dating you. I know he cares for you but he did it for me."

"I know…he told me that your…well…that your fiancé had married someone else and that you needed him."

Mia pulled on her lip.

Ashleigh caught the action and it alerted her senses. She thought of Keefe and the way he'd behaved when she found out he'd lied about his identity. She wasn't in the mood at the moment to hear more lies.

She had too many things right now to worry about, her main worry being the IRS. They were breathing down her neck, claiming she had not paid her taxes for the last four years. She'd turned the matter over to her accountant who was suddenly unavailable for her calls or visit.

Still, she smiled at Mia. She liked the pretty young woman, and had been happy that if she weren't going to get to wear her dream gown, that it would be worn by such a pretty and nice woman as Mia. However, it appeared that neither of them would get to wear the gown.

She couldn't help noticing how oddly Mia was acting. She had her eyes closed and had balled her fists as if she were in pain. She was also making strange sounds that she seemed unaware of. A lump began forming in the pit of Ashleigh's stomach. She recognized those traits. They were the same ones Keefe had displayed when he'd broken up with her. She braced herself, knowing now that whatever Mia had come to tell her was bad.

"Mia, you okay?" Ashleigh asked. "Is there something wrong with your brother?"

Mia opened her eyes and stared at Ashleigh for a moment before answering. "Keefe isn't seeing you because of me. I didn't want him to."

"Why? We don't have any problems." Ashleigh was curious, but her stomach was doing flips, because she was suddenly positive she wasn't going to like whatever it was Mia had to tell her.

"I'm in love with Damien." Mia waited and when Ashleigh didn't answer, she repeated herself. "I'm in love with Damien."

For a split second Ashleigh thought she was in a dream. She stared at Mia, unable to prevent the frown that tugged at her features. *I don't believe this*, she thought. *This can't be happening.*

"My Damien?" she managed to ask at last.

"Technically no, but since I know what you're asking me, yes, it's the one and only, the infamous bad boy."

Ashleigh sipped her water. If she didn't she would be tempted to smack Keefe's little sister. "Your brother knew about this? You mean that's another lie he told me?"

"He didn't know about it in the beginning. When he found out he got angry. He didn't want me to see him."

Ashleigh was looking at Mia, loathing for the young woman making her skin crawl. She glanced around the crowded restaurant and for a moment she actually pictured physically reacting to what she was feeling and slapping the hell out of Mia. She envisioned her stretched out on the floor. But no, that wouldn't do. She was, after all, in a public place. She wouldn't make a scene. She glared at Mia, knowing that the woman had counted on her not wanting to make a scene in public. That knowledge almost made Ashleigh forget her resolve.

"All the time your brother was with me, you were seeing Damien behind my back?"

"No, not the entire time. We broke it off and didn't see each other for several months. Then when I got the letter from James saying he was married, I didn't see any reason why I shouldn't be with Damien. Except that I felt guilty about you and buying your wedding gown. Keefe still didn't want me with him, but I was so miserable that he gave in. Ashleigh, I didn't set out deliberately to hurt you."

"Neither did Damien," Ashleigh answered at last. "At least that's what he told me. You two deserve each other. How the hell did you get hooked up with him anyway?"

"The day I bought your gown he was waiting for me when I came down. He asked me to go and have a drink, so we went to McDonald's and stayed there talking for hours."

Ashleigh glared at Mia, and then began tapping her fingers rapidly on the tabletop to relieve her mounting tension. "You bought my wedding gown, then went downstairs and went out with the man who'd used me and yet you didn't intend on hurting me. Unbelievable. What were you thinking?"

Ashleigh pushed away from the table to stare at Mia in disgust. "What were you thinking?" she asked again.

"I wasn't thinking," Mia answered honestly, "not about you or the fact that I'd just bought your gown, or that I was engaged to get married." She shook her head. "And I refused to think what my brother would do if he found out, how he would feel." Tears slid down her cheek and she did nothing to wipe them away.

"Don't you dare cry," Ashleigh almost shouted, knowing she would have if other customers weren't sitting so close to them. "You aren't the one who gets to cry here, Mia. I can't believe you."

"Ashleigh, let me try and explain, please. I'd never before felt anything like what was happening to me, not in my entire life. I knew instantly that I loved him; that we belonged together. I knew it in your apartment when he looked at me. For a moment when he was looking at me, everyone in the room disappeared. When I got downstairs and found him waiting for me, I knew I would leave with him. If he hadn't asked me, I would have asked him. I love him, Ashleigh."

"And I suppose he loves you?"

"He does. He truly does."

"Mia, the guy is a loser and a user. You're young, maybe because you were lonely…" Ashleigh frowned. "How much money have you given him?"

"You sound like my brother. I haven't given him a dime; he hasn't asked me for money. Matter of fact, the very first day I told him I would give him no money, that I wouldn't take care of him, that I was not like…" Mia caught herself. "I told him I was not like his other girlfriends, that I wouldn't support him."

Ashleigh couldn't stop glaring at the uppity young woman. She needed to be brought down a peg. "Then if you're not giving him any money, you must be very good in bed."

"I hope when the time comes I will be."

"What are you saying?"

"I haven't had sex with Damien. I'm a virgin."

Ashleigh stared at Mia. "I don't believe you." She'd decided she didn't have to be polite to the young woman who'd stolen her ex and her dream.

"You don't have to."

"Damien wouldn't be with a woman he wasn't sleeping with." She thought of the last four months of their relationship and knew that was a lie. He hadn't touched her, not even to kiss her. Ashleigh didn't know now if she should be angry or warn Mia. She decided to try to talk some sense into her.

"Mia, do you want to know the thing that finally made me kick Damien out of my apartment? He took my charge card and took a woman to a hotel with my money. Mia, I had to pay for that. Now do you really think he's going to be true to you?"

"Yes. I'm sorry he wasn't true to you, Ashleigh, but that's not my fault. He loves me."

"You're a fool. He told me he loved me too."

"And he does love you. But he's *in love* with me."

"Mia, your brother is right."

"No, he's not and neither are you. I know Damien's heart. He's a good man, really he is."

"Mia, he's a womanizer. I can guarantee you that if he's not having sex with you he is with someone. I'd advise you to get him tested before you do decide to sleep with him."

"He's already been tested, and I'm not sleeping with him, not until—well, I'm staying a virgin until I'm married."

"And you think he's going to marry you?" Horror filled Ashleigh, and then changed quickly to anger. "You're going to marry, Damien, in my dress?"

It didn't matter that Mia had paid her more than she had asked. Now, in her mind, the woman had practically stolen it. Apparently

Mia knew what she was thinking.

"Ashleigh, the gown, you can have it back."

"I don't want it. You keep it. I couldn't wear it now anyway."

"Neither can I."

That was something. At least the woman wouldn't wear her gown to marry Damien. Ashleigh looked away as the waitress arrived and put the food on the table. She couldn't believe just how civilized the two of them were behaving.

As soon as the waitress left, Ashleigh stared hard at Mia. "He's going to hurt you, Mia, just like he hurt me. I was with him for more than two years. I know him a lot better than you do. You think you're the light of his life. Mia, you're not. He's going to disappoint you the same as he did me."

"I don't doubt he'll disappoint me at some time, Ashleigh, the same as I'll disappoint him. In fact, I already have, when I stopped seeing him. But we're human. That didn't make him stop loving me and when he does disappoint me, it won't make me stop loving him."

"Mia, you sound so mature, but you're being naïve. I should have kept receipts for the amount of money that he took me for."

"I'm sorry about all of that, Ashleigh, but he's going to make things right with you."

Ashleigh thought of the checks Damien had been sending her for the past months and a stab of pain hit her in the chest. She looked past the guilt she saw in Mia's eyes. Mia was in love with Damien. Of that she was sure. She thought again of all the money Damien had returned to her and she knew Damien loved the young woman sitting across from her.

"I wish you luck in that case, Mia. Just remember that I tried to warn you, and," she almost choked on a sob, "and your brother, he

159

tried. Mia, if I'd had someone in my life that loved me as much as your brother loves you, I think I would never have given Damien a second look." Mia was almost smiling, giving her a knowing look. "Well, at least I don't think I would have let it go on for as long as I did."

"Tell me the truth, Ashleigh. Are you really still in love with Damien?"

Ashleigh knew what the woman was asking. She wanted to walk away from the meeting guilt free. Maybe she even wanted to have her fall in love with her brother. Then her conscience would really be clear. She could do as she damn well pleased. Ashleigh wasn't so sure she wanted to give her that.

"Yes, Mia, I'm in love with him still, so now what? Are you feeling bad enough that you're going to give him up?"

"No."

"So why are we here?"

"I guess since you're still in love with Damien, there is no reason for me to be here. I was mistaken. I thought you and Keefe...never mind." Mia stuck her fork into her chicken salad and pretended not to be watching Ashleigh.

"Mia, I was going to marry the man. Do you think it's that easy to forget?" She turned away, then back. "That's right, I forgot. You did forget about the fact that you were going to get married, didn't you? For me, it's not that easy."

"Can I ask one more thing?"

"What?" Ashleigh answered in a cold voice.

"Did Damien ask you to marry him?"

What a strange question, Ashleigh thought. "What do you think, that I imagined the entire thing?"

"No, it's not that." Mia hesitated. "It's just that Damien told me that he'd never asked you. That you wanted to and somehow before he knew what was happening a wedding was being planned."

Ashleigh stared in shock before laughing. "He never asked me? Is that what you want to believe?" She saw the doubt creep up on Mia, doubt that she knew Mia wanted her to dispel. Who did this woman think she was? Of course Damien had asked her to marry him. She remembered it well. She had been…they had just… The woman's question had her flustered. Try as she might, she couldn't remember just when Damien had asked her to marry him. Why had she forgotten it? No woman would ever forget a proposal. She saw a tiny smile pulling at the corners of Mia's lips and she got angry.

"He was telling me the truth, wasn't he?" Mia said. "He never asked you?"

"What difference does that make? We were still going to get married."

"To me it makes all the difference in the world. It proves I was right to trust him. Ashleigh, I know you have no reason for wanting to help me, or to want me to trust Damien, but I liked you the moment I met you. I don't think you're a vindictive woman or my brother wouldn't like you so much. So yes, what you said before is true. I'll admit that part of the reason I'm here is the guilt I feel that you and my brother might have had a relationship, that because of me it didn't happen."

Ashleigh was staring at her. "I don't think your trust is as great as you pretend or you wouldn't have to confirm it with me. And that was what you wanted just then, right? For me to tell you that Damien was telling the truth, that he'd never asked me to marry him."

"I suppose you're partly right. I do want to prove to myself and everyone else, including Damien, that love makes a difference."

"Did you tell him to pay me back? Are you the one I have to thank for Damien's sudden attack of conscience?"

"No. You have Damien to thank for that. He's sorry for the way he treated you, he wanted to make amends."

"He's been sorry before but he's never given me a dime. It had to be you. Why? Is that the condition you put on being with him?"

"Not a condition. I just mentioned that he needed to try to make amends with you for what he'd done."

"And that is supposed to make everything better?"

"Not better, but balanced." She paused and took a deep breath before going on. "I don't think you would be happy married to a man who wasn't in love with you." Mia saw that Ashleigh was taking offense at her words and rushed to add, "Being in love is so different from simply loving someone. Ashleigh, believe me, I know. When you're in love everything's involved, not just your heart, but your soul and that's the way I love Damien and the way he loves me."

Mia's eyes took on a dreamy look and she smiled, thinking of Damien. "I'm not apologizing for loving Damien. But I'm apologizing for the awful way that things happened. If I could go back and change things, the only thing I would change would be my buying your gown. But since that's how fate brought him into my life, I guess I wouldn't even change that." She looked at Ashleigh and smiled. "Despite our best intentions, the soul longs for its other half, the person who will make them whole. Damien and I are that for each other. Otherwise my brother would have changed it all long ago. The heart loves whom it loves."

For the first time since they'd begun this ridiculous conversation, Ashleigh smiled. "I hope you enjoy this pretty dream of yours, Mia. I can promise you it won't last. It never does."

Ashleigh got up and threw some bills on the table, glancing at

Mia. There was no way in hell she was going to let Mia treat her to lunch. "That should cover my portion," she said, then turned and walked out of the restaurant.

CHAPTER THIRTEEN

"Can you believe the nerve, I mean, can you?" Ashleigh turned sharply, knocking over the vase, drenching the floor with water and scattering the flowers. She glanced at the vase that hadn't broken and almost wished it had.

"Nicki, answer me. You haven't said a word." Ashleigh was getting angry with her best friend who was watching her with a cool smile on her face, a smile as annoying as the one Mia had worn through most of their talk. Almost as if they both shared the same secret.

"Ashleigh, why are you acting like this? Damien wasn't in love with you, even you know that."

"But my dress."

"Yeah, it stinks, but she didn't come here planning to meet Damien and fall in love with him. Why are you blaming her?"

"She was here for the cleansing. How could she buy my dress, then meet him downstairs and go out with him? She knew who he was, how he'd hurt me."

"Did you see the way he looked at her in your apartment, Ashleigh?"

The memory pissed Ashleigh off. Of course she'd seen the way he'd looked at Mia. Not once since she'd known him had he ever looked at her in that manner. "He only did that to get back at me. He was just being his usual dog self. It meant nothing."

Nicki shook her head. "Now you know I believe he's a dog, but the way he looked at her, Ash, that wasn't his usual self and every woman in the room knew it. Something happened between the two of them."

Ashleigh glared at Nicki. "Why didn't you say something about it before?"

"Why? You'd finally come to your senses and dumped him, he was out of your life. Listen, Ashleigh, you can be competitive and I didn't want you letting Damien come back into your life simply because he'd fallen for Mia right in front of your face."

"Nicki, you're not being any help. You're being a smart ass."

"Listen, for the last few weeks you've been mooning over Mia's brother. When she called you a couple of days ago, you thought that somehow it would lead to your getting back with him. Now all of a sudden you want to act as though she's stolen your man. She didn't. You dumped him. He was up for grabs. Be happy that he's not your headache any longer. You know he's not going to change."

Ashleigh frowned and rolled her eyes. "That's where you're wrong. He has changed or rather, he's in the process of changing. Can you believe she had the nerve to call me a fool?"

She saw the change come over Nicki. At last her friend was coming to her side.

"She called you a fool? Who the hell does she think she is?"

Nicki's defense made her feel a little better but not enough that she would continue with the lie. "To be honest, I asked her how much money she'd given to Damien, and she said she wasn't a fool. But," Ashleigh rushed to explain, "saying it like that meant she was calling me a fool."

This time Nicki didn't rush to her defense but looked down.

"So what, are you calling me a fool also?"

"No, but you can't be mad at Mia if she didn't fall for Damien's line."

"She said he's never even asked her for any money."

"You're kidding. Damn, she looked so innocent. She must really be good in bed."

"No, she told me she's still a virgin, that she's saving herself for her husband. From the look in her eyes I know she believes her husband will be Damien."

"That's what got you so upset?"

"Nicki, I was with him for over two years. Why didn't he ever try to impress me? He's got a job and he's keeping it."

"Is he still sending you money?"

"Every week."

"Then that says something. He must care something for you or at least be sorry for being so damn sorry." Nicki laughed.

"*Sorry.* I'd like to think that's what it is. But that's not it. He's sending me the money because Mia told him he had to make things right with me."

"You're telling me that she's the one that has Damien acting like a man taking care of his obligations? Then I'm sorry, Ashleigh, but my hat's off to anyone who can make that lazy ass Damien hold onto a job. Maybe he is in love with her."

Ashleigh glared at her friend.

"Come on, Ash, you know you're not in love with Damien, not any longer, and I don't know if you ever were. So what gives? What's really going on here?"

"This whole thing, it's all too weird. Okay, I'll admit I was hoping Mia could clue me in on what's going on with her brother. I mean, we were into each other even though we had a rocky start."

"And a rocky middle," Nicki laughed.

"Okay, but I really thought, I mean, the last time we were

together it was so right. He left here happy and when he came by to tell me that he couldn't see me anymore because his sister needed him he was miserable."

"Did Mia explain that?"

"Yes, she said he did it because of her, all right. It seems she felt guilty about Damien and she didn't want Keefe to tell me and he didn't want to continue lying to me. So he chose his sister over me."

"That's the way you see this whole thing?"

"That's the way it is."

"Maybe you could look at it as a man being loyal and, ah, just maybe he's known his sister a little longer than he's known you. You know they say you can usually tell if a man's any good by the way he treats his mother and his sister."

"Does that really work?"

Nicki smiled. "I don't know but my mother always says it, so hey. Why don't you call him, tell him you know that his sister is with your ex, tell him it doesn't matter, that you don't blame him."

"I'm not begging him. If he wants to get with me he needs to make the call, but I don't know now if I want that. I swear, think about it, Nicki. If something comes of it, how can either Mia or Keefe stand knowing that they're with people who slept with the other's partner? I don't think I want to keep looking at Mia and thinking, 'She's with my ex.' Maybe it's better this way. Maybe I should just leave well enough alone."

"Is that really what you want?"

"You know it isn't."

"How am I supposed to know? You keep changing your mind. Try telling me straight out what you want, Ash."

Ashleigh smiled, then grinned. "I want to know that Keefe has been as miserable as I've been. I want him to come to me on his knees, crawling over broken glass to get here. I want him to be the man I thought he was when he looked into my eyes after making love to me. That's what I want. And I don't think I'm asking for too much."

"Neither do I, Ash. Neither do I." Nicki said.

"Mia, damn it! I told you to stay out of it. Why did you talk to her?"

"Because I didn't want to blow your chances with her. I just wanted to help."

"Did you?" Keefe glared at her. "Or did you make her think I was a little boy who needed his sister to run inference for him?"

"Keefe, it's my job to help people. It's what I do for a living, I have a degree…"

He stopped her. "I'm well aware what your degree is in. I paid for the degree, remember? Mia, you're a social worker, you're not qualified to fix my life."

"I'm a school counselor."

"My apologies. You're still not qualified to run my life."

She was hurt. "I'm going to be a psychologist, Keefe. I'm almost done."

"Then why don't you wait until you have that degree and why don't you wait until I come and ask you for help? I didn't ask you to help, Mia. In fact, I know that I told you to stay out of it."

"You've been so unhappy."

"And you care?"

Mia looked at her brother, puzzled at his comment. "What are you talking about? Of course I care."

She watched as Keefe walked away, wondering what he was going to do. He stopped in front of a mirror.

"Hmm," he said. "That doesn't look like Damien." He peered closer. "Nope, Mia, it's not Damien, just me."

Keefe turned back to face his sister, not knowing why he was behaving the way he was. He wished that Mia were qualified to help him, tell him why he was doing everything in his power to push her away. He wanted to hug her, tell her he liked the way things were with him being her hero, taking care of her. She was growing up way too fast and he didn't relish the idea of being left behind. He didn't relish the idea of losing his position in Mia's life. Was that his problem? he wondered.

"Keefe, you have no reason to be jealous of Damien. You're my brother. No one could ever replace you in my heart."

"I'm not jealous, Mia." His voice sounded tired, the way he felt. Tired.

"Yes you are, Kee, and there is no need."

"Don't you have a date with Damien tonight?" He was sick of this conversation that wasn't getting them anywhere. "Did Ashleigh ask about me?" he suddenly asked.

Mia wondered if she should tell her brother that Ashleigh had said she was still in love with Damien. It could have been said just to hurt her. She wasn't sure, but there was one thing she was sure of: she felt her brother's pain. There was no need to tell him what Ashleigh had said.

"I think she was too busy being angry with me. We didn't talk much about you. I just told her the truth."

Keefe didn't want to admit it even to himself, but Mia's meddling had stirred up the longing in his heart to a feverish pitch. He couldn't get Ashleigh out of his mind or his thoughts. He dialed her number a dozen times, hanging up before she could answer.

Keefe was disgusted by his own behavior. He couldn't believe that he would not even talk to her. He looked down at his hands, surprised to find them trembling. He dialed again, determined that this time he would stay on the line.

"Keefe?"

"How did you know?" Keefe asked.

"Caller ID. You didn't block your number."

He hadn't thought of that. Now he truly felt like a fool. "Ashleigh, can we talk?" he sighed. "Can I take you out to dinner?"

"Why? Your sister explained she was lying to me and you were helping. Is there something that I got wrong?"

"You have it all wrong, Ashleigh. I wasn't lying to you and neither was Mia. She's a good kid. She was trying not to hurt you."

"Then why didn't you tell me?"

"She didn't want me to; she felt guilty."

"She should have."

"Why?"

"Why? I can't believe you even have to ask that question. She has my wedding gown, and she's with Damien."

"You were selling the gown. You had an ad up in the laundry room. Don't blame Mia for that."

"What about Damien?"

"What about him? She didn't come between you, she didn't know either of you. He fell in love with her. Period. And she returned the feelings. She did nothing wrong."

Keefe couldn't believe it. As much as he'd ranted and raved in the past few months about his sister's relationship with Damien, he was now defending it and her. Keefe was standing on the edge of indecision. He wanted to see Ashleigh again but he would not listen to Ashleigh or anyone else put his sister down.

"You're not calling to apologize, so why are you calling?"

"I'm attracted to you and you're attracted to me. I made you a promise the last time we were together that as long as we were together, I would not lie to you. I kept that promise."

"What about Mia and Damien?"

"What about them? They're adults. I can't tell my sister what to do or who to date and, believe me, I tried."

"What did your sister have to say about your calling me?"

"I don't know. I didn't ask her permission."

"Then maybe you should." Ashleigh was remembering that she'd told the woman that she was still in love with Damien. Surely Mia had not repeated that to her brother. She started to tell him, tell him that she'd only said it to hurt Mia but thought better of it. He was protective of his sister. Besides, he needed a dose of his own medicine. He needed to know how it felt when someone kept something from you.

The moment Ashleigh hung up the phone she regretted not telling Keefe about the conversation with Mia. She pushed away the feelings that were trying to invade her thoughts. And she wrapped her arms around her body to stop the sudden chill.

If she were smart, she would call Keefe right back and tell him. Everything always had a way of coming back to bite her in the behind.

As she closed her eyes, Ashleigh prayed for a miracle. Why not? With the luck she'd been having she was due for one.

As Keefe waited for Ashleigh to open the door, he tried to breathe deeply to still the pounding in his chest. He had it all figured out; he was going to act cool, maybe not even go inside the apartment. Just take her out to dinner, talk, then see where they would go from there.

The door opened and all Keefe's plans were shot to hell. He looked past the hesitancy in Ashleigh's eyes and saw hope. He knew that look; he was hoping too.

He smiled and lifted a finger to brush away the hair that fell over her left eye. He felt her tremble and before she could complain, he had her in his arms. Her lips were just as he'd remembered, soft, lush and warm. Her arms wound around his neck and the next moment they were on the other side of the door closing out the world.

Her kisses matched his for hunger. He was glad she wasn't playing games. He needed her, needed to hold her close, feel her warmth. He needed to make love to her.

One of her hands was on his pants, pulling on the zipper. As the other tugged the material below his hips, it occurred to him to assist her, but his own hands were far too busy pulling Ashleigh's sweater over her head, then her pants from her narrow hips.

"Wait," he said, breathless, "if I don't take off these damn shoes I'm going to trip." He made quick work of his shoes and pants as he watched Ashleigh kicking off her own shoes and trousers. He noticed that they'd both left on their underwear and smiled. *Oh yes*, he thought, *just enough to cover, a little mystery*. He leaned down, planted his legs wide apart and lifted Ashleigh into his arms. In two seconds flat he had her on the bed and his hands buried beneath the silk of her panties, in the silky hairs guarding the entrance to her most private of secrets.

Suddenly her hands were wrapped around his back, caressing him, her nails digging into his flesh just enough to send shudders of desire coursing through him. And he wanted to enter her then. He'd wanted her for so long that it would only take a matter of minutes for him to hit the peaks.

"Ashleigh." He called her name, but her eyes were glazed over with need. He'd intended to tell her that he'd take it slow but from the way her hips were grinding into his, he could tell she no more wanted to take it slow than he did. This was something they both needed and they needed it now.

"Keefe," Ashleigh moaned, forgetting her resolve. She'd had every intention in the world of making him leave her apartment wanting her, of turning him on, then backing away, but the moment she opened the door her heart had begun doing a strange dance. When he touched her face she'd melted. If he had not initiated the kiss, she surely would have, for she'd dreamt of him every night since the last time they'd made love.

He was kissing her and she wanted to cry out from the joy she felt in her heart. She'd never felt this way about a man, even Damien. Despite what she'd told Mia, she wasn't in love with Damien. He'd never made her feel she belonged to him, that she was home when she was in his arms. With Keefe that was the exact way she was feeling. She was home and she liked the feeling. She hoped never to be apart from him again.

She felt his fingers slip inside her and her entire body shuddered at the sensation. Then she moved her right hand from his back, moving it lower, to find his arousal. She wrapped her hands around him, needing to touch him, to assure herself that he was real, that he was in her bed.

"Keefe," she sobbed, "now. I don't want to wait any longer."

Then he was above her and he was groaning as he entered her. For a moment a picture of Damien and Mia came to her but she let it go. She was determined nothing would spoil this moment.

He filled her and the feeling of being home only intensified. "God, how I've missed you, Ashleigh."

She thought that was what he whispered into her ear, but she wasn't sure. She couldn't tell him how deep she believed her feelings were for him until he said it first.

She didn't want to be just a booty call to Keefe.

"Ashleigh," he whispered, "open your eyes."

She hadn't even realized they were closed but did as he asked and opened them, looking up into eyes filled with want, with need, and, yes, she thought, with love. She felt his thrusts deep inside of her body and she welcomed them and him. She held him to her, never wanting the moment to end, feeling the sensations with her whole heart. Keefe came with a deep roar that she heard come up from his belly. Then she was flooded with warmth, the hot fluids seeping out around them, and Ashleigh gave in and on the crest of Keefe's orgasm she came.

They lay for the longest time in each other's arms, just breathing, not talking, just holding on to each other as if they were afraid that if they didn't hold on tight to each other someone would come in and take away their happiness.

"Keefe."

"Don't talk," he whispered.

So he did feel it too, Ashleigh thought.

A short time later she tried again. "Keefe."

"No, he moaned. "We'll only fight and I want to make love to you, Ashleigh. I've been so hungry for you, for your body. Just let me get my fill; then we can talk."

He cut off any protest or further words with a kiss, his tongue invading her mouth, his teeth nipping at her lips. She understood what he meant for she'd been famished and now it was time to feast. She lost all notion of talk when his mouth moved from her lips and fastened on her breast. What exquisite pleasure. Then once again she felt his hand moving down the inner part of her thigh and she trembled with knowing. She could already feel the opening of the gates for this man who'd brought her home.

Keefe couldn't get enough of Ashleigh's body. No, he thought as he suckled her, it wasn't just her body. It was the woman inside, it was Ashleigh. His heart pounded loud in his ears and he almost whispered aloud, *my woman*.

In silence they made love over and over. Then they fell asleep in each other's arms.

CHAPTER FOURTEEN

Reluctantly, Ashleigh woke as the last vestiges of sleep pulled at her, keeping her pleasantly drowsy. Still, Ashleigh realized there was something different. She breathed in the faint lingering smell of sex. She took another breath and a masculine scent invaded her nostrils, mixed with a light dusting of the dying fragrance of her own perfume, a baby powder smell. She reached her hand over slowly and before she'd moved an inch her fingers came into contact with warm skin.

Even an inch was too far away from her. She readjusted her position so that his hard body was spooned against her soft curves. She'd thought he was sleep but he turned ever so slightly to smile at her and kiss her on the cheek.

"Good morning," she said at last. "Can we talk now?"

He smiled in return and attempted to pull her even closer. "We can talk for a little while. I'm getting hungry again," he whispered.

"Last night, does it mean anything?" Ashleigh's heart was hurting and she found it difficult to keep her voice even. This felt so right, Keefe in her bed, her in his arms. They'd satisfied their intense hunger and it still felt right. She waited for him to answer.

He was kissing her forehead, his fingers brushing the side of her face lightly. "It means that I haven't been able to get you out of my mind. I think of you constantly."

"We've got problems," she answered, "your sister for one."

"My sister is not our problem."

"You're getting angry," Ashleigh whispered, not wanting the feeling of closeness to evaporate. "Keefe, she's in love with Damien. I lived with the guy. You're a man, tell me. Are you going to be able to be with me knowing that?"

"I don't see what Damien has to do with us." He was getting annoyed. Yes, he knew what Ashleigh meant. He knew it would be hard. "Okay," he admitted at last. "I can't stand the guy. That alone is a big problem. And do I like knowing that you slept with him? Hell no. Will I be adult enough to handle it when the four of us are forced to be together? I can only hope so."

Then he turned her face toward his, so he could look in her eyes. "You *are* over him, aren't you?"

"Yes," she answered without hesitation. "I'm over him." Somewhere in her soul she knew she should tell him the truth, that she'd lied to his sister, told her that she still loved Damien, but only to hurt her.

She heard the sigh of relief from Keefe and changed her mind. If Mia had not mentioned it to him, perhaps she never would. There was no need, and she really didn't think Keefe would understand either way. The thought that she'd done something deliberately to hurt his sister wouldn't sit well with him.

She shivered in his arms. And as his arms closed tighter around her, she had to believe she was making the right decision. She'd call Mia later and they would fix things. She'd tell the young woman that she'd lied, that she didn't love Damien. *Yes, that should do it. She would talk to Mia.*

"No more talking, we've talked enough."

As much as she wanted to agree with him, have his hands touching her, bringing her again to orgasm, she knew there were still things that they should talk about.

"Just a couple more things. You called me a gold digger." She looked directly at him. "Don't do it again."

"I won't." He kissed the tips of her fingers, pulling each digit into his mouth to nibble. "I told you I'm getting hungry."

Ashleigh laughed softly but she was determined not to let him distract her. They needed to talk. "Keefe, I need to know what happened. Who hurt you?" He let her go. She'd expected that much. Men never wanted to talk, but she'd gotten into too much trouble in the past from not talking.

"Keefe," she was insistent, "tell me about it."

"If you tell me why the hell an intelligent woman would take care of such a no good bum, how she could fall in love with him."

"Ask your sister." The words were out before she had a chance to censor them. He glared at her and moved even farther away, but at least this time he was still in her bed. "I'll tell you what. You tell me about her and I'll tell you about Damien. Agreed?"

He was frowning at her and she didn't know if he would answer her or not. She waited, trying hard not to push him, breathing as quietly as she could, until she felt his fingers brush the sides of her naked body. Then they found hers and curled her hand into his strong one. He wasn't looking at her but that was okay. She heard him sigh and knew what he was going to tell her was hard for him to do. She gave his arm a stroke with her free hand to encourage him.

"Treece, Treece Williams," Keefe began as his mind wandered back to the time with her. She hadn't been his first but she was the first one that he had fallen in love with. It still hurt even now to think of her. She was everything that he'd wanted in a woman, loving, fun, beautiful. She'd gotten along well with Mia. And that had been one of his main requisites. Even now he remembered how nervous he'd been when Mia had met her for the first time, how his heart had pounded, hoping his sister would approve, that Treece would like her in return. He'd wanted to marry Treece, have babies with her.

Mia had been as captivated by Treece as he had been. For several months he was happier than he'd ever been in his life. He was making tons of money, Mia was doing well in school and he was in love.

Then the day came that ended it all. Treece had come to him in tears, saying that she needed twenty-five thousand dollars; that her parents' home was about to be taken from them. When he'd attempted to get more information she'd broken down and cried and Mia had told him to stop badgering her. He could still picture the scene now, Treece crying and Mia holding her, crying also.

"Kee, give her the money," Mia had cried. "We have it."

It wasn't the money. It had never been the money. He'd only wanted to know more about what was happening. He would do anything for Treece and for Mia. They'd both turned teary eyes toward him and he'd gotten his checkbook and written out the check, pausing only a moment when Treece said to make the check out to her.

"But shouldn't I make it out to the bank?"

"Kee, leave her alone. Just do as she asks and make it out to her." That had been Mia. He'd looked at his sister. He trusted her implicitly. She had good instincts and she adored Treece. So he'd written out the check and ignored the sudden fuzzy feeling in his brain, the twittering in his psyche that something was wrong.

It had been over a week before he realized that something was wrong. Treece wouldn't return any of his calls, then suddenly her phone was disconnected. When he'd gone to her apartment he found it empty and an angry man outside the building cursing at her empty window.

After some macho posturing the two of them had figured out they both had been in love with the same woman, had both been taken was more accurate. They talked and investigated and when everything was over, there were seven different men involved, seven men she'd scammed. Keefe felt a shiver claim his body as he relived the events for Ashleigh.

He looked at Ashleigh with the raw pain. "You know something? All of us would have gladly given her the money." He half snorted, half laughed. "Hell, we did give it to her. And I think all of us would have taken her back but she wanted none of us. She'd used us and used her body to get money to try to get her boyfriend out of jail. A boyfriend that she'd taken care of, lived with, a boyfriend who had peddled drugs and had peddled women. She'd used all of us for him. She cared nothing about any of us."

The words were sticking in his throat now as he fought back the pain, the tears. "I could have lived with her hurting me, Ashleigh, but she hurt Mia. She was the first woman in our lives who appeared to care about Mia. And Mia needed that. There was only so much a brother could do for her. What she did to my sister I could never forgive. For months Mia mourned her. She cried all the time, and for the first time in her life she failed a class. She felt tremendous guilt for urging me to give Treece the money and wouldn't believe me when I told her I would have given it to her even if she had not told me to. We both went to counseling for several months to get through that. That's when Mia decided to become a psychologist, so she could help others. Still, it was hard."

He bit his lips. "My sister's very important to me, Ashleigh. I won't allow anyone to hurt her ever again, even a woman that I love." He made sure she understood what he was saying before he continued. "For our entire lives it's been just the two of us looking out for each other. Even if we make mistakes, in the end we know we can count on each other. Now you know," he ended.

Ashleigh licked her lips, a surge of love for the man who'd bared his soul to her filling her heart. "What about your parents? Who raised you?"

"I did. I'm the only parent Mia has."

"You're not that much older than your sister. How could you—"

"Because I had to."

"Are your parents dead?" Ashleigh whispered.

He stared at her a moment before answering. "I have no idea about our father. As for our mother, for all the good she did, she may as well be. We…Mia needed her. She wasn't there. End of story. That's the last question, Ashleigh."

Ashleigh waited for him to ask her to tell him about Damien but he didn't, though they both knew she would have to. After hearing him out, Ashleigh realized it was more important than ever that she get to Mia, convince her that she wasn't in love with Damien. It wouldn't do any good to tell any of that to Keefe. He wasn't ready to listen to that.

At least she knew why he hated Damien so much. "Keefe, even without your telling me all the details I know you and Mia went through rough times with your mom. She saw him grimace, gave his fingers a squeeze, and continued. "Having your parents around isn't always the easiest thing in the world either. Nicki and I both came from similar families. They had done nothing but work all their lives. They had no dreams and didn't know how to give support to their daughters with dreams. In fact, they did the opposite. They told us we'd gotten big-headed, that we would return home soon and prove them right."

Ashleigh glanced up at Keefe to see how he was taking what she was saying so far. "I'm just beginning to understand some things about myself. Nicki and I talked after I saw Mia and she reminded me of a few things."

"Like what?" Keefe prompted.

"She reminded me that when we left home I made a promise that I would always understand the dream in a person. And I guess she was right. Even before Damien I was pretty much drawn to men with big dreams." She smiled. "Trouble is, none of them had an ounce of talent and none of them worked toward pursuing those dreams. They were all talk. Then I met Damien and he was different. He had tons of talent and at first it did seem he was trying."

"So what happened?"

"I decided to manage him, manage his career and manage his dreams. For a while it was fun. Then it got to the place where I was the only one that gave a damn about Damien's singing. He didn't seem to care." She hesitated, not proud of what she would say next. "Once when I yelled at him that he wasn't trying hard enough, he looked at me and said, 'Why should I?'

"I thought at the time that meant he thought he was not going to make it anyway. Now I think he meant that I was doing it all, so why should he."

"That doesn't make him any less a bum."

Ashleigh saw the hard glint that came into his eyes and defended Damien a little. "He didn't do all the things that Treece's boyfriend did."

"He laid up on you and allowed you to take care of him."

"That was my fault as well as his." She licked her lips. "I'm the one who insisted that he move in with me. He was perfectly happy living at home with his mother." She worried her lips even more.

"He told Mia that he'd never asked me to marry him. I was angry when I talked with Mia. I told her it was a lie," she looked down, "but it wasn't. After I thought about it, I realized Damien never did ask me to marry him. He was just going along with my plans, being carried away by all my preparations."

"He told me the same thing," Keefe admitted. "Still, if he didn't want to marry you, he should have had the balls to say so, not string you along."

"I think he was trying to tell me, Keefe, and I wasn't listening. I think maybe all the womanizing was a way for him to get out of the relationship. Maybe he didn't want to tell me he didn't love me."

"You're making excuses for him. Are you sure that you've over him?"

"I'm sure," Ashleigh said and made up her mind to tell him the thing that had been hardest for her to admit, the thing that she'd not confessed to Nicki.

"Keefe, Damien stopped touching me. For months he slept in the bed beside me and didn't touch me."

"Did he say why?" Keefe asked.

"No. And I convinced myself that he was just tired or that he was too depressed, and that after we were married things would improve. They would be different."

"I'm the first man you've had since Damien?"

"Yes, and I know what you're thinking. I don't sleep around, Keefe. I was horny when we got together that first time, but it was because I was attracted to you."

"You're not using me to get back at Damien?"

"No."

"And you're not in love with Damien?"

"No. And Keefe, I don't have any hidden agendas. I'm not

Treece. I don't need your money. I have my own business."

She neglected to tell him that though she had her own business she didn't know for how long, that the government had laid claim to her belongings. Unless her accountant came up with her cash, her dream would go up in smoke. That would be the one thing she would never tell him. How could she? As much as she wanted to be completely honest with him, that bit of information would destroy them before they could really begin.

"No more demons?" Keefe said.

"No more demons," Ashleigh answered.

"And Mia?"

"I'll talk to your sister. I do understand how important she is to you. And before I found out you were brother and sister, I liked her. Don't expect miracles, Keefe, but I'm willing to try to make it work."

"That's all I can ask." He kissed her, licking her lips with his tongue. "Now are we done talking? I'm hungry again."

When Keefe left Ashleigh's apartment, he was happier than he'd been in a long time. Staying the night with her and making love to her this morning had been just what he'd needed. He'd yelled at Mia for butting in but knew if she hadn't he wouldn't have made a move. He turned his car in the direction of his sister's apartment. Glancing at the clock on his dashboard, he hoped that she would be home alone.

No such luck. The moment he walked up to the door he heard the laughter from inside. "Damn." He unlocked the door and went in, determined not to allow Damien to spoil his mood.

He stood there for a long moment watching his sister. She was glowing. Despite his wishes, it was evident Mia had given the man her heart. The thought of Damien possibly hurting Mia filled him with so much rage that a little of it spilled out in the direction of the one causing the problem.

"So Damien," Keefe began, ignoring his sister's smile, the pleading in her eyes to be nice. "How's the job?" He walked toward the kitchen before Damien could answer, the quick flash of disappointment in Mia's eyes forcing him to retreat.

"The job's fine," he heard Damien shout. Keefe cursed softly under his breath, wishing he wouldn't allow the mere presence of the man to get to him. Keefe opened the fridge to get some juice and felt his sister's presence.

"Kee," she admonished, "try, okay?"

Then before he could ask her, "Try what?" she was calling Damien into the kitchen.

"I want the two of you to stop snapping at each other. I'm going out." She glanced at her watch. "Can I leave the two of you in here for fifteen minutes without worrying about you killing each other?" She didn't wait for an answer, merely grabbed her purse and left, leaving both Keefe and Damien to stare after her, then at the closed door.

"Just what does she hope to accomplish with that little stunt?" Keefe looked at Damien and frowned. "What are we supposed to do, kiss and make up?"

Damien grinned, "Don't think so, man, but Mia wants us to get along. I can't see any harm in trying. Besides, I have nothing against you other than the fact that I'm in love with your sister and I can't figure out why you hate me so much."

Neither could Keefe. The things he'd said to Ashleigh came surging back. Maybe he was trying to make Damien responsible for the things Treece had done. But he could think of nothing to say, no way to begin.

"I'll start," Damien offered. "I've been sort of wanting to talk to you anyway."

Keefe fastened his eyes on Damien's face. "First, tell me how you feel about Ashleigh? Do you still have feelings for her? I mean, if she wanted you back, would you go?"

Damien frowned, then shook his head. "It's easy to see you and Mia are sister and brother. You think alike. She asked me the same thing and I'll tell you what I told her. I care for Ashleigh, that's all. Even though I dogged her, she was a real friend to me. She helped me out so many times," he ignored Keefe's raised brows, "not just with money. She believed in me and she did that at a time when I didn't and I'll always be grateful for that. But I'm not in love with Ashleigh." He lowered his head and his voice. "I know how this will make me sound and I already know your low opinion of me, but I was never in love with Ashleigh. I know that now."

For a few moments both men were silent. Then Damien again broke the silence. "I'm in love with Mia. Keefe, this is real, it's true love," he said and a huge grin split his face. "I want to ask Mia to marry me."

"Now?" Keefe was staring in shock at Damien. "That's why you're here?"

"Not tonight, in three weeks. I have a big surprise for her and I'm using it to ask her. I just want to make sure you're cool with this."

"And if I'm not?"

"I'll ask her anyway, but it would make all three of our lives easier if you were. I know you hate it, but Mia loves me. Sooner or later you're going to have to accept that fact," he paused, "just as I had to accept that to her you're the sun, moon and the stars. In her eyes you can do no wrong. I know I can never replace you in her life and I'm smart enough not to even try. It's enough that she's willing to share her love with me." He looked at Keefe and grinned. "It's not like wishing you away is going to make it happen." He started laughing and to his surprise Keefe joined in.

"Well, I guess we do have one thing in common. We both know that wishing doesn't make things happen." They both laughed again.

"We have two things in common," Damien amended. "We both love Mia. Can we try for Mia's sake to get along?" He stuck out his hand and once again surprising both of them, Keefe took it. "Don't blow my surprise, okay?" Damien asked as they heard Mia's key in the lock.

"You sure I can't try wishing you away again?" Keefe asked and laughed. And in the middle of their laughter Mia returned, gazed at the two of them, looked pleased as punch, then kissed each of them and sat on the sofa with an I-told-you-so look that made both Keefe and Damien start laughing again.

For several days everything was smooth sailing. Keefe made a bundle on some stocks despite the slump in the market. Everything was looking up, he was spending as much time as he could with Ashleigh and it had the feeling of rightness. That thought alone should have been enough to clue him in that the universe was about to tilt and once again he would be on the wrong end.

"Oh God, Nicki, I'm scared."

"You said he gave you a week to get the money. Maybe your accountant didn't steal it. Maybe he'll come up with it."

Ashleigh glared at Nicki. "Get real. Do you know how I got that extension? When that man from the IRS came into my shop, I begged, pleaded, everything. I told him it wasn't my fault; that my accountant took care of my taxes. He wouldn't listen, Nicki. I even cried. Nothing worked until I flirted with him."

"You didn't go to bed with him?"

"No, I didn't. But I did go out to lunch with him and he made me pay. Can you believe it? Here I don't have money to pay my taxes and this creep knows it, and what does he do? He tells me, 'You've got this, right?'"

"Ashleigh, I hope Keefe doesn't find out."

"There's nothing to find out. I went to lunch with that creep to save my store."

"Why don't you just ask Keefe for the money? The guy's loaded."

Ashleigh couldn't believe the words her friend had uttered. She would have thought Nicki needed no explanation. She was well aware of their history, that Keefe had called her a gold digger. She'd even confided to her about Treece. "Are you crazy?" she asked angrily.

"But, Ashleigh, you need help. You need money and fast."

"I would rather lose the shop than have Keefe think that I'm like

Treece. I won't have him thinking I want him for his money. God, Nicki, I love him. I'm not going to lose him by asking for his help."

"Well, my offer to have some brothers kick the shit out of your accountant still stands. Just say the word."

Ashleigh attempted to smile as she accepted Nicki's hug. "I just may take you up on that offer," she moaned.

A knock sounded on the door and Ashleigh glanced at Nicki. "It's not Keefe. He called me; he's not coming over tonight."

Please God, don't let it be the IRS man. She looked toward Nicki, then answered the door. Damien.

She should have known. Her life was quickly spiraling downward. When it finally bottomed out, it seemed only appropriate that the man who'd started her on the path should be there to witness it. Why had she bothered wasting her time dreaming of a happily ever after?

Damien had been pacing since he'd come to Mia's. He'd kissed her absentmindedly and had even asked Mia about Keefe's whereabouts.

"Damien, what's wrong? Tell me what's going on."

He turned toward her and his eyes had a haunted look. "It's Ashleigh," he managed to croak out, and she moved even farther away, this time physically.

"What about Ashleigh?" she managed to ask, her voice not even sounding like her own. Evidently Damien couldn't tell because he continued talking.

He turned to face Mia. "Ashleigh's going to lose her business.

The government has seized her shop. They said she hasn't paid her taxes for four years. And unless she comes up with the cash, that's it. All gone. Her dream goes up in smoke."

"What is she going to do?"

"I don't know," Damien answered. "She didn't want me to know. I went over to talk to her face-to-face, make amends like you said, and she was upset, crying. Nicki was there and she told me what was going on. I want to help her but I have nowhere to get that kind of money." His eyes took on a wild look. "I don't even know anyone with that kind of money who would be willing to help her."

"I think you know one person with that kind of money." Mia moved across the room. "Keefe has that kind of money." She stood against the wall, bracing her back for support. She was watching his face, his action. She saw the leap of hope spring up in his eyes and something died within her. Her brother had been right. Her body ached. She felt pain as she never had before and she wanted to scream, sink into the floor and scream until the pain went away. She lost her battle to stand. Her legs gave way and she found herself sliding toward the floor. Damien was lifting her, concern in his eyes, and she pushed away from him.

"I'm not going to let you do it."

"Do what?" he asked, puzzled.

"You're not going to hurt my brother, either of you."

"What the hell are you talking about? I haven't done a damn thing to your brother."

"I'm not going to let you hurt him, Damien. No one's going to ever hurt him again, not as long as I can stop it." She pushed herself away from Damien. "Ashleigh's not going to use my brother and neither are you."

Angry, Damien stood glowering over her. "Tell me what you're talking about, Mia. Now."

"You, you and Ashleigh," she screamed. "He's not giving her any money." Though tears streamed down her face, she still saw the disbelief, then the hurt and at last the anger rest on Damien's face.

"You think that I'm here to try to get money from your brother?"

"Yes. Why did you ask about him? You never have. Why today?"

"Because I wanted to talk to you in private, tell you about Ashleigh and I didn't want what just happened to happen with him. God, I know how the guy is about money and his distrust, but not you, Mia. I thought you trusted me."

"I trusted someone before, Damien, and all it got was my brother hurt. I'm not going to let it happen again," she repeated. "My brother is not giving Ashleigh money."

"You didn't hear me ask him to, Mia. That wasn't what I was doing. I was just telling you that I was worried about her." He glared at Mia, at the tears streaming down her face and wished things could be different. He loved her with his entire heart and the thought of living without her was something he didn't want to face.

"Mia, you're more like your brother than I would have ever imagined. I don't like it. And I'm not going to spend the rest of my life jumping through hoops for you. No more, Mia. If money is so damn important to you, why don't you just wrap yourself up in it? Use that to keep yourself warm. You don't need a man. You don't have room in your life for anyone other your brother and I'm not playing second fiddle to him anymore. You tell your brother to take his money and shove it up his ass and the both of you can go straight to hell and stay there. It's over, Mia."

As he opened the door to leave, there stood Keefe. "Wishes do come true," Damien said and left.

CHAPTER FIFTEEN

Keefe stared after Damien, trying to decipher his cryptic message and the anger mixed with pain he'd seen in Damien's face. No doubt about it, something was wrong. Keefe rushed into his sister's apartment and found her sobbing. "Mia, what's wrong?" he asked. "Did he do anything to hurt you?"

She clung to him, whimpering over and over that she was sorry. All he wanted was to get her to calm down.

"You were right, you were right all along." Mia lifted her face and her misery tore him apart. Damn Damien for hurting her. He'd find him and when he did, he'd kick his ass. "Mia, stop crying and tell me what he did to you."

"He tried to hurt you," she sobbed even harder, "but I wouldn't let him."

"Mia, what are you talking about?"

"Ashleigh. Damien came here and told me that Ashleigh's losing her shop, that the IRS is seizing it, something about her accountant. He said her taxes haven't been paid in over four years."

A cold chill raced down Keefe's back and he wished like hell that he was any place besides his sister's apartment. God, how he wished this was all just a bad dream.

"How did he find out?"

"He went to Ashleigh."

"Why was he at Ashleigh's?"

"I don't know. I told him a few days ago what Ashleigh told me, that she still loves him and wants him back."

Keefe closed his eyes against the sudden onslaught of pain. He stood there for a moment, reeling, listening to the sound of his sister's continued crying. He didn't want to yell at her but he needed her to stop crying. She'd just dropped a bomb on him and it was hard for him to be compassionate about her pain when he had so much of his own.

At last he opened his eyes and the sight of his sister sitting there crying, her heart breaking, had the same effect on him that it always had. He had to make things right for her before he could wallow in his hurt.

He sat next to her. "Mia, are you sure that's what Ashleigh said?"

She sniffled indignantly. "Of course I'm sure. I told Damien. I asked him what he would do if she wanted him back. He told me he didn't love her, that he loved me. Now today he tells me that she needs money."

"Mia," Keefe said patiently, "that's a long leap. Did he ask you for the money?"

"No."

"Then how?"

"He asked me where you were. He wanted to ask you for the money."

"Did he say that?"

"He didn't have to say it. I said it for him. That's when he got angry. I told him that I wasn't going to let him hurt you and I won't, Kee. I won't ever let anyone hurt you again."

Mia wound her arms around him so tightly that she was choking him. She was trembling, and he knew what she was afraid of. His head ached suddenly, and images of Ashleigh filled his thoughts. He was falling in love with her. He had to believe she wasn't like

Treece. This couldn't be happening again.

"Mia, maybe you're wrong. I didn't tell you but I've been seeing Ashleigh again. She didn't mention anything about any problems. Maybe the entire thing is something that Damien cooked up."

That he didn't mind believing, but he didn't want to believe that Ashleigh had lied to him, that she still loved Damien.

Mia lifted her head and stared at her brother. "You don't believe me?" she asked. "Or you don't want to believe me?"

"Damien told me that he loves you, Mia."

"And Treece told me that she loved you."

Keefe rubbed his eyes, his fingers tearing through his hair. "Did Damien say how much money she needed?"

"No. I didn't give him a chance." Fear struck her heart. "Kee, you're not thinking about giving her the money, are you?"

"I have to talk to her, Mia. I have to see if it's true."

"Do you think I would lie to you?"

His pain-filled eyes connected with hers and she knew he was thinking of her lying about Damien. "Kee, do you think I would lie to you about something this important? Ashleigh told me that she still loved Damien. I didn't tell you before because I didn't see the need. You told me to mind my own business. I didn't know you were seeing her again."

He thought of the past week he'd spent with Ashleigh. He'd even gone to her shop several times and taken her to lunch. Mia was right. He didn't want it to all be a lie, but he couldn't help doing what Mia had done: compare the situations. He'd been unbelievably happy with Treece. There was a lump in his throat making it hard to breathe, much less talk any more about it.

"I have to ask her about it, Mia, I have to ask her," he said softly.

"And if she tells you that I'm lying?" Mia was piercing her brother with her stare, not believing that he would take Ashleigh's word over hers.

"If she tells me that you're lying, it's over, Mia. I believe you. Don't I always?" He attempted to smile. "I'm sorry about Damien. I really thought he loved you."

"Yeah, so did I."

Keefe spent the night at Mia's. They pretended to be engrossed in the situation comedies on TV but their laughs were hollow and their pain showed through. When Mia finally kissed him on the cheek and went into her bedroom, he heaved a sigh of relief. He was worried about her. She loved Damien. That much he knew, and she was behaving as though he didn't exist. He remembered Damien saying he wanted to marry Mia, that he had a surprise for her. None of it made any sense.

He fell asleep and dreamt of Ashleigh, of making love to her. When he woke he wished that he could pretend as his sister was doing. He wished Ashleigh didn't matter to him, but she did, and it was only now that he was beginning to know just how much.

He had thoughts of giving Ashleigh the money she needed. If she needed it, he would give it to her in a flash. If she didn't…if it were only a scam… Keefe didn't want to think about the possibility of that.

He made coffee and again he worried about Mia as she headed off to work with no mention of the previous night, still pretending that nothing had happened, that Damien had never existed. One look at her dead face and he much preferred the tears.

Keefe waited in Mia's apartment until Ashleigh's shop opened. He didn't want to go to Ashleigh's apartment, not now, not in the mood that he was in.

He stood inside the door to Ashleigh's shop staring at her, trying to read any signals that she might be giving off, listening for sounds from the back. With a shock he realized that he was listening for sounds of Damien. He'd asked her straight out if she had feelings for Damien and she'd told him no, but he knew Mia had not lied.

Ashleigh was watching him, a nervous smile on her face, and he knew she'd seen Damien. Again. He watched as she walked toward him and he bit the inside of his cheek to ground himself. He wanted to reach for her, beg her to not let it be true, tell her how he felt. But Mia was right. He couldn't let either of them be made a fool of again.

"I didn't ask Damien to ask you for money, Keefe."

"So it's true?"

"It's true that my accountant has not been paying my taxes. It's not true that I wanted money from you. Damien told me that he never asked Mia for money. He told her about my problem because he was worried about me, about my losing my shop."

"So the two of you are friends now?" Keefe glared at her.

"It's not like that, Keefe."

"Then tell me how it is. Did you tell Mia that you were still in love with Damien?"

Ashleigh wanted to cry. She should have known something would happen to mess things up, but this, this big lie she'd told because she was angry—she had known nothing good would come from her ex being involved with the sister of the man she was falling in love with.

DYANNE DAVIS

Not only that, but for God's sake, why had Damien mentioned her financial problems to the one person he shouldn't have?

Ashleigh didn't blame Keefe or Mia for thinking that she and Damien were working a con. She looked at Keefe and winced, the look in his eyes striking fear in her heart. She thought for a moment to lie, just tell him that she'd not told that to Mia. But she knew his mind was made up already. He believed his sister and if she lied now, there would be no chance for them to make it right.

"Keefe, do you really think after the week we've spent together, I could betray you like that?"

"You still haven't answered my question."

"And you haven't answered mine. Tell me, Keefe, do you think I would betray you after all the things we said to each other?" She was praying he would say no, but the cold look on her face squelched that hope.

"Ashleigh, did you tell my sister that you are still in love with Damien?"

"Yes, I told her that, but Keefe, I didn't mean it. I was just so angry with her."

"For what? If you don't love Damien, why should you have been angry with Mia?"

"She had everything that I'd dreamed about. Don't you under-stand that? She had my dream gown and she had the man I was helping to reach his dreams. She had everything that belonged to me and I was angry."

"I asked you if you still have feelings for Damien and you lied to me."

"I didn't lie."

Keefe snorted, "You lied to either my sister or me."

"I lied to Mia, Keefe. I wanted to hurt her. I didn't tell you that

197

before because I know how much you love her. I knew you'd be angry that I'd tried to hurt your sister, so I didn't tell you."

Keefe looked at her hard. "Why would you tell Damien that you needed help and not tell me?"

"I didn't tell Damien. He came over to my apartment a couple of nights ago, and Nicki was there. She told him."

"Why was he there, Ashleigh?"

"He wanted to salvage our friendship, tell me that he was sorry."

"Are you sure that's all he was trying to do? We both know how the guy is. One woman isn't enough for him. Maybe sleeping with Mia isn't enough. It wasn't enough when he was sleeping with you."

She slapped him. "You're a fool, Keefe. Damien isn't sleeping with your precious sister or me. Or with anyone else from what he says and I believe him. He loves Mia. But the two of you have been waiting for him to screw up. God, I wish he'd cared about me even a fraction of the way he cares about Mia. She's wrong about him and you're wrong about me. I don't want your money. I never did. How many times do I have to tell you that?"

She walked away, went behind the counter and rumbled through some drawers, pulled out a paper, and walked back toward him and flung the paper in his face. "Here Keefe, this is from the federal government. Or maybe not. Maybe besides being a gold digger, I'm also a master forger."

Keefe took the paper and looked it over. It was real. A demand for seventeen thousand dollars. He looked at the date. Ashleigh had only a few days to come up with the money. "I can give it to you."

"Don't you dare...don't you dare." Her voice was low but the words were filled with anger. "I can forgive you in time because I know why you're behaving like this. But don't you dare offer me money, Keefe. I'll fix my own problem. I always have. I always will.

I'm not a gold digger. I don't want your money. And you want to know something funny, Keefe? Neither does Damien. He only wanted to help me. Never once did he question me or disbelieve me. You think he's such an awful person, someone your sister is too good for. Well, right now I'd say she would be lucky to have him.

"You have loyalty and love for one person, and one person only, Keefe, and that's Mia. That's both of your problems. No one will measure up to your ideal. Where are your friends? I'll tell you where. Neither of you has any. Why? Because you only need each other. Too bad you can't marry each other. Then maybe you'd both be happy."

Keefe felt as if Ashleigh had slapped him for the second time. It was true, at least some of it. He and Mia didn't have many friends and he knew it was due in part because of the betrayal of people in their lives. They'd been able only to count on each other.

He dug into his pocket, and took out his checkbook and wrote a check for the entire amount and laid it on the counter. Ashleigh glanced at him and the check and ripped the paper into shreds.

He wrote a second check and again put it on the counter. "Ashleigh, you need the money. You're going to lose your shop. Take it."

"I'd rather lose it," she answered as she ripped the second check into shreds.

"Is it over, Ashleigh?" Keefe asked as he looked at her. "Are you saying that you can't forgive me?"

He watched as she turned away, his heart skipping a beat. Then she answered, "In time I'll forgive you, Keefe. Like I said, I understand your motives, but unlike you, I don't expect perfection. I'm not your sister, Keefe. I'm not perfect. So maybe you need to decide if you can live with that. If not, then maybe you should do as I suggest and just stay with your sister."

He stood there for a moment longer before turning to walk away.

"Keefe, I'll call you when I've forgiven you. Don't bother coming back until then."

Ashleigh stood behind her counter, trembling from Keefe's assumptions. Sure, he had his reasons. But after all they'd been through she'd expected more. Still she knew given time she would forgive him. She loved him and despite his suspicious nature, she believed he was falling in love with her also.

She looked at the tax bill still lying on her counter and gritted her teeth. Damn it all to hell. She wasn't going to leave the future of her business or her relationship with Keefe in anyone's hands but her own. She was done waiting and hoping that her accountant did the right thing. It was time she took some action. With that thought in mind she picked up the phone.

"Nicki, were you jiving or can you really get me some muscle?"

Silence.

"Nicki?"

"What are you asking exactly? I mean...I was sort of kidding."

"I don't want anyone to do anything illegal. I just want some backup. They don't even have to talk, just stand behind me and look intimidating. I'll do the rest."

"What are you going to do?"

"I'm going to go and get my damn money."

"You go, girl."

"Nicki, I'm serious."

"I know you are. I have an idea. Why don't you take Damien. The deep sound of that brother's voice strikes fear in a weak man as much as it makes a woman wet."

"Nicki!" Ashleigh screamed. "Stop playing. I'm serious."

"What happened, Ash?"

"Keefe came down. He wrote me out a check."

"I suppose you were too proud to take it."

"I couldn't take it, Nicki, I love him. If I took money from him now, he'd never believe that. I would rather lose the shop than take a chance on losing Keefe."

"That serious huh?"

"That serious."

"I'll call Damien and a couple of other guys," Nicki promised.

Keefe went to his office, wrote out a third check and mailed it to Ashleigh's store, knowing that she wouldn't cash it but not knowing what else to do.

He didn't get much work done that day and would have gone home to his own apartment when he finally called it quits except he was worried about Mia. He'd called her several times during the day and he didn't like the way she was sounding. Her voice was still devoid of emotion. He wondered if she was trying to be strong for him.

He'd picked up dinner but neither of them had an appetite. He'd ask Mia questions and she'd answer, but not with her usual vivaciousness.

Finally he broached the only subject that was on his mind.

"I went to see Ashleigh today."

"I know."

"How did you know?"

"I felt it," she said without looking in his direction.

"She admitted that she told you she was still in love with Damien." He waited for a reaction. Getting none, he continued. "She said she did that only to hurt you. She was angry with you. Even you said that, remember?" Still nothing. She wasn't even looking at him.

"Mia, Damien didn't lie. Ashleigh showed me the letter from the IRS. It's true."

"Too bad," Mia said. Still no emotion.

"Mia, are you okay?"

"Yes." She smiled at him, finally looking in his direction, but her smile frightened him even more than her dead look.

"Kee, I forgot to mention to you, don't write any checks. They won't clear."

He heard her but it took him a moment to focus on her words. There was something more than strange happening here. "Mia, what are you talking about? There's plenty of money in the checking account."

"No, there isn't," she insisted, "and there isn't any in your savings either. So don't try that."

"What did you do, Mia?" he asked, knowing immediately what she'd done.

"I took most of it out."

For one moment Keefe panicked. He'd mailed Ashleigh another check. What if she attempted to cash it and it bounced? She would think... Then he calmed down. Ashleigh wouldn't cash the check.

"Mia, why did you do that? I wrote Ashleigh a check this morning."

"I figured you would, that's why I did it."

"She tore it up."

"It doesn't matter." She was still smiling at him and it was freaking him out.

"Mia, you had no right to do that. That's my money and you can't tell me what to do with it. Besides, I took away your checkbook. How did you do it?"

"You didn't take my name off your accounts, Keefe. I'm not going to let anyone hurt you." She smiled and turned away from him to watch television. "Not even you yourself. I'm going to take care of you like you've always done for me."

"Mia." Keefe clicked the off button on the remote control. "Honey, you're wrong. Ashleigh wasn't trying to hurt me, and neither was Damien."

"Good," she answered and turned the television back on.

"Mia, you're not listening to me. You misjudged Damien. He loves you. He wasn't asking for money."

She wasn't answering him, giving him more reason for fear. He couldn't yell at her anymore about taking the money from his accounts. Because it didn't matter. Maybe Ashleigh was right in saying they put too much emphasis on money.

For the next few days Keefe alternated between worrying about Ashleigh and worrying about Mia. One night he even went by her class. She looked at him oddly, as though he were the one with the problem, and asked why he was there. When he told her he was worried about her, she laughed it off and told him not to, that she was fine. And on the surface she behaved as if she were. If only in his heart he believed that she was.

She was too old for him to fool with gifts bought by him and given to her on the pretext that their mother had sent them to her. Besides, even if he wanted to buy her a gift, she had control of his money and was doling it out to him. He allowed her to continue doing it because he didn't know what else to do.

Ashleigh had asked that he leave her alone until she called. He'd tried but he found the need to hear her voice overwhelming, so he gave in.

"Ashleigh," he rushed on as she answered, "I know what you said and I respect it. I just wanted to know that you're doing okay. I'm worried about you."

Ashleigh sighed. She'd been thinking about Keefe and the fact that he could listen to her and go away so easily. Despite her wishes at the time, she'd been annoyed that he hadn't called.

"You don't have to be worried about me, Keefe"

"Did you get everything straightened out?"

"Not yet. But I have a plan."

"Ashleigh, I miss you. I'm truly sorry for what happened."

"I know."

"Have you forgiven me?"

"Yes."

"Ashleigh, I'm falling in-"

"Don't say it, Keefe."

"Why not? It's true."

"Now's not the time. There're too many things happening right now, too many problems that have to be taken care of. Besides, I don't want to hear it like this, when everything's topsy-turvy and you think I'm mad at you."

"Do you think there will ever be a perfect moment to tell you?"

Ashleigh closed her eyes, holding the phone to her ear and rocking her body. She sure hoped so. As much as she wanted to hear Keefe tell her that he loved her, she wanted it right. "Yeah, I think there will be a better time. There has to be."

"And if there isn't?"

"Let's just get through one crisis at a time."

"Are you sure I can't help?"

"I'm sure, but thanks for asking. I already have people lined up to help me with my plans." She wondered if she should tell him that Damien was helping. Before she could weigh the pros and cons, the words tumbled out. "Damien's helping me.

"I see."

She heard the hurt in his voice. "I didn't have to tell you."

"Why did you?"

"Because I wanted you to know. And, Keefe, there is nothing for you to worry about. Damien wants to help and he's perfect for my plan."

"Are you going to tell me your plan?"

"It's better that you don't know."

"Ashleigh?"

"No, Keefe, its better that you don't know. I'll call you in a couple of days."

"You'll call?"

"Yes. I promise. I'll call." Ashleigh hung up the phone, wishing she could have Keefe beside her when she implemented her plan, but she couldn't involve him. Technically what she was going to do could be considered kidnapping and extortion, but she was doing what she had to do to get her money back. And if things backfired on her, she didn't want Keefe to get hurt. She loved him.

Ashleigh had forgiven him. That was the one bright note he carried with him from their conversation. He knew she would call him. She'd promised. Besides, he didn't really have time to make things right with her at the moment. He was too busy worrying about Mia's sanity to do much good in any other area of his life.

He was trying desperately to find a way to bring some sunshine back into both of their lives. What they got instead was a visit from the *last* person Keefe expected to help.

CHAPTER SIXTEEN

Keefe heard voices inside Mia's apartment and his stomach turned. He didn't have to go in to know who was inside. It was their mother. Since Mia had always been a soft touch for her and since Mia now had control of his money, he wondered how much his mother would hit them up for this time. This was just what Mia needed. Another disappointment in her life.

"Keefe, look who's here," Mia called to him as he entered the room. He eyed his mother warily, then sighed and took a seat. "Why are you here?" he asked at last.

Before she could answer, Mia answered for her. "I forgot to tell her that James and I aren't getting married. She came to help."

Keefe rolled his eyes and shook his head. He had told Mia he would take care of it, but had delayed, not wanting to talk to his mother. Now he wished he had. She was once again back in their lives and as surely as she was standing there, she would wreak havoc, leaving their lives in worst shambles and Mia in worse pain. Just as she'd always done. And as always, he'd be the one left behind to pick up the pieces. *Damn,* he thought, *why now?*

Keefe eyed his mother angrily. Despite everything she'd been through, the woman was still beautiful. She was much taller than Mia, nearly as tall as Keefe. Still slim, perfect makeup, as always. Her expensive clothes were perfect too. He could feel his neck knotting and glanced at his mother's face, at her honeyed complexion, so like his own, and her warm brown eyes. As much as he'd wished it in the past, there was no denying the woman was their mother. He looked at the new shortened hair she was sporting and grimaced. Their mother was beautiful. Then again, why wouldn't she be? She was a narcissist. She was her own one true love.

"Hello Keefe," his mother said.

He grunted. It wasn't a hello but it was more than he wanted to give her. He glanced at Mia, hoping that she'd not told the woman what was going on, told her what she'd done, or within days they'd both be broke.

"Mia, can I talk to you in your room for a minute?"

"Don't worry, Kee, she answered, "it's okay. And stop looking at me that way. I haven't gone crazy."

He arched his brows. "Mia, I really think we should talk."

"Not now," she answered and sat down.

He glared at their mother, then at Mia, determined that he would not let their mother learn anything from him.

"You're looking good, Keefe."

He didn't answer.

"Mia told me about James, that he married someone else. You should have called me; I would have come."

"Why?"

"To help out. Mia needed me."

"You've never been here before when she needed you. What on earth would have made me think you would be here for her now?" He saw his mother flinch and Mia tilt her head to stare at him. She wasn't giving him her look of disapproval and that more than anything told him that she wasn't okay.

"Listen, Mia and I got through it same as we always do, so don't worry."

"I was only saying that I would have come to help."

"I don't believe you."

"You don't have a reason to believe me, I know. But I'm still sorry that you and Mia had to go through it all alone."

"What else is new?" Keefe sighed, taking another good look at the woman who'd given birth to him. God, she looked so much like Mia it was eerie. And her voice—If he didn't know better and if he closed his eyes, he would swear it was his sister's. They had the same soft musical tones. Two women who couldn't be more different. One he adored, one he couldn't stand. How he wished that neither he nor Mia resembled the woman. It would be so much easier to hate her, more satisfying.

"Are you over James?"

Keefe turned in Mia's direction, wondering how his sister would answer that question.

"There was nothing to be over. I was never truly in love with him."

"Then why on earth did you agree to marry him?"

"He asked."

Keefe sat up straighter, staring at his sister, chills capturing him. Sure, he'd known that she'd never felt overwhelming passion for James, but still he'd thought she loved him in her own way.

"Mia, you said yes to a man you didn't love?"

"Why not, Mom? Isn't that what we do?"

Keefe watched as for the second time their mother winced from the words spoken by one of her children. Only this time she really appeared to be hurt. Mia never said mean things to her. He was the one who did that.

"Mia, I was never with a man that I didn't love."

Before their mother could finish, Mia began laughing hysterically. "Love, you have no idea what that means. You've been married…

What? Seven times? Or is it eight? My God, I've lost count of the men you've lived with. You're going to tell me you loved all of them?"

"I always thought I did."

Keefe looked over at the woman he'd always hated and suddenly he felt pity for her. She apparently believed what she was saying, but that wasn't what worried Keefe. It was what Mia was saying or rather what she wasn't saying.

"Mia," Keefe said, and she smiled sweetly at him.

"My dear sweet brother, my hero. You've always been there for me, haven't you? You've always known, haven't you? That's why you've tried so hard. You knew I was going to turn out just like her, didn't you, going from man to man?"

She was smiling but she was trembling so hard that Keefe could see it from where he sat.

"What's going on, Keefe?" their mother asked, and he noted the worry in her voice. That didn't make him feel any better. Mia had to be really near the edge to make their mother feel even the smallest amount of worry.

"Don't ask Keefe, Mom. Ask me, I'm right here. Besides, Keefe won't tell you. He's still too busy trying to pretend that I'm perfect, that I'm not just like you, but he thinks it. Right, Keefe?"

"Mia, stop," he said but she continued.

"Mom, while I was engaged to James, I managed to fall in love with someone else. Only now I know it wasn't love. How could it be? How could I possibly think I loved him? I don't think I'm capable of love. What do you think, Mom? Do you think I'm capable of loving anyone? I mean, look at you. You don't even love your own children."

There was no anger or bitterness in Mia's voice, only amaze-

210

ment. *Shit*, Keefe thought. He'd known his mother being there would cause problems. But this he'd never counted on.

What a God-awful way to end a horrible week. "Mia," Keefe snapped at her, "cut it out now. You're hurt, I know that, but you're wrong."

"Keefe," she answered, sounding like a little girl, "you said I was just like her. Don't you remember? You were right."

"I didn't say that."

"Yes you did," she answered him, "and don't worry, Kee. I'm not angry with you about it. You were telling the truth."

"If I said it, Mia, it was in anger, although I don't think I said it. But either way you aren't."

Her eyes were glazed over and she continued talking, not listening to Keefe.

"You tried to warn me about Damien. I should have listened. It's my fault for cheating on James."

Keefe looked toward their mother. He didn't want to have this conversation in front of her. "Mia, let's talk about this in your room." He attempted to pull her in that direction but she refused to budge.

"I should never have looked at Damien. Everything that's happened is my fault, Kee."

"No, Mia, it's not. You can't help falling in love. Besides, it was meant to be. James married someone else."

Again she smiled at him and shook her head. "Kee, what are you talking about? You hated Damien from the beginning. You saw right through him. I didn't and I almost failed you again."

Keefe looked toward their mother, knowing she was more than curious, that Mia was on the verge of telling her that she'd taken control of his money. But surprisingly it didn't matter. If Mia would just stop acting like a zombie, his mother could have every dime he owned. He didn't give a damn. All he wanted was his sister back to normal.

"Listen to me, Mia, I was wrong. I was wrong about Damien. He loves you. I believe him."

"It doesn't matter. Even if he does, I don't love him. Look at me. I'm not upset at about our break up. It's not bothering me. How can I have loved him? I don't feel anything."

Keefe wanted to cry. He was looking at his sister, not knowing what to do. He looked to his mother, hoping against hope that for once in their lives she could give Mia the mothering she so desperately needed.

"Mia, you're wrong. Neither of you are anything like me. For that I'm grateful. I've always admired and envied your relationship, your love and loyalty for each other. You don't think you can love? My God, how wrong you are. Not love? What about your brother? I know you would die for your brother." She looked in Keefe's direction.

"I also know why you agreed to marry James. You thought it would please your brother. You love him. You'd do anything to make him happy and as far as your brother goes, why do you think he hates me so much? Because of his love for you. I hurt you and he hates me for it. There are few things in my life I can be proud of, but giving birth to the two of you and choosing names for you, that I am proud of. Now I don't know if the names are a curse or a blessing.

Keefe was staring at his mother, who for the first time in his life had his attention. "What are you talking about?" he asked her.

"You probably don't remember but I told you," she said, looking directly at him. "I looked in a baby book and found your name. I liked the meaning: handsome, noble, gentle and lovable. And then when I was pregnant with Mia you would hug my belly and say that's mine, and I looked up words that meant *mine*, and found Mia.

"Even then I knew the two of you would take care of each other, do the things that I couldn't. I knew you'd take care of her and she'd take care of you. So, Mia, if you don't think you know how to love, look at your brother and tell me you don't love him."

Mia turned toward her brother and tears rolled down her cheeks. "I do love you, Kee. I love you so much it hurts."

Keefe went to her and held her in his arms. "And you love Damien. Don't be afraid of loving him. He loves you. He wasn't trying to hurt me; it was all a big mistake."

He held her and allowed her to cry, knowing his mother's words were what she'd needed, what he'd tried for the past week to say. He looked over Mia's head at their mother, the woman he'd spent a lifetime hating and he said, "thank you," as tears ran down his own cheeks.

"I do love him, Kee, but it's too late. I didn't trust him and now he doesn't want me anymore."

"Honey, you're wrong. It's never too late. Damien loves you. I know he does. You're going to work things out with him. And I'm going to work things out with Ashleigh."

He held her, rocking her, letting her cry it out, and when she was done, his sister was back. And for that he had his mother to thank.

Keefe's eyes connected with his mother's. She had a look that at first he didn't understand. Then it dawned on him that she wanted to comfort Mia. There was such longing in her eyes. For only a nanosecond old feelings flooded him and he questioned why he should relinquish Mia. His mother had never comforted her before. Why should she have that privilege now? He was the one who'd been there. As the look intensified in his mother's eyes, he understood she would not intrude. He felt Mia's shudders and his residual anger drained away. Mia needed this and this time he had the power to give it to her.

He glanced in his mother's direction and nodded his head toward her. Her mouth opened in surprise but he nodded his head again and she mouthed a thank you to him as she came and took her daughter in her arms. Mia's face lifted and she looked at her brother for a long moment. Keefe couldn't help the tears that ran down his own cheeks. He nodded to Mia, then stood back and watched as Mia allowed her mother to comfort her. He wondered where all the tears were coming from but knew instinctively that she was crying for all the years she'd never gotten to cry in her mother's arms. As their mother crooned to her, brushing back her hair, kissing her forehead, her cheeks, something happened to Keefe.

Whatever his mother might ask him for in that moment he would gladly give her. This was the one gift he'd been unable to give to Mia. A lump formed in his throat. For this moment, for this pain, she had a mother. No matter how much he loved his sister, having their mother there was the best medicine she could have.

Keefe looked at his sister finally getting what she needed. It was time for him to have what he needed. He went into his room and made the call. "Don't stop me," he said, when she answered. "When this whole nightmare is over I intend to tell you that I love you. I need you, Ashleigh," he whispered.

"I need you too, Keefe," she answered. "Don't worry, it's almost over. I'll call you tomorrow."

In spite of the problems yet to be solved, Keefe felt hope at last.

He rubbed at his eyes that now felt gritty and went back out to be with Mia and his mother.

A few hours later Mia was curled up in their mother's arms. Her tears had dried but it appeared that Mia didn't want to give up the comfort of her position. Keefe didn't blame her. They both knew this opportunity might never come again.

"Listen, I know I'm the last person in the world to give advice to anyone-"

Keefe glanced in his mother's direction but didn't make any snide remarks, which was a surprise to the three of them. She'd helped with Mia and for that he was willing to grant her a certain leeway. "Speak your mind," he offered and noted the look of gratitude in her eyes. Something akin to guilt pierced him. He'd never given much thought to the pain he'd heaped on his mother through the years—he'd always thought he was justified.

"Mia, honey, your brother's never going to stop loving you; no matter what you do. Even if you turn out to be exactly like me, he's going to always love you. So stop being afraid of that. You can't lose his love. And he's never going to fully approve of any man that you love. Down deep he has to love the fact that he's the most important person in your life." Their mother glanced from one of them to the other.

"Don't get angry, Keefe. You wouldn't be human if you didn't enjoy the power you have over your sister. It's the same with Mia. She has that same power over you and she knows it. From the time she was a baby she had you wrapped around her little finger. If she cried you would drop everything and do her bidding, no questions asked."

Her eyes dropped down to her daughter and she smiled. "Honey, it's hard enough finding a man that you even think you love without trying to find one's that's going to please your brother. He's never going to want you to replace him."

"No one could ever replace him," Mia interrupted.

"And that's the problem. You're going to have to learn to open your heart. I mean really open your heart to more people than Keefe. If you don't love a man, you can't be happy with him simply because your brother finds him acceptable. It's a good thing you didn't marry James. You would have been miserable and you would have made James miserable. Probably the only person who would have been happy would have been your brother."

"What are you talking about? How can you think I would be happy with Mia in an unhappy marriage?"

"Because she'd still need you. She'd come to you, cry on your shoulder and you'd be the one to try to fix things for her, be her knight, as you've always been."

For a moment no one said a word. Then their mother asked the next question. "Mia, how does your brother feel about Damien?"

Mia didn't answer and their mother smiled. "Don't worry, I know. He hates him. Why, Keefe?"

"Because he's a womanizing low-life scum that lives off women and cons his way through life."

"Not any more," Mia defended.

"Keefe, are you sure that it doesn't have something to do with the fact that Mia for the first time truly loved another man, that you could see it and it scared you a little bit?"

"That wasn't it. He was no good. I had good reason." He looked toward Mia for help. "Am I lying about the way he treated women?"

"Well," Mia smiled, "he had a bad reputation."

"Bad reputation," Keefe sputtered. "Come on, admit the guy was bad news."

"Okay, I guess if I had been the big brother I would have been worried, but he never treated me with anything but the utmost respect." She bowed her head a little and blushed. "Well, respect and love. He really did love me." Mia tilted her head. "He loved me enough that he was determined to try to make you like him." She smiled at her brother. "He knows how much I love you, so I guess that's why he told us both to go to hell when he left."

Their mother laughed and they joined in. "Oh yeah, I don't think I'd want to be the one that tried to come between the two of you. Now, Keefe, do you mind if I ask you about the woman you're seeing?"

Somehow in the hours of comforting Mia they'd gotten around to giving their mother all the details from the wedding gown to Ashleigh and Damien telling the two of them to take a hike.

Keefe had been the one to confess to her that Mia had taken all of his money and put it into different accounts. That had surprised Mia as well as Keefe. He wasn't worried about the money. For once in his life he didn't care. It was not his main worry. Mia was. And having her back to normal was worth whatever amount of money their mother needed this time around.

"Okay, one question," he gave in.

"You really called Ashleigh a gold digger?"

"That was a while ago, but she was acting like one. She thought I was the janitor and she didn't want anything to do with me because of my job, or what she thought was my job."

"And she forgave you?"

"It took some doing and Mia butting in, but yes, she forgave me."

"Then you went back again and offended her?"

This time Keefe didn't answer, just stared at his mother and Mia.

"I really messed you kids up, didn't I?" their mother asked. Neither Mia nor Keefe answered her.

"Treece helped," Mia said at last. "We both thought she was wonderful, that she really loved Kee." Mia sighed, "It looked like the same situation all over again."

"How much money did Treece take from you, Keefe?"

"Twenty-five thousand dollars."

"Before that, did she make you happy?"

"Yes," he answered, not wanting to remember that the months he'd spent with Treece had been among the happiest of his life. He glanced at Mia.

"That was the first time I ever thought of you as my brother. Usually you behaved more like my father, or my mother," Mia teased, but when you were with Treece you were so young, so care-free."

"You really liked her then, Mia?"

Mia looked at her mother. "Yes, I really liked her, and I wasn't jealous that Keefe had someone. I was happy for him."

"Then let it go," she advised them. "Keefe, you've remade the money and it's over. And you both loved her. Let it go. Don't let that color the rest of your lives. Both of you need to stop being afraid."

The room became quiet and she looked at the two of them. "Okay, I can see I've said enough and for the first time that I can remember, no one has stormed out of the room, so I think I'll go to bed now." She kissed Mia and smiled at Keefe.

Keefe knew she wanted to kiss him, have him embrace her but he wasn't ready for that yet. One step at a time.

CHAPTER SEVENTEEN

"Mia, do you think she's right?"

"She's been in enough relationships that she should have learned something." Mia cocked her head toward the door. "I can't believe you were nice to her."

"I can't either," he answered. "It just happened I was grateful to her."

"Yeah, I know. You thought I had lost it." She stopped. "You were right, I had. It didn't feel like it though. I thought I was being rational. I was determined to save you and...I...I...didn't care what you thought about it. I'm sorry, Keefe."

She rose from the sofa, went to the desk and pulled out several bankbooks, including a new checking account, and handed them over to her brother. "I think I went a little nuts for a few days. Great psychologist I'm going to make."

"And that's the reason you *will* make a great psychologist."

"Why, because I'm nuts? I had a total meltdown."

"Yes, but now you can recognize the signs, know the feelings behind them. You know one thing Mom's right about? We have to expand our lives, Mia. I never thought about it before but neither of us has any friends outside of our jobs. No one that we spend time with. I think we need that."

"So what do we do, take out an ad?"

He smiled at her. "I think maybe we should both worry a little less about what the other one is going to feel about people we care about. I think that would be a start. I think we need to stop being afraid."

"You think we're holding each other back from finding love?"

He didn't want to admit it but he knew they had. He'd broken things off with Ashleigh because he didn't want Mia to feel guilty. And as for Damien, Mia had gone behind his back and dated him because she was worried what he'd say. Oh yeah, they had unknowingly sabotaged the other's relationship.

For a long time they stared at each other

"How could a woman who've never done a thing for us could come in here and point out all of our flaws?"

"Whether or not we like it, she is our mother. And, Kee, you're wrong. She did give us something. She gave us each other. I don't know what I would have done if you had not been in my life."

Keefe went to his sister and hugged her. "You're right, she could have gotten rid of us. As vain as she is I'm surprised that she didn't. You are going to be great as a psychologist, Mia. That was totally insightful. I am grateful that she gave me you to love and to take care of. Who knows? If I had not had you to care for, maybe I would have never accomplished the things that I have."

"Are you saying that you're going to forgive her?"

"I think I'm ready to work on forgiving her."

"I never thought this day would ever come. Wow, Keefe Black, forgiving his mother."

"Okay stop it. I didn't say I've got the warm fuzzies for her, and I didn't say I forgave her, just that I'm thinking about it. Her helping you…I think now maybe she did what she could. She's a flake and she's narcissistic, and a bit of a slut, but she can't help who she is. I suppose in her own way maybe she cared a little bit. It doesn't excuse what she did to us but I think I'll stop beating her up every time I see her."

"You know, I was thinking about that. She always managed to pick guys who were at least nice to us. No one ever abused us."

"That's true and Jerry did help us even after Mom left," Keefe admitted. "In fact we owe a lot of what we have now to Jerry. He's the reason we were able to leave foster care. Yeah, Jerry always kept in touch with us and came over to make sure we were doing okay. That's a lot more than our relatives did. You're right, Mia, she could have done a lot worse."

And this time he didn't add that she could have done a lot better.

Several days had passed since their mother had left and this time she hadn't had to ask for a handout. Keefe had written her a hefty check. She'd looked at him in amazement and asked him if he was sure. He'd told her that he was and he'd told her how grateful he was for what she'd done for Mia.

She'd wanted to hug him. He could tell by the look in her eyes, but he still wasn't ready for that. But he had managed to tell her to take care of herself and that was a big start.

Now it was time to begin taking care of the woman he'd fallen in love with. He decided to go by his apartment and check his answering machine. The first message hit him like a bolt of lightning. The sexiest voice he'd ever heard purred, "Mr. Black, it's all over. I desperately need a plumber. My drain is clogged."

Hot damn! To hell with the rest of the messages. He grabbed the phone and punched out Mia's number. "Mia," he said when she answered, "don't look for me tonight. I'm going to Ashleigh's and I have a lot of making up to do."

"Good luck," she answered.

"Thanks." He smiled as he headed out the door to buy the biggest bouquet of flowers he could find. For once Mia wasn't uppermost in his mind.

Ashleigh had the door open only seconds after he knocked. He lifted her in his arms and spun her around. "I didn't think you were ever going to call me."

"I thought you deserved to wait," she answered, taking the flowers from his hand and tossing them on the counter. "Just kiss me, Keefe. Kiss me and let's start over."

With her still in his arms he kissed her, closing the door with his foot. "Is everything alright? Did you find a way to pay your taxes?"

"Yes." She moved her head from his chest. "Damien was a big help." She watched Keefe's face, saw the faint signs of jealousy and touched his cheeks. "He helped me get my money back, Keefe, that's all."

"How?"

"We used his size. Nicki got a couple of guys and the four of us paid a little visit to my accountant. We escorted him to the bank and I insinuated that they would kick his ass if he didn't return my money."

"You're lucky the guy didn't have you all arrested. I'm surprised he didn't think of that. I mean, three big guys in the bank waiting for him to make a withdrawal."

"We thought of that too. And no one wanted to go to jail. I was the only one who went into the bank. The others hung around outside.

"Did they rough him up before he agreed to go to the bank?"

"Actually, nobody even touched him." Ashleigh smiled up at Keefe. "I eyed his crotch and asked him if he ever wanted to have sex again in his life. The guys never said a word, just stared at him. He just assumed they were there for muscle. That's all it took. I made him give me back all my money, not just for the taxes, so that's even better. We even took pictures of the cashier's check and me handing it to the IRS agent.

"Why didn't you let me go and be your muscle? Why Damien and not me?"

"Let me show you something." She pulled him over to her desk and pulled out a box of papers. "Damien has been paying me back out of each check." She showed Keefe the ledger she was using to record Damien's payments and copies of his pay stubs. "He owed me, Keefe. It was another way to pay me back, by helping me get back my money."

"It's true. He really has changed. Mia told me that he was paying you back. I thought it was just another lie."

"Yes, he has changed and I found out he was doing it because of Mia. He loves her, Keefe. You were both wrong to treat him that way."

"I know," Keefe answered miserably. "Does he still love her?"

"Of course he does."

"Then why hasn't he called her?"

"He said if she wants him she's going to have to make the first move. He's determined, as determined as he was to keep that job you got for him. He wanted to prove you wrong."

Keefe laughed, "He told you about that huh?"

"Yeah, he did. Shoveling shit at the zoo, Keefe? That was a bit mean, don't you think?"

"Not at the time I got it for him. I thought the guy was so full of shit that he might as well work with it for a living. But he did surprise me by keeping it."

Ashleigh smiled. "Well, here's another surprise. He likes it. He likes working with the animals, being outdoors. He said he writes his songs while he works and guess what? He's finally on his way. He has a job singing at Mr. Sal's three nights a week. I can't believe it. He went after his dream and he finally made it. He wanted Mia to be proud of him."

Keefe was looking at her in amazement. "You're happy for him, aren't you?"

"I am, that's all I ever wanted, for someone to realize his talent, for him to fulfill his dreams. You know what? All of this has taught me a big lesson. You can't go after another person's dreams for them. They have to do it for themselves. Since falling in love with Mia, Damien's changed."

Keefe nibbled on Ashleigh's ear. "You really believe that, don't you? I guess I do too. She's miserable without him, really miserable. I never thought I would be wishing for the day when I would walk into my sister's apartment and find her there laughing with Damien, but that's exactly what I want." He nibbled Ashleigh's ear again.

"Maybe there's something we can do. Maybe we can come up with something to get her and Damien back together."

"Maybe later," Keefe answered, lust filling his eyes and his voice. "Right now it's not my sister's love life I'm worried about."

"No?"

"No," Keefe growled, "it's mine." And he lifted Ashleigh in his arms, buried his lips in the soft flesh of her neck and carried her to the bedroom.

"Amen to that and hallelujah," Ashleigh answered. "It's about time." She intended to show him just how much Mia and Damien weren't on her mind. She was going to make love to him the entire night and she was going to do her best to not make any more mistakes, but she knew if she did, Keefe would forgive her as she would forgive him for his. She wasn't looking for perfection. She was looking for love.

Ashleigh woke in the morning for the first time in years feeling that she wasn't under a curse. She looked over at Keefe and grinned. He was watching her.

"How long have you been awake?" she asked.

"For a while. I just wanted to look at you. We came so close to losing this, Ashleigh."

"No we didn't, Keefe. I wasn't going to give up on us that easily." She kissed him. "Tell me what you were doing while I was out being a bad ass."

"My mother came for a little visit."

She waited for the pain and anger that had been in his voice when he'd mentioned his mother before, but she didn't hear it. "Are you okay?"

"Yeah, this time she actually helped."

"I'm glad." Ashleigh lay on his chest wanting to ask him to tell her everything about his mother and his childhood, not leave anything out but she didn't want to bring up painful memories, not now.

"You've made peace with your mother," she said instead.

"For now," he answered. "She helped Mia and for that I'm grateful. But Mia needs more help."

"Do you want me to help?" Ashleigh asked, uncertain.

"Yeah, baby, I want your help."

He smiled and his smile warmed her all the way down to her toes. "Then, Mr. Black, you have it. Between the two of us, I'm sure we'll get the two of them back together."

"I love you, Ashleigh."

"And I love you, Keefe Black, and I'm willing to help your sister get her life back on track so that you can concentrate on me."

"In that case you need to stop talking and focus on me. I'm not thinking about anyone but you. My concentration's entirely on you. Tell me, how does this feel?"

"Good." Ashleigh moaned as he buried his lips in her neck. Mia and Damien's problems could wait a while longer. For now she wanted to make love. Again. To the man she loved.

Ashleigh and Keefe watched Damien as his co-worker pointed toward them. He ambled over and Ashleigh crossed her fingers. Hopefully her presence would diffuse some of the male testosterone.

"So, Keefe, have you found a new job for me?" Damien asked.

Keefe laughed. "I'm not here to cause you any problems, Damien, I just wanted to thank you."

"Thank me?"

"Yeah, I talked to Ashleigh and she told that you helped her with the tax situation."

Damien shook his head slightly, then laughed. "I didn't do it for you. I did it for Ashleigh. I owed her that much."

Ashleigh could tell that Damien wasn't wild about talking to Keefe but she refused to allow that to dissuade them. They'd come for a specific reason and they weren't leaving until they'd had their say.

"Was there anything else?" Damien asked, starting to leave.

"Yeah one more thing," Keefe answered before Damien could take off. "Mia, she's miserable."

Damien stopped, his eyes hard. "And you're telling me because?"

"Because she misses you and I don't know why you haven't called her."

"Well, Keefe, I don't think it's any of your business. I mean, you're Mia's big brother, not mine. Then he cocked his head to the side. "Tell me something, Keefe. Why *are* you here? You should be celebrating the fact that we aren't together."

Keefe was getting angry. Ashleigh could sense it. She'd promised him that she would help. She should have known it wouldn't be easy. She couldn't say she blamed Damien. He had no good reason to listen to Keefe.

"Damien, Keefe didn't want to come here. I told him you would listen. What have you got to lose? Just hear him out."

Damien glared at Keefe before turning to her. When he smiled at her, she knew he would do as she asked and listen.

"Okay, Keefe, go ahead. Say what you came here for.

"Like I said, Mia's miserable. And I don't like to stand by and see her unhappy without trying to help."

"I'm sorry to tell you this, Keefe, but this one time you're going to have let it ride. You have no control over this situation."

"Damien, you told me that you love Mia, that you wanted to marry her. Don't you miss her?"

Ashleigh saw an immediate change. Damien's neck muscles stretched taut and he chewed on his lips.

"Miss her? Hell yes, I miss her, but I'll learn to live with that."

"Why? All you have to do is go to her."

"Listen, I've done all that I plan on doing. I told her I loved her and she told me to back off until her fiancé came home. On top of that, she ordered me not to date." He half laughed at the memory of that. "Man, I didn't. I didn't even think about talking to another woman." He shook his head again. "I can't believe it. She offered me nothing, just told me to wait and I did. Then after everything that we'd been through together, she thought I was trying to con her; that I was trying to take you for money. I can't believe it," he repeated. "Maybe I have you to thank for that because I know your opinion of me was always low, but, man, that's pretty damn bad."

"Damien." Ashleigh touched his shoulder. "There's a very good reason why Mia behaved that way. Don't be too hard on her. Give her another chance."

Damien stared at her for a moment. "Why are you helping him, Ash? He's treated you as shabbily as his sister treated me."

"I love him," Ashleigh stated. "I forgave him."

For a moment the three of them stood looking at each other. Ashleigh touched Damien's arm once more. "Don't give up on her, Damien. You never would have found yourself if it hadn't been for her. We both know you never tried to change for me. Just give her a chance; she had her reasons. You have to be patient if you want a future with her. That's all that matters."

"Didn't my loving her matter?"

This was proving much harder than Ashleigh ever anticipated.

She turned to Keefe and whispered, "Tell him about Treece. Maybe it will help."

Keefe swallowed. Ashleigh knew he didn't want to. Damien was watching him. "Go ahead, Keefe," she coaxed, "tell him."

Keefe was left with no choice. He relayed everything that had happened with Treece. "Mia wasn't trying to hurt you, Damien. She was looking out for me and you must admit she had good reason."

Damien looked directly into Keefe's eyes. "You have good reason, my man, for not trusting women. I don't blame you, not one little bit. Hell, if some woman took me like that I don't know if I'd ever trust one again."

"So you understand then why Mia got so upset?"

"I said I understood why you would. Mia? Now that's a different story. I love her and she knows it. She made her choice that night. She chose you and I'm not going to be in constant competition with you."

"You're not."

Damien laughed. "Come on, Keefe, don't lie. We both know that if Mia and I got back together and you found a reason for her to not be with me next week she would blow me off. I'm done."

"That's not going to happen. I can almost guarantee it."

"How? Did you order her to get back together with me?"

Both men stood watching each other warily, sizing up the situation. "Mia loves you, Damien," Keefe said at last.

"And I love her, but in order to have a relationship with her I guess I have to have one with you and I'm not taking any more orders from either of you."

"What if Mia comes to you?"

"I can't make any promises."

Keefe stuck out his hand. "I'm sorry. I misjudged you." He waited, wondering if Damien would take his hand. After several seconds Damien did.

"You didn't misjudge me. You were right on the money. I was no good, a dog, and I'll be the first one to admit it, but I've never been that with Mia. From the moment I met her I knew she was the one." Damien glanced toward Ashleigh. "Can you believe in all of these months I haven't had sex once?" He shook his head and glared at Keefe. "Not even with Mia. I guess you wouldn't have approved."

Ashleigh stepped between the men, the look on Keefe's face breaking her heart. She'd told him this would work. They needed it to work. Mia needed a life in order for her brother to find peace. She shook her head slightly at Keefe, then looked again toward Damien. "That's not Keefe's doing. He didn't even know that Mia was still a virgin."

She saw the look that crossed Damien's face and couldn't prevent her gasp of surprise. "You didn't know? You didn't know," she repeated, "and still you didn't cheat on her. My God, Damien, I had no idea just how much you really do love her." She looked at Keefe, hoping he would know what to say to Damien.

"Damien, my sister and I...we don't talk much about her sex life. Hell, I never even wanted to think about it. That's my baby sister. She was engaged, I just assumed...I didn't know that she was...that she'd never...," Keefe stuttered. "And I'm not saying if I could have influenced her decision I wouldn't have tried."

"You did influence her decision, Keefe." Damien glanced at Ashleigh before lowering his eyes. "I didn't know that she was a virgin. She never told me. I just thought that it was me, that she didn't think I was good enough for her to make love with."

"I'm happy for you, Damien," Ashleigh smiled, "that you found someone you loved enough to give up your favorite pastime. I knew you loved her, but it's only now that I know just how much. You respected and loved her enough to not even ask for a reason. Wow!"

"I'm sorry that I made things even harder for the two of you," Keefe said. "It was just hard for me to believe that you truly loved her. I believe it now, if that helps."

Damien smiled a sad smile in Keefe's direction. "Not really, man. This is one thing you can't fix, but thanks anyway. I can tell you that without a doubt, Mia's the only woman I've ever loved. I know I changed because I thought she deserved something better. Hell, I knew she deserved something better than what I'd been in the past. So I decided to become the best me that I could because that's what Mia deserves. But in the process I discovered something." He stopped and smiled. "I discovered that I deserve the best a woman has to offer also. I deserve for her to love me completely and unconditionally, not give me the scraps her brother doesn't want. Yeah, I deserve better." He smiled at Keefe and walked away. "See you later Ash, he called over his shoulder.

"What now?" Keefe asked as he looked at Ashleigh.

"Don't worry," Ashleigh assured him. "We'll think of something."

"Ashleigh, tell me why you're busting your butt to help Keefe get Mia and Damien back together?" Nicki asked.

She was suspicious. Ashleigh could tell from her tone. "Okay, I'll admit I have an ulterior motive. But I also want Keefe to be happy. His sister's happiness is very important to him and he's important to me."

"And?"

"And when Mia is back with Damien, Keefe won't have to divide his attention. Okay?"

"That's better," Nicki laughed. What's the plan? Maybe I can help."

"Right now I don't have one. Keefe's just working on trying to get her out of the house. She's refusing to go any place other than work and school."

"I've got it," Nicki snapped her finger, "the perfect solution."

"If it's perfect, tell me." Ashleigh was daring to hope.

"Damien's opening. If you can invite Mia and get her to come, then I think when the two of them see each other, nature will take over and do the rest."

"She won't come. Keefe keeps asking her to go out. Aren't you listening to me?"

"Maybe you should try asking her."

Ashleigh kissed her friend on the cheek. "Great idea. I'll do that." She smiled to herself as she thought of an uncomplicated future with Keefe. Oh yes, she was more than willing to work to ensure that future.

CHAPTER EIGHTEEN

"Mia, you need to get out of the house, do something. Maybe you should call Damien, see if you can work things out." It was a long shot and Keefe knew it but he had to try something.

"Listen, stop worrying about me. I'm not in that zombie state anymore."

"But you're letting someone go that you love and I wonder why. I thought we talked about this, that we were both going to at least try and open our hearts."

Mia glanced at her brother. She knew he was worried about her. Ever since her meltdown he'd become even more protective than he'd been in the past and that was saying something. He was close to suffocating her.

"Mia, something has to be wrong. Just tell me. Maybe I'll let it go," Keefe said, knowing that he wouldn't, not until he'd at last gotten Mia and Damien in a room together. If he managed that and nature didn't take over, then maybe he'd leave it alone.

"Keefe, I've had some time to think about it, and I wonder if pursuing things with Damien would be the best thing for me to do. I mean, so much has being happening so fast around here that I don't want to rush into things. Now that I've thought about it, it would be a little weird being around you and Ashleigh if I were with Damien. So I've decided to let it go, wait for something or someone who will not make my life more complicated."

"Are you saying that you're not going to try and work things out with Damien because I'm with Ashleigh?"

She didn't answer.

"Mia?"

"I don't know," she said at last.

"You're a liar. You're still afraid, you're afraid that your feelings for Damien may not last. I saw your face when Mom was here. You're still worried that you're like her. So what if you are? Maybe she's right, maybe it doesn't matter. If you love Damien and he loves you then let now be enough. Don't worry so much about the future. There are no guarantees, Mia. Not in love. In love we have to grab it where we can find it and hang on because who knows, in the blink of an eye it can be taken away from you."

Mia smiled at her brother. "Talk about replicas, you're your mother's son. You sound just like her. I never in a million years thought I would hear that speech coming from your lips."

"I was wrong. He ignored her look of shock. "I was wrong about a lot of things and one of those things I was wrong about was Damien. He does love you."

"He'll get over it and move on the next woman he meets."

"I'm sure he'll get over it, but you have to ask yourself if you want him to. Do you want the man you love to move on to the next woman?" He kissed her cheek and walked out of his sister's apartment. He was going to Ashleigh's. He'd almost lost her. Twice. He wasn't about to allow that to happen again.

Ashleigh was cuddled in Keefe's arms. They'd made love until they were both exhausted. Now he was simply holding her. "Any luck with Mia?" she asked.

"Nope she's still being difficult."

"Do you mind if I call her?"

The look of gratitude that crossed Keefe's face made Ashleigh wish she had asked him sooner.

"You don't mind?" he asked.

"I'd love to. And I have a feeling it might be harder for her to say no to me. If she tries, I'll make her feel guilty. Don't worry," she said, noticing the change of expression on Keefe's face. "She'll agree."

There was no time like the present to do it. So she did. "Mia. Hi, this is Ashleigh. If you have no objections I was thinking that it would be nice if we got together. I want us to get along."

For a minute Mia didn't answer, so Ashleigh called her name. "Mia, are you there?"

"Yes," Mia said at last.

"I want to go to this new club. I've badgered your brother into taking me on Friday. Would you please join us?"

"Thanks, that's nice of you, but…well… I'm not in the mood for going out. I have a lot of things to do."

"Please, Mia. Keefe won't have a good time if you're home alone and I really want to get out." Ashleigh glanced in Keefe's direction and shrugged. Sometimes it took a good dose of guilt to accomplish your goal.

"Okay," Mia finally agreed.

"Good. You're going to enjoy yourself, Mia. See you Friday. Ashleigh turned toward Keefe with a grin. "Leave it to a woman to get things done," she teased.

When Keefe left Ashleigh's it was with a plan. Mia had agreed to go to the club. Ashleigh was taking care of things with Damien, asking him to reserve a table for her and some girlfriends, a front row table. Keefe could hardly wait for Friday. He punched in Mia's number. "Wake up, I'm coming over."

"Why?" Mia looked at the clock on the bedside table. "Kee, it's four in the morning. This couldn't have waited?"

"Don't be such a grump. I'm on my way over."

"And again I ask, this couldn't have waited? Why are you so happy?"

Keefe laughed. "Why do you think?"

"So why didn't you stay over?"

"I wanted to talk to you before you went to work."

Mia glanced again at the clock. "You had another three hours."

"I know." He laughed again. "I'm happy and I wanted to talk. Is that a crime? Hey, Mia, how about getting up and scrambling me a couple of eggs. I'm hungry."

"Why didn't Ashleigh feed you?"

"She did," Keefe answered. "But now I need food. See you in ten minutes."

Mia forced herself from the bed. She was awake now. She wanted to be annoyed at her brother, but she wasn't. She was truly happy that things appeared to be working out for him and Ashleigh. She went to her closet and pushed back the huge bag that had started the ball rolling. The wedding gown that neither she nor Ashleigh would probably ever wear. She headed for the shower, remembering the way Damien had looked at her as she modeled the gown.

She was showered and dressed and had the coffee on before her brother's key hit the lock. He came in the door singing. Mia glanced toward him. Before she could get out a word he had lifted her in the air and was twirling her around.

"So you're in love, huh, big brother?"

"Does it show?"

"Yes, it shows," she smiled, "and it looks good on you."

"You don't mind?" Keefe stopped to check out his sister's response, wanting to know her true feelings. "I mean, that it's Ashleigh? You're okay with it?"

"Listen," Mia answered, "I'm all for anyone who can make you happy. You deserve it."

"So do you. We both deserve it, and we're both going to be happy."

She eyed him curiously. "I thought we'd agreed that we would stop trying to control the universe, that we were going to allow each other to find our own happiness. We're not going to meddle, right?"

"Right," Keefe answered, "we're not going to meddle. But, Mia, I don't think I can actually not be concerned about your happiness. I want you to feel the way that I do right now." He stopped, leaned back and looked at her. "I'm sorry. You did, didn't you? I guess I didn't want to see it."

Mia didn't want any reminders; she didn't need any. Damien was never far away from her thoughts. "It's okay," she told her brother. "If it had been meant to be, it would have worked out. I guess it just wasn't in the cards for us to be together."

"Sometimes fate might need a little push," he said, then smiled and poured them both a cup of coffee.

"What are you planning, Keefe? I'm not into blind dates if that's what you have in mind. And to be honest, I don't really want to be a third wheel while you and Ashleigh coo over each other."

"It's not a blind date and I promise you won't be a third wheel. I want to spend the evening with my sister. What's wrong with that?"

"Nothing except I don't know if I believe you."

"Mia, I've never lied to you and I don't think I'm going to start now, so do you think you could wait until Friday? And you promised Ashleigh that you would come so you can't back out. Now, would you please fix me some breakfast? I really am starved."

Friday found Keefe back at his sister's apartment. He looked her over with a critical eye. "Mia, is that what you wore to work?" he asked with just a hint of disapproval in his voice, knowing that the outfit was not one she would have worn to work but wanting her to change.

"No, Keefe."

As expected, Mia looked down at her clothes, black silk pants and a plain black sweater. "What's wrong with my clothes?"

"Well, the club we're going to is…well, it's a very nice place…and well, I just want you to dress like you give a damn. I know I'm only your brother but damn, Mia, a little makeup won't kill you."

Mia stared at her brother, trying to decide if her feelings were hurt, or if she was just a little miffed. "Okay, I'll change," she said and headed back to her bedroom.

"This time try and find something that shows you tried to pay attention to how you look, as if maybe you care about your appearance," Keefe yelled out to her.

His last comment solved Mia's dilemma. She wasn't miffed, she was pissed. She took another look at her outfit. There was nothing wrong with what she was wearing. She sighed. Since she was doing this to please Keefe, she might as well go all out and do as he'd asked.

When she came back out, her brother let out an appreciative whistle and Mia smiled. "I guess that means you like what I'm wearing?"

"Much better," he answered. "Now come on, let's go. I don't want to walk in in the middle of the show."

Mia walked out with her brother, not wanting to admit that her change of outfit had changed her mood as well. The black had merely reflected her attitude, ominous and dark. Now with the glittery gold top she wore, she felt like the top. She sparkled. And she'd piled her hair atop her head and fastened it with a gold art deco barrette that fought her top for sparkle. She'd even taken the sparkle to her lips with the new lipstick she'd never worn. And Keefe had been right about that also; the makeup was making her feel like a new woman.

Another thing Keefe was right about was the club's very festive atmosphere and clientele; a smooth beat of the music had Mia feeling good as she rolled her upper torso slightly in tune with the music. She saw Keefe looking around as though looking for someone and her suspicions returned that it was a setup. She saw Ashleigh waving at them before Keefe spotted her and she glared at her brother. "That table Ashleigh's at is for four. I told you not to fix me up. I thought you wouldn't lie to me."

"I thought you would never lie to me either, so now we're even," he said as he grabbed for her hand, held on tight and pulled her toward the table Ashleigh had reserved.

Mia noticed there was no one else at the table and hoped that just maybe she was wrong, that they weren't planning on springing a blind date on her. She could take being a third wheel better than she could a blind date.

She smiled cordially at Ashleigh, answering the questions she asked, refusing to look at her brother. She was glad when the emcee finally came on stage to announce the coming act.

"Please, everyone, put your hands together and let's welcome our next act. This is his debut performance at the club but he's going to be a regular here three nights a week. Ladies and gentlemen, please, a big round of applause for Damien."

Mia's mouth dropped open and she closed her eyes, her heart beating a mile a minute. "Did he tell you to bring me here?" she asked, but neither Ashleigh nor Keefe answered her or if they had she wasn't listening. She was focused on Damien. He walked confidently out on the stage. He owned it before he even opened his mouth. When he did begin singing a surge of pride filled her. She smiled at Ashleigh, then at Keefe. "I told you he was good," she said. "Do you think he knows that I'm here?"

A moment after she asked the question, Damien stopped singing. He was staring at their table, in her direction. The background music played on while Damien walked toward them.

"He knows you're here now," Ashleigh said as Damien stopped on the stage directly in front of Mia.

He was staring at her and the look he gave her was even more intense than the one he'd given when she'd first seen him at Ashleigh's and had fallen instantly in love with him.

Keefe stood and held his hand out to Ashleigh. Come on, let's go."

"Aren't you staying?" Mia asked.

"No." They both grinned at her. "You're on your own."

Mia turned toward her brother's direction. "You did set me up. You knew."

"Of course I knew," he whispered.

"I thought you weren't going to meddle?"

"Another lie," he answered proudly. "I told you I'd do whatever it took to make you happy."

"Do you think he's forgiven me?" Mia asked anxiously.

"What do you think?" Ashleigh asked. "Mia, please believe me when I tell you that not once in all the time I was with him did Damien ever look at me like that. He loves you, Mia."

"It doesn't bother you?" Mia asked.

"No, really it doesn't. I wanted Damien to fulfill his dream and he has. Mia, he would have never done this if he had stayed with me. He had no incentive to be better. He went after his own dream because of you. He loves you and he wanted you to be proud of him."

"I am," Mia smiled. "I am so very proud of him," she repeated. As tears slid beneath her lashes she reached out her hand and her brother gave her a reassuring squeeze.

"Don't be afraid of loving him, Mia," Keefe added. "You deserve to be happy. Now, if you don't mind, it's time I showed Ashleigh just how much she means to me."

With that Keefe kissed his sister's cheek and walked out of the club with his arm around Ashleigh.

"What do you think is going to happen?" Ashleigh asked.

"Frankly, my dear, at this moment I don't care. We got them this far. Now it's up to them."

"I can't believe you're not dying to know how this turns out."

He grinned back. "Believe it. There are more important things on my mind at this moment, and baby, you head the list."

"So, what's on your mind, Mr. Black?" She saw the lust in his eyes. "Besides that?"

"You'll see," he said as they stepped through the door.

Shivers of delight coursed through Ashleigh. Her heart thudded in her chest, and she dared to dream.

"Over here." Keefe was leading her to a black stretch limo. The driver opened the door as they approached, stunning Ashleigh.

"How did you...? When did you have the time?"

"I made the time." He kissed her and ushered her into the luxury limo. The fragrance of flowers filled the interior and she looked around.

"Keefe," she whispered. "This is so nice."

"This is just the beginning, Ash. I want to give you your perfect moment. All of our problems are solved. Now I want to tell you again how much I love you."

Keefe put a finger under her chin and lifted it until her lips were in perfect position. He peered into her eyes. "So this is what true love feels like."

Another shiver claimed Ashleigh on hearing Keefe's words. So much had happened to them. It was hard to believe it was finally almost over. She closed her eyes and hugged Keefe close to her. She thought briefly of Mia and Damien. Damien had his dream and he'd achieved it without her help. She couldn't deny that Mia was the catalyst for the change in Damien, for his growing from a boy into a man. She'd seen the way Damien had looked at Mia and she'd felt momentary envy. No man had ever looked at her in that manner.

"Ashleigh, I love you," Keefe repeated.

She opened her eyes and stared at him in surprise. Keefe was looking at her the way that Damien had looked at Mia. A little cry escaped her. "Keefe, Keefe, I love you too."

He lowered his lips and kissed her and she knew for certain she was where she belonged. His kiss returned her home. Home was in

Keefe's arms. At last she admitted to herself that there was only one man in the world who could bring completion to her soul. And she was in his arms. Life and love took some strange turns, she realized. She had sewn a wedding gown for a love that wasn't real and a marriage that was not to be. Yet somehow it had all led to this moment with Keefe. Theirs was anything but a perfect relationship, but what was the fun in that? They would have missed out on all that making up.

"I love you, Keefe," she repeated. "I do love you." She gave herself over to the kiss. He'd completed his job as Mia's protector. Damien would fill that role quite nicely. Without reservation she surrendered her heart to Keefe, knowing that she was the center of his universe, and that he was the center of hers. And it had all happened because of an ad for a wedding gown.

THE END

AUTHOR BIOGRAPHY

Dyanne Davis was born in a small town in Ala. Moved to Chicago when she was eleven, with her mother and sister, where she remained. She's happily married to William Davis, her newest critique partner. They live in a nearby Chicago Suburb with their only child, William Davis Jr. A love of the written word began at the age of four when she began reading. Her passion for reading carried over into a desire to write. Dyanne retired from nursing three years ago with her husband's encouragement to pursue her dreams of writing full time.

ACKNOWLEDGEMENTS

As it will always be in my life, God is honored above all.

To everyone that wasn't mentioned by name before, I love you. John and Ernestine Ross, Ongela, Tanya, Mikey, Kim, Quensell, Cassandra, Kathy, James, Michael, Marcus, Andrew, Kayla, Makela, Tanisha, Gloria, Mr and Mrs. O'Hara, Anne, Brianna, Colin, Andrew, Maria, Dr. Akl, Dr. Meah, Dr. Vania Ilham, Debbie, Edie, Hoselita, Johnny, Tony, David, Mala and everyone else in my life. Edna Adduci, thank you for your untiring efforts on my behalf.

Fatima Gomez, my sister not of blood but of love. Thank you for sharing your family, your love and your life. You've enriched me on every level and I will love you always.

Leila Akl, a mainstay in my life, a friend that I can count on no matter what. I love you. Your family has become an extended family and will always be such and you will always be my sister.

Beth Spandonidis, for defending my dreams and believing in me always even when others didn't. I respect you for your honest opinions of what I write. Don't ever stop giving that. You hold a special place in my heart and I love you dearly.

Ann Banks and Gloria- what a wonderful display of support. Thank you. And yes Ann- I love the both of you also.

To everyone who read and liked The Color Of Trouble. I thank all of you who took the time to write and tell me that you enjoyed the book. I also thank the ones of you who wrote to say you didn't. The potshots keep me humble and the scales balanced.

To Sidney Rickman,my editor. You have to be the greatest editor alive. You're a wonderful writer and a bit psychic I suspect. You always seem to know where I'm heading even when I've forgotten. Thank you.

Brigid Darden, Wow!!! What a party. It was definitely worth the wait. I know you know how special you are to me, but this is in case you don't. I love you.

For Olivia Holton, for giving the idea to Barb Deane who willingly gave it to me.

I began with acknowledgements to God, and will end with the two most important people in my life, my husband and son, Bill Sr. and Bill Jr. I would not have written my life any other way. You two are first and foremost in my heart and in my life

EXCERPT FROM

CLASS REUNION:
CLASS OF '68
BY
JOHN OJO

On a sunny Sunday afternoon on our farm, in the cotton fields of Alabama, I calmly walked inside our house and began packing my bags for college. It had always been said in my family that I would go to college, so much so that, when the day finally came, I heaved a heavy sigh of relief, realizing that my parents would now have to find another topic of conversation around our dinner table.

The college I chose to attend was Glendale University. The University had produced several generations of businessmen and leaders, including a president. It had just been ordered by the courts to begin admitting black students and it had agreed to provide scholarships for the top two students at each black high school in Alabama. I qualified for the scholarship as I was the valedictorian of my high school.

As far back as I could remember my father Samuel had stressed that I had to do well in school. His own lack of formal education, he felt, had restricted him to a lifelong career as a cotton farmer, enabling him to support himself and his family, but not much more. He was seventy years old now, worn and tired, having lived and labored on his farm all his life Samuel had married Agnes, my mother thirty years earlier, a few weeks after he turned forty. She gave birth to me several years later, a very difficult birth that had left her frail and sickly. The doctors told her that she would probably not be able to conceive again. She carried this burden as she carried all others, by putting her faith in the Lord, waiting for Him to look upon her with favor, so that she might have another child.

Agnes's barrenness continued for years, during which she went from one church to another, singing songs of deliverance, kneeling, weeping, and crying out for mercy before many preachers. She attended many gatherings and sermons where it was claimed that the preacher could perform miracles. She struggled and fought among the multitudes that gathered to get to the podium, so that the preacher could lay his healing hand on her. Yet, after several years of endless prayer, the Lord had not seen it fit in His heart to lay down her burden. Her faith faltered, and she sought other remedies for her barrenness. Agnes sought out men and women who sacrificed animals before altars, and claimed to be in communion with the spirits. They performed rituals and sacrificed numerous animals to appease evil spirits so that they might see it fit to lay down her burden. Yet, after countless rituals, her barrenness continued. Then one night she had a terrible dream. In her dream, she had died and stood before the Lord's judgment. She was cast among the company of devil worshippers, pagans and heathens, condemned to suffer eternal damnation in hell. She awoke from this dream terrified, so she fled from these people and turned back to the Lord, seeking forgiveness and salvation. A year later, at the age of 45, she gave birth to twin daughters Tracy and Nancy. I had just turned ten a few days earlier. The birth of the twins brought great jubilation in our household. Neighbors, friends and relatives from afar came to rejoice and praise the

Lord for the great work he had done. Samuel was filled with pride and joy, but soon it occurred to him that these twins were the children of his old age. Although it was never discussed, I knew that my father who was already 56 yrs old would be long dead by the time my sisters were old enough for college. My father had worked tirelessly all his life, yet he had little to show for it. The low price of cotton had condemned us to a subsistence lifestyle, never saving any money and often in debt.

Recent crop failures had forced my father to borrow heavily against the farm, so much so that losing our farm and home to the bank was a real possibility. My father never complained, but simply expected prayer to solve his problems. He could not now discard the blind faith that had sustained him all his life, the faith that I feared would lead our family to ruin. Frequent crop failures had done nothing to convince my father of the futility of remaining a cotton farmer. He gave increasing amounts of money to his church and began holding daily family services at our home. But I wondered if it had ever occurred to him that all farmers suffered in a drought, whether they were sinners or not, and that when it rained, rain fell on the righteous as well as the sinful, just like the bible said.

I picked up my bags and began walking to the bus stop by our farm. My mother and sisters followed me as did my father, who joined us late. I remained silent, while my parents chatted happily, obviously pleased that their son was going off to college. As we reached the bus stop, my father spoke to me softly "I have this feeling that you can be somebody, that you can move on up. Make us proud, son. Make us proud. "

As my bus took off along the dry, dusty road to Glendale, I glanced back at my mother and sisters, who smiled and waved as my father looked on. In a way, I was their only hope. Their survival depended on my success. I had an overwhelming feeling, deep inside, that I just could not lose. I had to overcome. There was no other way home.

2003 Publication Schedule

January	Twist of Fate	Ebony Butterfly II
	Beverly Clark	Delilah Dawson
	1-58571-084-9	1-58571-086-5
February	Fragment in the Sand	Fate
	Annetta P. Lee	Pamela Leigh Starr
	1-58571-097-0	1-58571-115-2
March	One Day at a Time	Unbreak My Heart
	Bella McFarland	Dar Tomlinson
	1-58571-099-7	1-58571-101-2
April	At Last	Brown Sugar Diaries & Other Sexy Tales
	Lisa G. Riley	Delores Bundy & Cole Riley
	1-58571-093-8	1-58571-091-1
May	Three Wishes	Acquisitions
	Seressia Glass	Kimberley White
	1-58571-092-X	1-58571-095-4
June	When Dreams A Float	Revelations
	Dorothy Elizabeth Love	Cheris F. Hodges
	1-58571-104-7	1-58571-085-7
July	The Color of Trouble	Someone to Love
	Dyanne Davis	Alicia Wiggins
	1-58571-096-2	1-58571-098-9
August	Object of His Desire	Hart & Soul
	A. C. Arthur	Angie Daniels
	1-58571-094-6	1-58571-087-3
September	Erotic Anthology	A Lark on the Wing
	Assorted	Phyliss Hamilton
	1-58571-113-6	1-58571-105-5

October	Angel's Paradise	I'll Be Your Shelter
	Janice Angelique	Giselle Carmichael
	1-58571-107-1	1-58571-108-X
November	A Dangerous Obsession	Just an Affair
	J.M. Jeffries	Eugenia O'Neal
	1-58571-109-8	1-58571-111-X
December	Shades of Brown	By Design
	Denise Becker	Barbara Keaton
	1-58571-110-1	1-58571-088-1

Other Genesis Press, Inc. Titles

A Dangerous Deception	J.M. Jeffries	$8.95
A Dangerous Love	J.M. Jeffries	$8.95
After the Vows	Leslie Esdaile	$10.95
(Summer Anthology)	T.T. Henderson	
	Jacqueline Thomas	
Again My Love	Kayla Perrin	$10.95
Against the Wind	Gwynne Forster	$8.95
A Lighter Shade of Brown	Vicki Andrews	$8.95
All I Ask	Barbara Keaton	$8.95
A Love to Cherish	Beverly Clark	$8.95
Ambrosia	T.T. Henderson	$8.95
And Then Came You	Dorothy Elizabeth Love	$8.95
A Risk of Rain	Dar Tomlinson	$8.95
Best of Friends	Natalie Dunbar	$8.95
Bound by Love	Beverly Clark	$8.95
Breeze	Robin Hampton Allen	$10.95
Cajun Heat	Charlene Berry	$8.95
Careless Whispers	Rochelle Alers	$8.95
Caught in a Trap	Andre Michelle	$8.95
Chances	Pamela Leigh Starr	$8.95
Dark Embrace	Crystal Wilson Harris	$8.95
Dark Storm Rising	Chinelu Moore	$10.95
Designer Passion	Dar Tomlinson	$8.95
Eve's Prescription	Edwina Martin Arnold	$8.95
Everlastin' Love	Gay G. Gunn	$8.95
Fate	Pamela Leigh Starr	$8.95
Forbidden Quest	Dar Tomlinson	$10.95
From the Ashes	Kathleen Suzanne	$8.95
	Jeanne Sumerix	

Gentle Yearning	Rochelle Alers	$10.95
Glory of Love	Sinclair LeBeau	$10.95
Heartbeat	Stephanie Bedwell-Grime	$8.95
Illusions	Pamela Leigh Starr	$8.95
Indiscretions	Donna Hill	$8.95
Interlude	Donna Hill	$8.95
Intimate Intentions	Angie Daniels	$8.95
Kiss or Keep	Debra Phillips	$8.95
Love Always	Mildred E. Riley	$10.95
Love Unveiled	Gloria Greene	$10.95
Love's Deception	Charlene Berry	$10.95
Mae's Promise	Melody Walcott	$8.95
Meant to Be	Jeanne Sumerix	$8.95
Midnight Clear	Leslie Esdaile	$10.95
(Anthology)	Gwynne Forster	
	Carmen Green	
	Monica Jackson	
Midnight Magic	Gwynne Forster	$8.95
Midnight Peril	Vicki Andrews	$10.95
My Buffalo Soldier	Barbara B. K. Reeves	$8.95
Naked Soul	Gwynne Forster	$8.95
No Regrets	Mildred E. Riley	$8.95
Nowhere to Run	Gay G. Gunn	$10.95
Passion	T.T. Henderson	$10.95
Past Promises	Jahmel West	$8.95
Path of Fire	T.T. Henderson	$8.95
Picture Perfect	Reon Carter	$8.95
Pride & Joi	Gay G. Gunn	$8.95
Quiet Storm	Donna Hill	$8.95
Reckless Surrender	Rochelle Alers	$8.95

Rendezvous with Fate	Jeanne Sumerix	$8.95
Rivers of the Soul	Leslie Esdaile	$8.95
Rooms of the Heart	Donna Hill	$8.95
Shades of Desire	Monica White	$8.95
Sin	Crystal Rhodes	$8.95
So Amazing	Sinclair LeBeau	$8.95
Somebody's Someone	Sinclair LeBeau	$8.95
Soul to Soul	Donna Hill	$8.95
Still Waters Run Deep	Leslie Esdaile	$8.95
Subtle Secrets	Wanda Y. Thomas	$8.95
Sweet Tomorrows	Kimberly White	$8.95
The Price of Love	Sinclair LeBeau	$8.95
The Reluctant Captive	Joyce Jackson	$8.95
The Missing Link	Charlyne Dickerson	$8.95
Tomorrow's Promise	Leslie Esdaile	$8.95
Truly Inseperable	Wanda Y. Thomas	$8.95
Unconditional Love	Alicia Wiggins	$8.95
Whispers in the Night	Dorothy Elizabeth Love	$8.95
Whispers in the Sand	LaFlorya Gauthier	$10.95
Yesterday is Gone	Beverly Clark	$8.95
Yesterday's Dreams, Tomorrow's Promises	Reon Laudat	$8.95
Your Precious Love	Sinclair LeBeau	$8.95

ESCAPE WITH INDIGO !!!!

Join Indigo Book Club©
It's simple, easy and secure.

Sign up and receive the new releases
every month + Free shipping and
20% off the cover price.

Go online to www.genesis-press.com and
click on Bookclub or
call 1-888-INDIGO-1

Order Form

Mail to: Genesis Press, Inc.

1213 Hwy 45 N
Columbus, MS 39705

Name _____
Address _____
City/State _____ Zip _____
Telephone _____

Ship to (if different from above)
Name _____
Address _____
City/State _____ Zip _____
Telephone _____

Credit Card Information
Credit Card # _____ ☐ Visa   ☐ Mastercard
Expiration Date (mm/yy) _____ ☐ AmEx   ☐ Discover

Qty.	Author	Title	Price	Total

Use this order
form, or call
1-888-INDIGO-1

Total for books _____
Shipping and handling:
  $5 first two books,
  $1 each additional book _____
Total S & H _____
Total amount enclosed _____
Mississippi residents add 7% sales tax